THE MAN WAS TAUNTING
FOR A FIGHT

Austin stiffened. Every instinct demanded that he teach the rowdy a lesson on manners. No man ought to be allowed to speak to another man that way. If this had been Texas instead of Arkansas . . .

The slaver laughed as Austin turned away and stepped into the stirrup.

"Gutless pile of dog shit."

Anger flared white hot and exploded in his brain, blinding Austin to the peril of what he was about to do next. He spun on him like a top and in a heartbeat his fists flew out. Startling fast, Austin plowed into the slaver. Pent-up anger raged through his fists as the man shrank beneath his quick and powerful blows. Austin buckled him with a low jab and followed it with a bone-shattering uppercut that snapped his head back. Teeth jarred together, blood flowed, and the slaver dropped.

Out of the corner of Austin's eye, he saw Jim sawing at the reins of his startled horse.

Up on the wagon seat the driver grabbed for the pepper-box in his belt.

"Look out!" Austin shouted.

Jim's hand stabbed for the Walker. It cleared leather and boomed. . . .

Praise for
CRIPPLE CREEK:

SHADOW ROAD

DOUGLAS HIRT

BERKLEY BOOKS, NEW YORK

SHADOW ROAD

A Berkley Book / published by arrangement with
the author

PRINTING HISTORY
Berkley edition / August 1999

The Penguin Putnam Inc. World Wide Web site address is
http://www.penguinputnam.com

ISBN: 0-425-16992-8

BERKLEY®
Berkley Books are published by The Berkley Publishing Group,
a division of Penguin Putnam Inc.,
375 Hudson Street, New York, New York 10014.
BERKLEY and the "B" design are trademarks
belonging to Penguin Putnam Inc.

PRINTED IN THE UNITED STATES OF AMERICA

10 9 8 7 6 5 4 3 2 1

For Jim and Mary Sublette
who taught me much more than
''close only counts in horseshoes
and ichthyology.''
My best and fondest wishes.

ONE

Laconia, Arkansas, June 1860

Four weary mules hauled the heavy freight wagon up the dusty street, their heads hanging in the hot, humid air, their plodding slow but steady. They hardly flinched at the crack of the driver's long bullwhip, and stubbornly ignored his fiery curses that turned the muggy air blue. They had only one speed left in them this late in the day.

"Damn your mangy hide to hell, you worthless sack of bones." The whip cracked above the offside mule's ear. "Catfish cuttings is what you'll be if you don't liven your step. Think I ain't tired, too?"

On the seat beside him, a man with a shotgun across his knees managed a grin. An outrider mounted upon a tall chestnut rode to the left of the freighter, his eyes straight ahead, a rolled-up whip grasped in his right fist. He did not smile.

In the bed of the wagon huddled eleven blacks; old men, young children, and a few in between. The blank looks upon their faces were their first line of defense, masking their true thoughts. But their round wary eyes were in constant motion; the drab, clapboard buildings, the white, vaguely curious faces watching them from the sidewalks, the dogwood trees in the town square—all fodder for their apprehensive brains. Whatever thoughts they held, their expressions weren't revealing them.

At the Buster G. Calhoun Saloon, Leroy Walton pushed aside a batwing door and stepped out onto the sidewalk. As the door swung back, Theodore Marcs's fist caught it. The sidewalk's boards creaked behind Walton. He took two cigars from his vest pocket, handed one over his shoulder. Fishing for a match, he struck it against the turned column of the awning overhead, put the fire to their smokes, and nodded at the passing freighter that had drawn them outside in the first place. "Slavers come to town, Teddy," he said around the cigar in his mouth, flicking the match into the street.

Two or three other men from the Buster G. Calhoun Saloon stepped out to watch, too.

"Don't you know, there is going to be an auction next week, Cousin Leroy."

"So I hear. Saw a handbill tacked to the telegraph pole." Leroy returned the silver matchsafe to his vest pocket, removed a gold watch, and glanced at its porcelain dial. "Seven-thirty already."

Teddy doffed his tall, silk hat and brushed at an imagined spot. "Lordy, where did the day go?"

Leroy expanded his lungs until the buttons of his silk vest strained. "Smell that river, Teddy."

Marcs's hand slapped to his neck and he showed his cousin the blood splotch upon his palm. "Skeeters out already. The sonuvabitches are big as horseflies this year. You can thank the Mississippi for that."

Both men chuckled. The freighter with its cargo of slaves continued up the street, its doubletrees, harness traces, and chains rattling as the tall iron-rimmed wheels rumbled lowly. The evening air was beginning to cool as the freighter worked its way up the single narrow street of Laconia and some of the men returned to the saloon.

"We have time for another beer, cousin."

Leroy made a face. "I have had enough of Calhoun's warm beer."

"Well, what do you want to do?" Teddy yawned briefly and returned the hat to his head. Another swat produced another bloody spot, on the back of his hand this time. "Damned skeeters."

Walton leaned against the awning post, drawing thoughtfully on the cigar, watching the freighter rumble softly to the edge of town, to the livery there. "Let's go see what Everly has brought in with him this time."

Teddy frowned. "What do you want to go look at a bunch of coloreds for?"

"What else to do in this flea-bitten town?"

"We can go down to the river and watch the steamers pass by."

Leroy made a face, stepped down off the sidewalk, and started across the street toward the end of town. Teddy shuffled after him. "We can ride over to the Westfalls' place," he offered. "Maybe sit on the porch swing with Wanda Loo?"

"Wanda Loo? Wanda Loo Westfall is as frigid as an arctic winter. What do you want to waste your time with her for?"

The freighter had pulled to a stop in front of Samuel Hawthorne's Livery by the time they caught up with it.

"You niggers climb on down here and stand in line," the driver, Peter Deats, was shouting. "Get you black asses moving! Ain't got all day here!" As the slaves clambered off the back gate, Deats made a tick upon a paper on a board.

"Evening, Mr. Deats. Got yourself a wagonload of darkies I see."

Deats looked over. He was a short man with the body of a bull and a shock of red hair like a carrot patch. "Why, if it ain't young Mr. Leroy Walton, and his cousin Theodore. Yes, sir, we do got us a wagonload full. For the auction next week."

"Figured as much."

"What are you two doing in town—here, straighten up that line. Hurry it up. You, boy! Stand right there."

"Polishing the bar stools at Calhoun's." Teddy grinned. "Not much else to do in Laconia."

"That's a fact," Deats agreed.

The man on horseback, Franklin Everly, had dismounted and was handing leg irons to the fellow who had ridden shotgun. Leroy knew him only as Hobey, and whether that was his given name or a family name, he could not say.

Deats continued, "This is only the half of 'em. We are going back out in the morning. Expect to pick up another fifteen or twenty by time we get back. It should be a fine auction."

The slaves climbed out of the wagon one after another, some quite young, some looking too old to bring even a widow's mite of a bid at auction. Leroy's view stopped upon the face of a striking young black woman. There was a spark of anger in her dark eyes, unlike the docile down-turned cast he was used to seeing in a slave. She was a slender, finely proportioned woman in a blue cotton dress that had seen better days—striking! Leroy reckoned her to be his own age, or a year or two younger. Perhaps twenty-two at the most. She stood tall and straight, and when her eye caught his she did not immediately look down, as was the practice of slaves. There was a lively spirit hidden within this one, and that attracted Leroy almost as much as her beauty.

As Hobey fastened a shackle around her ankle, Leroy stepped in front of her, looking her up and down as if he was examining one of his father's prized racehorses.

"What's your name?"

Her eyes flashed with fiery anger.

Walton grabbed her chin and wrenched her head up and their eyes locked. "I asked you a question, wench."

The hard leather handle of a blacksnake whip rapped his wrist. "You can look at 'em but don't touch," Everly said. "If you like what you see, you will have a chance to bid on her next week, along with everyone else."

"I asked her a question."

Everly shot the girl a glance. "Tell him you name."

Her jaw worked tightly.

Everly unfurled the long black whip and let its tip curl upon the ground at his feet.

"Savilla."

"Savilla what?" Everly said.

"Savilla, suh."

"That's better." He glanced at Leroy. "Satisfied?"

"Yes, thank you."

Franklin Everly continued down the line with Hobey, shackling the slaves.

Walton grinned at his cousin. "Savilla," he said. He nodded his head in approval and turned to Deats. "Why is her master sending that one to the block, Mr. Deats?"

"Hmm?" Deats looked up from the board. "Oh, well, let's see." He flipped a couple sheets of paper, read, then chuckled. "Seems her owner has a son who had taken to dallying with the wench. Reckon he didn't want no mulattoes running around the place."

The men laughed.

"You don't say?" Walton drawled softly, his interest piqued even more. "She's a sporting wench, heh?"

"Don't know as I'd go so far as to say that. All I know is the old man wanted her away from his son." Deats gave him a wink. "I have to admit, she's a right handsome filly—that is, if you like dark meat."

"She's got spirit, too. I like that."

Deats frowned. "Whenever you find spirit in a nigger, best you beat it out of her before she goes to making trouble for you. That's the last thing anyone in these here parts needs, a nigger with spirit."

Leroy and Teddy lingered until the slaves were marched into Hawthorne's big barn. After the tall doors had been rolled shut the two cousins wandered among the lengthening shadows down to the wharves and spent fifteen minutes watching slaves load crates onto a riverboat tied up there. Later that evening they returned to Calhoun's Saloon, sipped whiskey until late into the night, somehow found their way back to their carriage, and drove home.

Texas, six weeks earlier

"More coffee, Mr. Fandango?"

"Yes, ma'am, Mrs. Caywood. Did I ever tell you that you

make the finest coffee in all of Texas—and that covers a lot of territory.''

Juanita Caywood took the pot from her stove with a quilted hot pad. ''Oh, at least once a day,'' she said, and filled the china cup Austin Fandango had set upon the table. She looked up at her husband. ''And you, Mr. Caywood?''

Jim Caywood was tall as a good-size door, and just about as broad at the shoulders, although over the last twenty years his middle has been reaching in that direction, too. He grinned, gave his foreman a wink, and said, ''With an endorsement like that, how can I pass it up? It isn't often a man gets to have a taste of the 'finest coffee in all of Texas.' ''

Juanita Caywood was a remarkably attractive woman. True, her once coal-black hair was now shot through with streaks of gray, and her face showed the strain of frontier living—showed it in the creases radiating from her eyes and the corners of her mouth. What else could one expect after a lifetime of battling a fierce Texas sun and the hot winds that sucked moisture from flesh just as surely as they did the rank grass and the watering holes scattered across the JC Connected range?

Jim Caywood's hand surrounded the fragile cup, his finger being too large to comfortably navigate the tiny handle of Mrs. Caywood's finest china.

Austin Fandango was nearly as tall as Caywood, but lacked a good fifty pounds on the older man. He glanced back to the notes on the sheaf of papers he had brought with him to the ranch house, a native-sandstone-and-log dogtrot that Jim had built twenty-five years earlier. It was a good house. It had seen them through windstorms, gullywashers, and droughts, had stood solid against dust devils and blistering summer days. Had fended off Comanche attacks and Mexican marauders. Jim and Juanita raised two children within its strong walls. They buried the son in the family plot out back and sent the daughter back east to school, where she met a man and stayed. Now it was only the two of them, and a dozen or so permanent employees . . . and Austin, who was more a son than an employee.

"We made a count and came up with seventeen hundred and eighty-seven head." Austin looked up from the paper and grinned. "Biggest herd yet, Mr. Caywood. We will fill the stockyards at St. Louis with JC Connected beef this year."

From another part of the house came a woman's light laughter followed by the low voice of a man. Juanita frowned and shook her head.

Jim and Austin grinned.

"Only a few more months," Jim said, as if reading his wife's thoughts.

"These girls," she said. "They get marriage in their head and they are at once useless around the house."

Austin said, "If it is any consolation, Mrs. Caywood, we will be taking Walter with us on the drive. After today you will have Betsy back—at least for the next eight weeks."

"Yes, and then the wedding." Juanita shook her head and returned the coffeepot to the stove. "So much to do." She looked at her husband and came as close to scowling as Austin could ever remember. "You finally find good help and then what? They meet a man, get married, and leave. We will have to find another girl to help around the house, yes?"

"We will have to find another girl, yes," Jim replied, his craggy face creasing into a smile, his brown eyes glinting in the sunlight through the kitchen window. Jim's skin was tough as old boot leather, burned nut brown by the sun. Sometimes Juanita would joke that she could hardly tell him apart from their foreman, but always Austin would chime in and announce that Mr. Caywood still had a long way to go before equaling his fine hue.

"Walter is not half-bad at wrangling either," Jim pointed out. "We will be losing him, too."

"But not until we get back from St. Louis," Austin added, gathering up his papers. "Anything else we need to discuss before tomorrow?"

Jim set his coffee cup on the table. "I don't think so—" Juanita's expression stopped him. "What is it?"

"Will you be coming right home after the drive?" she

asked. From the concern Austin heard in her voice, he knew what was on Juanita Caywood's mind.

Jim said, "No, not directly."

"The Shadow Road again?"

"I've been taking it back every year now going on twenty, I see no reason why I should not this year."

"I wish this year you would not."

"Why?"

Juanita shook her head. "I do not know. A feeling?"

Austin did not particularly want to ride the Shadow Road this year either—not that he ever really wanted to. But there were bitter troubles roiling just below the surface these days. More so than usual. Talk of secession was becoming widespread, even in Texas, and especially in the Deep South. It was the last place a black man would care to find himself—even a free black man. But Austin had ridden the dark trail with Big Jim Caywood for twenty years, and if he intended to do it again this year, Austin was prepared to remain at his side.

"I have to. You know I promised—"

"Yes, I know," she said, interrupting him.

In twenty years Austin had only heard pieces of the story. Jim had never once spoken plainly of it to him. The only person still alive who knew the full of it was Juanita. All Austin knew was that it had something to do with the scar that lanced Jim's chest above the heart, made by a Comanche arrow, and a promise given a stranger and never broken. Beyond that, it was just as much a mystery to Austin as it was to every other man and woman who worked on the JC Connected. But a mystery that every year compelled Big Jim Caywood to ride the Shadow Road, to buy slaves at auction, and a job on his ranch.

Juanita nodded. It was impossible to argue with a man like Jim Caywood. "Very well, I know you do what you must." She gave Austin a sideways glance. There was hidden meaning there, he was certain, but it only made the mystery so much deeper. "If you must go, then maybe you will try to find a nice girl to take Betsy's place, yes?"

Jim took Juanita's hand into his huge paw and smiled. It

was about as close to affection as he ever allowed in public, although Austin knew Jim and Juanita loved each other deeply. "I will look for a girl for you, yes," he said. Just then Betsy giggled from the back room.

Jim laughed.

Juanita shook her head.

Austin grinned as he took his hat from the peg by the back door. "I'll have the men ready to move out tomorrow bright and early, Mr. Caywood." He gave Juanita a wink. "There is just no keeping young lovebirds apart, ma'am, but Walter will come to his senses again once on the trail a day. And so will Betsy—leastwise until we get back."

"Austin," she said, looking at him the way a concerned mother might regard her only son. "Speaking of lovebirds, is it not about time you find yourself a nice girl? It's not good for a man to be alone, and you are no yearling. You will need someone to look after you in your quiet years."

"Juanita," Jim said, "you bring this up every year."

"Well, what better time or place for Austin to look, yes?"

Austin gave her a broad, toothy grin and shook his head. "Not me, ma'am. I'll not be put to harness by any gal, and that's a fact. A man stuck with love is about as worthless as a barrel of shucks."

"Austin," she said disapprovingly.

He grinned at her, stepped out into the bright, Texas morning, levered his hat onto his head, and strode away toward the barn.

The spring drive began early the next morning; eight cowboys, eighteen hundred head of mixed cows and calves, and a rangy old steer named Bobalong—a veteran of a dozen trail drives, in the lead. Bobalong knew his business. He kept the cows moving at a steady pace that allowed them to graze along the way and, if all went as planned, add a few extra pounds between the open ranges of Texas and the cattle pens at St. Louis.

A horse wrangler name Phillip Warren looked after the sixty-horse remuda that Jim had bought at twelve dollars a head and intended to sell in St. Louis for eighteen. The

brand-new Studebaker chuck wagon was manned by a
middle-aged Mexican named Pedro Ortiz. This spring drive
up the Shawnee Trail had become a tradition with Ortiz, and
he hired on each year because of a long-standing friendship
with Jim Caywood. The rest of the year he made saddles and
harnesses in a shop behind his adobe house that he sold to
a store in San Antonio, a hundred miles to the south.

When the drive was over, Ortiz, Warren, and two or three
wranglers would return to Texas with Bobalong. The other
men had hired on only for the duration of the drive and
afterward were free to sign on with other companies. A few
would work their way north to Chicago—some as far east
as New York City. But they all eventually ended up back in
Texas in time for the spring roundup the following year.

A week into the drive the men and the cows had settled
comfortably into the routine of trail life. A month later, as
they were nearing the Red River and Indian Territory, they
came across their first Indians.

TWO

Willis stepped tentatively upon the wide brick walkway and with growing trepidation lifted his wide eyes to the tall white house with the green shutters at each window. It was made of wood and small, compared with some Willis had seen, but imposing nonetheless when judged against the dirt-floor shack that he, his mother and father, and sister lived in.

The house had three stories and was fashioned after the style of a Southern plantation house. Six chimneys sprouted from its roof, and a wide shuttered porch hugged three sides of its second floor. Yes, compared with his own hovel, Master Thomas Hill's house was fit for a king . . . maybe even the king of Canada!

Ahead loomed the tall, wide door; an imposing thing for Willis even though it was only the back door—painted green to match the shutters. Being a back entrance, used mainly by the kitchen slaves, it was simple and sturdy, constructed of wooden planks bolted together, having a single small pane of glass set into it. Through this window Willis caught a glimpse of movement in the house; a black face above a white apron was all and then the fleeting figure was gone.

Willis gulped down a lump the size of a patroller's fist.

This wasn't the first time he'd been summoned to the big house. And each time he had stood in the master's presence, it had been followed by a stern bawling-out and extra tasks piled on top of his regular workload.

"To pay back the damages you have caused me, Willis," was always Master Thomas Hill's reason. "Willis, why must you always be so careless and break things?" the rotund white man would lament.

At least Willis had never been bucked and whipped, not like some slaves he had heard tell of who belonged to other men. Master Thomas was a Christian man who did not believe in whipping. But Hill put up with no foolishness, and Christian or not, it did not stop the man from working his colored folks to a tattered end!

With feet of lead, Willis started up the walkway. He half considered wheeling around and running away. But he knew he'd never make it past the patrollers. Toward Canada he would have gladly turned his steps—that is, if he only knew where Canada was. Up north someplace, he had been told once. Maybe just the other side of St. Louis? Willis had heard a passel of wonderful things about St. Louis, but it was Canada that was mostly whispered about by the field hands during the hot workdays. Most all the older slaves talked wistfully about Canada, with its freedom, where the Fugitive Slave Law did not threaten to drag a runaway back to the shackles he had escaped.

Willis suddenly frowned. If he ran away he would have to leave his family. At least Thomas Hill did not believe in breaking up families . . . not unless he had to. Running away was something always dreamed of but never really contemplated—except by a few brave and hearty souls.

Willis would never be one of them.

"Likely bust a foot in de trying. And dem pattyroller would come and tie me in a bundle and drag me back. Then Marster Thomas would pile even *mo'* work onto po' Willis's shoulders."

The door grew closer and Willis's steps heavier. "It warn't my fault dem blamed mules went to high-bucking jest when I got to taking Misses Alice's new dressin' mirror off it."

Snatching the ragged straw hat from his head, Willis raised a hand, hesitated, then rapped upon the door. Not a loud rap. Maybe no one would hear? But someone did hear.

The door opened and Marcella, one of the Hill's three house slaves, stood there in her black dress and white apron. Her fat black face was pinched in a smirk, and there was a taunting lilt in her high voice. "What you want here, Willis? Why ain't you out hoeing dem rows? Or is it 'cause you went an' busted up young Misses Alice's birthday mirror dat you stand here with your hat in your hand and your face lookin' like your mama done give you cast'r oil?"

Willis never much cared for Marcella and her haughty better-than-thou attitude, just because she was a house slave and no longer a field hand. He did not much care for Lilly either, although for different reasons. Lilly was always bustling about and fretting over this and that, and wielding her feather duster like the world would come to an end the day a speck of dust was to light upon *her* settee, or *her* dining table.

Of the three house slaves, it was only Old Samuel, Master Thomas's boy, that Willis got along well with. Old Samuel was a fastidious director of all of Thomas's personal affairs. He daily polished Hill's boots to a spit shine, and brushed his suits with Lilly-like zeal, but he never ever called them *his* suits. He was a reliable confidant to the master of the house, a sage in time of trouble, a walking, talking catalog of all that was going on in the master's life. But more than that, Samuel knew his place and never strayed from it. Even though he carried more authority than all thirty-eight of Thomas Hill's slaves all rolled together, Samuel understood that he was still a slave himself and he never allowed his position of authority to go to his head. His first allegiance was always to the other black folks on the farm, and when he could, he would sneak small favors to them.

Willis remembered a day last fall when Thomas Hill, his wife, Louise, and their daughter, Alice were away visiting family in Natchez. Old Samuel invited Willis down into the cellar, where he had a jug of whiskey, and the two of them proceeded to get rip-roaring drunk.

Willis grinned at the memory now. That had been the highlight of his whole life—all eighteen years of it!

"Well, what are you here for, boy?"

The pleasant thought shattered against the stony shores of Marcella's scowl. "Marster Thomas send word he want to talk to me."

"Hmm. He did? Well, I ain't surprised." Her scowl deepened. "Wipe your boots good an' clean. Don't want you tramping no dirt in on my swept carpet. Now follow me. An' don't touch nothin'!"

Willis trailed her broad black dress into a hallway where the three fire buckets hung upon the wall. They passed the inside kitchen where the food cooked on stoves in the kitchen back behind the house was made ready to serve the family. The hallway ran straight through the middle of the house. Ahead Willis saw the front door. The ladies' parlor lay to the right of the hallway, just beyond the dining room. To the left were the rooms where Hill kept his hunting rifles and where friends and business associates sometimes gathered to play euchre, talk politics, and sip whiskey.

Marcella did not take Willis that far into the house, however, wheeling instead down a hallway that passed a flight of stairs to the family's sleeping quarters on the second floor. They were grand rooms. Willis had seen them one day while carrying a package for Mrs. Louise. All the bedrooms conveniently opening out onto the veranda, where the shutters where swung wide in the early mornings and late evenings, and most all winter. It was only the summer months when they would be closed during the heat of the day.

The passageway led to the east wing of the house, where Hill had his office and library. A door in one wall connected with the game room. It was presently closed.

Marcella stopped in the doorway of Hill's office and waited for the white man to look up.

"Yes, Marcella?" he said, dipping a pen into an inkwell.

"Young Willis here to see you, suh. Says you ask for him?"

"Oh, yes."

Willis did not like the sound of that.

Hill set the pen down, powdered his drying ink, and pressed a blotter to it. "Come in, Willis."

Stepping around Marcella, Willis shuffled to the front of the desk, fingers crushing the brim of his dilapidated hat, eyes cast down at the brocade carpet beneath his feet. He was distantly aware of Marcella's heavy footsteps receding back down the hallway, then only the silence, a long-drawn-out silence broken only by the soft, steady *tick-tock tick-tock* of the banjo clock in the corner. A trickle of sweat formed on his forehead at the line of his tight black hair and trickled down his cheek. He was afraid to wipe it, so he just let it flow, and another, and another, until finally Thomas Hill spoke.

"Willis, Willis, Willis. Whatever am I going to do with you?"

"Suh?"

"Let's see. Two summers ago it was the window to the dining room."

"De ladder slipped while I was standing on it, suh. Dat window breakin', it couldn't be helped, what wid me fallin' through it like I done."

"Accidents happen to everyone, Willis," Hill agreed. "But then just a few months later you let a wagon load of lumber for the new barn roll into the kitchen. Took out the whole corner and we had to build a new one."

Willis grinned briefly. "Yo' done build yo'self one fine-lookin' kitchen. Ruth, she say it de finest kitchen in all of Arkansas, and de cornpones dat dat new stove makes is mouthwaterin'." He looked back at the toes of his worn-out boots, his smile fading. "De brake done slip on dat wagon, suh. I couldn't help it."

"And what about the hoist in the hay barn?"

"Worms in de wood done eat it clear through. Soon as it take on de weight of dat bale it snapped like a chicken-wing bone."

Thomas Hill steepled his fingers above the paperwork upon his desk, his eyes boring through Willis just like the termites had bored through the hay hoist. Willis dared not look up. He ached to wipe the sweat sliding slow and sticky down his forehead and over his cheek, salty at the corner of his mouth. His fingers worried the brim of his battered straw hat, crushing it almost beyond usefulness.

With a note of exasperation, Thomas Hill said, "And I suppose you have a good excuse why you allowed those goats into Mrs. Hill's rose garden?"

Willis shook his head. "No, suh. I . . . I just didn't see dem sneak away like dey done."

Hill considered a long moment before continuing. "And now this. That mirror which you broke was a birthday gift to Miss Alice. You know that, don't you?"

"Yes, suh," he replied softly.

"Do you know how disappointed she was seeing it lying shattered upon the ground?"

Willis nodded his head, eyes firmly fixed upon the toes of his work boots.

"Have you nothing to say?"

"De mule got spooky."

"Did it never occur to you to unhitch the mule, if it was skittish? Or at the very least see to it that the animal was securely tied to a rail?"

"No, suh. I didn't think—"

"Didn't think!" Hill exploded, driving his fist onto the papers on his desk. "That is the problem with you, Willis, you don't think! You *never* think! What shall I ever do with you? I've half a mind to take a blacksnake to you and beat some common sense into that dense skull of yours!"

Willis rarely saw Thomas Hill get so angry that his anger would burst from him, and this eruption instantly set him to quaking and wringing his hat until the straw fibers cracked in his fists.

As quickly as the storm came on, it passed, and for a long quiet moment the banjo clock in the corner ticked in antiphony with Willis's racing heartbeat. Soft footsteps entered the room and stopped behind and to one side of him.

All at once Hill drew in a sharp breath. The sudden inhalation was a hammer blow that made Willis jerk to attention. "Yes, Samuel?" he said, staring past Willis's left shoulder.

"Mr. Harold Ricter come to see you, suh. Him waiting in the parlor right now."

"Oh, yes. He has an appointment. I nearly forgot. Thank you, Samuel." Hill composed himself. With his voice firmly in control again he said, "You can go now, Willis. We will continue this at a later time."

"Yes, suh. Thank you, suh." Willis backed toward the door. Seeing Samuel's tight, unsmiling face was almost more of a blow than the bawling-out he had just received from Thomas Hill. Samuel's stern look told him that this infraction was a serious one, and that serious consequences could very well follow. At the doorway Hill's voice stopped him.

"Willis."

"Suh?"

"To pay for the mirror you broke, Willis, you will work extra hours. There shall be no more Sunday afternoons off. Directly after church services you will resume your tasks. Is that understood?"

"Yes, suh, Marster Thomas." He turned on his heel and started down the long hallway, listening to the voices in the room behind him as he hurried away.

"Samuel, when is Mr. Everly due through here again?"

"Mr. Franklin Everly, him say him come back to dese parts before the next auction in Laconia."

"And when might that be?"

"About six week, suh."

Hill's voice turned regretful. "Well, when Franklin shows up, tell him I'll have one he can take with him."

"Yes, suh."

That was all Willis heard before Marcella snagged him by the shirtsleeve and tugged him along the passageway to the back door and outside.

"What do you make of them, Mr. Fandango?"

"Comanche."

Jim nodded. "Pretty far east for Comanches, aren't they? Do you recognize that big buck in the front?"

Austin squinted and shook his head. "Too far off. Want me to see what they want?"

"I already know what they want." Caywood reined his horse around and rode back to the chuck wagon. Ortiz read the look on his face and reached behind the seat for Jim's heavy Colt Walker revolver.

"Better give me mine, too," Austin said. "And my rifle." Austin checked the caps on his Colt's Navy, shoved the revolver into its leather, and slid his long Sharps .52-caliber into the rifle boot on his saddle.

Walter Bidley rode up alongside them. "Want me to ride along with you, Mr. Caywood?"

"No. I want you to keep the cows here, Walt. Bring the stragglers up, bunch them, and let them graze. Mr. Fandango and I will go talk with those Indians."

"Think you ought to take some of the boys with you, Mr. Caywood?"

"Better to leave the men here. Some of those Comanches might get it in their heads to try and run the herd off."

"Don't look to be that many," Walter said.

Austin grinned and shook his head. "Don't let what you see fool you. Comanches aren't ones to go and show their hand too soon. Might be fifty waiting just on the other side of that rise."

"Mr. Fandango is right. Keep a sharp eye on those cows."

"We'll keep 'em bunched up," Walter assured Caywood.

Jim and Austin turned their horses toward the rise of land.

The Comanches remained astride their ponies, three or four hundred yards off. As the distance closed, Austin saw that the leader of this band was a man he knew.

"It's War Eagle."

Jim Caywood kept his eyes ahead as their horses loped across the Texas prairie. "The chief is far from his regular stomping grounds."

Drought was a common plague in this land and some years the Indians fared worse than others. Some years they traveled far and wide in search of game and water not made bitter by alkali. Already the grass needed rain, but Jim had his doubts this year would be better than last. Another hundred yards and he noted not only War Eagle's sharp features, his dark, drawn cheeks, but also the lean look of the other men with him.

Austin said, "Last time I seen War Eagle was three or four years back. He and his people were camped along the Canadian, over in New Mexico Territory."

The two men reined in and covered the last few yards at a walk. The Comanches were not wearing war paint, but a prudent man did not take chances. Austin's view skipped over the eight warriors. They were armed only with bows and arrows, and war lances. Their weapons were held across their knees in an open gesture of peace.

Jim lifted a hand and said, "War Eagle. It has been many seasons since we talked. I am pleased to see that you still ride and hunt."

"Big Jim. Yes, many winters from the council fires. I see you come now and much happy." He looked at Austin and his mouth lifted in a smile. "And Buffalo Man. I see you far off, know it you."

Austin laughed. "Not surprised. Even a Texas sun can't burn men to my fine dark hue."

"You're a long way from home, War Eagle." Jim looked at the handful of braves with him. "Where are the rest of your people?"

"We ride three moons, follow buffalo. Many days now we hunt." War Eagle's hands moved in unison with his words. Austin knew a little of the hand talk of the plains Indians, and that it was not uncommon for an Indian to use both signs and words. The chief shook his head. "Buffalo go away. No meat. Women hungry, little ones much hungry."

Austin glanced at Jim and got the small nod he expected. "How many people travel with you, War Eagle?"

The chief said that there were forty-seven, counting women and children.

Jim said, "Would three fat Texas cows help fill the hole in your people's bellies?"

The Comanche nodded his head.

"Thought so. Mr. Fandango, please cut out three head for the chief and bring them up."

Austin galloped back to the waiting men and passed on Jim's order. Ten minutes later he was driving the animals across the short grass to the waiting Indians. Immediately the Comanche took possession of the animals and two warriors drove them down the back side of the long hill and over another ridge.

War Eagle grinned and nodded his head. "You good friend, Big Jim." He looked at Austin. "Buffalo Man, him strong warrior. Friend of War Eagle, too."

"You and your people have yourselves a big feast tonight," Austin said. "And I hope that tomorrow you will find many buffalo and sweet water."

"You go that way?" War Eagle asked, indicating a northeasterly direction.

"We go to the place of the big lodges on the Mississippi. We call it St. Louis."

"Hmm. Keep scout eyes open, Big Jim. Many Cherokee lodges that way."

"I know. The Cherokees drive a hard bargain, but Mr. Fandango and I have the remedy they are looking for." Caywood raised his hand again in parting. "I wish you good hunting, Chief War Eagle, and many long seasons, many wives, and many children."

The Comanches turned their horses down the hill and in a few minutes were gone.

"That went easy enough," Jim said, starting back to the herd.

"Three cows is cheap insurance to pay for a safe passage," Austin noted.

"Only wish the Cherokee were as easy to pay off."

Austin laughed. "The Cherokee have been around you white men too long. Three beeves might satisfy a band of hungry Comanches, but it ain't worth a barrel of shucks to a bunch of commerce-minded Cherokees."

"No, the cutthroats want ten cents a head to cross their land. Reckon that must be why they are known as one of the 'civilized' tribes?"

• • •

The JC Connected herd continued north and east. They managed the Red River crossing with only a few head lost and no casualties among the men, for the river was low this year. In Indian Territory the Cherokee Light Horse police patrol extracted a one-hundred-seventy-five-dollar toll from Jim's purse of traveling expenses. After that it was an easy three weeks across the territory and through some of the prettiest Missouri countryside ever to meet the eyes of the travel-weary men.

When the cattle pens in St. Louis were finally reached, the cattle counted, sold, and the men paid their one hundred dollars each, they sailed their hats into the overcast sky and scattered to the shops, the saloons, and parlor houses.

The drive had been mostly uneventful. Walter Bidley was anxious to get back to his bride-to-be. Pedro Ortiz had his business to return, too. Phillip Warren had a wife and three kids. They, along with old Bobalong, would be heading back to Texas in a few days.

Jim and Austin had other plans. Their way back home would be by the Shadow Road, and this year for some reason—a reason Austin could not quite understand—that made him as uncomfortable as sleeping on a ticky mattress.

THREE

Although every state south of the Mason-Dixon was worried about the growing hostility in the North toward the problem of slavery, Missouri seemed to have been infected by the fervor of the debate over this "peculiar institution" more than all the others. Maybe it was because she rubbed shoulders with Iowa and Illinois, both strongholds of anti-slavery sentiment. Or perhaps it was the result of the growing Kansas Territory just to the west of her, where the debate over slavery was hot and heavy—some men in Congress wanted to repeal the Missouri Compromise altogether.

Even the citizens of Missouri were not of a like mind on the matter, torn as they were between the two camps. All in all, it made life for a black man mighty uncomfortable . . . not that life for a black man was particularly easy anywhere in the United States, North or South, Austin mused.

"Cut out two extra horses from that remuda," Jim had told Phillip Warren just before selling the entire string of animals to the horse merchant. "Pick good ones and put saddles on their backs."

Warren knew his horseflesh. He had selected two mares, a claybake and a coyote dun, so gentle that Austin figured they could be staked out on a hairpin.

When Jim and Austin rode down into town, one of the spare horses was carrying two saddlebags filled with the gold Jim had gotten for his cows. St. Louis was a sprawling city, stretching out in every direction. It was enough to give a man a kink in his neck just looking at all of it. Every year the town seemed to grow bigger. Austin tried to recall how it had been when he first saw the place, almost twenty years ago. Back then it was mainly a collection of streets running alongside the wharves on the river, still showing much of its Spanish ancestry.

Today St. Louis was about the biggest and busiest place on earth! Austin had heard rumors that Chicago was bigger, and that might be a fact, but he'd never been there to know the truth of it. The wharves were lined with steamboats as far as the eye could see, twenty blocks' worth of boats! A solid line of them tied up from Belcher's sugar refinery all the way to the Almond Street Landing.

The bustle of commerce was all around them, a hundred boats off-loading cargo, or taking it on. The air was gray with the smoke of their stacks, the sun only an indefinite glare through the heavy haze. Drays pulled by one or two mules rattled along the wharf road in an endless stream. Hundreds of half-naked black men with great burdens upon their shoulders marched up and down the gangplanks.

The sharp voices of men barking orders blended with the shrill of steam whistles, the clanging bells, steam hissing from valve cocks, and the swoosh of water splashing in the paddle boxes as paddle wheels beat the river into a dirty froth.

The confusion of activity was enough to make a simple cowboy's head spin. Given his druthers, Austin would have taken the quietness of a vast Texan prairie to this any day.

"Reckon we can find one to take us south?" Austin mused as they reined to a halt to watch it all.

"Suppose you and me find out?"

As they started their horses to the levee, Austin was aware of the eyes that glanced up and settled upon him. He straightened up a little taller in the saddle and urged his horse ahead until its nose stretched just a tad beyond Jim's horse.

"Feeling your oats, are you?" Jim said as they drew up on the wharves and swung out of their saddles.

"If they want to gawk, I figured I'd give them something to gawk at."

Jim grinned and handed Austin the reins to his horse and the spare. "Wait here for me. I'll go see about booking us passage down to New Orleans. And keep an eye on that." He stabbed a thick finger at the saddlebags.

"It's safe with me."

Jim climbed to the top of the wharf and stopped, studying out the river, up and down. He stood there with his hands on his hips, looking like an old gnarled oak tree that someone had planted right in the middle of all that traffic. Then he swept his hat off his head, ran fingers through his sparse gray hair, and tugged the hat back, low over his eyes. Austin saw Jim speak to a man passing by. The man pointed up the river and Jim bent his steps that way until Austin lost sight of him in the crowd.

Somewhere during the six weeks pushing cows up the Shawnee Trail, spring had become summer. Now the heat and humidity lay heavy along the river, like wet woolen blankets, smothering the levee, where it mingled with the odor of burning garbage, human sweat, manure, and the sickly-sweet odor wafting down from Belcher's sugar refinery. Searching for a spot of shade, Austin spied an alleyway that offered an escape from some of the heat. He crossed the levee road and brought the horses into the alley. It was only marginally cooler here. A breeze would have helped, but the air was dead still. At least the sun's hazy glare did not reach this place, and for a moment he was out of the traffic.

Leaning against the building, Austin fished up tobacco and paper from his shirt pocket and built himself a cigarette. He listened to the foot traffic on the boardwalk but paid it little attention as the match flared in his fingers and he put it to the cigarette. This St. Louis boardwalk was a beehive of activity; mostly heavy-booted boatmen dressed in rough, homespun, clothes, the occasional woman and child, smartly dressed businessmen, riverboat clerks, captain, firemen. More folks than Austin saw in all the ten months back in Texas.

He flagged out the match and flicked it into a muddy puddle just beyond the entrance to the alley.

"Newspaper?" a young voice called out. "Buy a newspaper. Only one nickel. Get yo' newspaper here!"

"Boy," a man said sharply.

"Suh? Yo' wont a newspaper?"

"Gimme one, boy."

Something in the man's tone piqued Austin's interest. He levered himself away from the building and peered up the sidewalk. A few feet beyond was a black boy not more than ten or eleven years old, looking up at two white men. The boy wore a tattered shirt, frayed trousers, and no shoes. He had a bundle of papers under one arm.

"Yes, suh." The boy peeled a paper from the bundle and handed it over.

The men looked to be in their mid-thirties. They might have been travelers, or simply workers from one of the steamers . . . no, travelers, Austin decided. The taller of the two carried a cardboard suitcase. The other, a thickset man with a narrow brown beard circling his chin only, had a canvas sack over his shoulder. Both wore broad straw hats that had seen better days.

The tall one set his suitcase down and snatched the newspaper away from the boy. He rifled through the pages, which amounted to only four or six, folded it over, and began running a finger down the page.

"That will be one nickel, suh," the boy said.

"Look here, Mitch," the tall man said, stabbing at the paper.

The bearded face leaned near and dark eyes narrowed. "Says the *Pride of Alton* is leaving at four o'clock. Looks like it puts into Laconia all right, Randy."

"Reckon that's the boat we ought to be on, then," Randy said.

"What we waiting for? I got just enough money left in my pocket for deck passage."

Randy grinned. "Come tomorrow we'll be back where folks treat us right."

"And pay us right."

The men laughed at what must have been a private joke. They still had not paid for the paper and the boy was getting nervous, shifting from foot to foot.

"Suh. I need my nickel."

Randy wadded up the paper, tossed it into the street, and grabbed up the suitcase. "See? I don't have your paper no more, boy," he said. "Be on your way."

"No, suh. My marster will whip me to a tatter if I don't bring back a nickel for dat paper."

A knot had begun to harden in Austin's stomach when the men laughed again and started across the street.

"Please, suh," the boy implored.

Mitch stopped and wheeled back. "Give the kid a nickel, Randy. Look, he's about to pee in his britches."

Randy grinned and drew a coin from his pocket. He held it out, but snatched it back at the last moment, and kept it just beyond the boy's reach. The men had a good laugh. Randy said, "Let's see you dance for your nickel, boy."

A crowd began to gather. Each time the boy would reach, Randy would yank the coin back and laugh.

"Damn," Austin whispered, and stepped out of the alley. Just then Randy tossed the nickel. It cartwheeled through the air and splashed into the muddy puddle of water at the toe of Austin's boots.

The boy made a dive for it.

"Leave it be, son," Austin said. The deep rumble of his voice brought the two men around and every eye was turned on Austin.

The knot tightened in his belly.

The boy went to his knees for the coin.

"I said let it be." Austin's stern command stayed the lad's hand. He shifted his view to Randy. "You fish that nickel out, mister."

Randy was too dumbfounded to speak at once, and when he finally found his voice, it was edged with disbelief. "Are you talking to me, boy?"

Austin stiffened. He had never been very good at holding back when his temper was up, and he felt it flaring now. Jim Caywood had warned him more than once to keep a tight rein on it, to count three and maybe more. Austin always tried, he really did, but sometimes it was like staying atop a bucking cayuse, sometimes all you could do was fly off.

Softly, Austin breathed, "One." He leveled his voice and said to Randy, "I haven't been a boy for over twenty years, mister. You heard me. Fetch that coin up and put it in this boy's hand. Then you can tell him how sorry you are for making him dance for his rightful due."

Randy's jaw dropped. Around him came chuckles as the crowd thickened, seething with anticipation. "What right do you have telling *me* what to do? Where is your master?"

"I'm my own master, and as for rights, I've got my fists and my gun to back up my rights." His hand came to rest upon the walnut grip of the revolver at his side. "You make the choice which one it will be."

Randy had not noticed the revolver. He stared at it now, then at Austin, and said, "Who gave you a gun? My God, Mitch," he said to his partner, "is it legal for a nigger to carry a gun?"

"Don't know, Randy. I ain't never seen such a thing happen before. But I don't think Sheriff Calhoun would allow such a thing down in Phillips County."

Randy was nearly as tall as Austin, but he lacked his weight. He'd not last long beneath Austin's bare knuckles. But Mitch was another story. He was a short bulldog of a man with a thick neck and a crooked nose that had been broken a time or two in the past. Mitch was a fighter. He would be hard to knock down.

Austin determined all of this in the half-dozen heartbeats that passed in silence. The crowd had backed away a few paces, wisely giving the three of them room if lead began to fly. The heat was so oppressive that few men wore coats, and Austin did not see a gun on the two gents, or on anyone else in the crowd. But that meant little. Vest-pocket derringers and revolvers were common enough.

Mitch stepped forward now. "You are an arrogant sonuvabitch, aren't you?" He dropped his canvas bag and came another step. You apparently ain't from these here parts, boy. Where you from?"

"Texas, where men don't taunt little boys who can't fight back."

"Texas?"

Someone in the crowd said, "He come in on that cattle drive the other day. I seen him."

"Well, someone down Texas way has been lax in your upbringing, boy. You drop that gun belt and I will teach you the proper way for a nigger to act around white folks."

The paper boy was jumpy as a long-tail cat in a room full of rocking chairs. "I'll just get my nickel and go," he said, peering up at Austin. "I do't want no fightin' on account of me. If my marster ever finds out—"

"Let the money be, son. One of these two white men will be fishing it out for you directly."

Mitch laughed. "Boy, you sure got a lesson to learn, and school is about to begin." His fists came up, bunched and hard, and he hunched forward as if he had done this once or twice before.

Austin was no stranger to the "gentleman's art," or the not-so-gentlemanly way men worked out their differences in barrooms or back alleys. He unbuckled his gun belt and put it over the horn of his saddle. "Son, hold these for me while I tend to this," he said, putting the reins to the horses in his hand.

Austin didn't hunch forward, nor did his fingers bunch into fists at once. He stood tall and limber as a steel spring. He was wiry enough to dodge Mitch's fists, and had reach over the shorter man. So for the moment, until a hole opened in Mitch's defenses, the two circled, neither throwing the first punch.

"Well, well, what have we here?" The voice boomed like thunder and the next moment Jim Caywood cut through the crowd like a tall ship parting stormy waves. He stepped between the two men and grinned.

"Austin, this is no time for having fun. We've work ahead of us." Though his words carried a faint undertone of humor, his eyes were deadly serious and warning.

Austin caught Jim's meaning. A brawl on the JC Connected would amount to no consequences, other than some blood and broken teeth or nose. Even in their part of Texas, where slavery was legal but not often practiced, and where Austin was known and generally liked by most of the folks, a bit of fisticuffs would be acceptable. But here in St. Louis, where folks took their slaving seriously, taking on this white man could have dire results.

"Is this your nigger?" Mitch growled.

Caywood wheeled around and looked down at the man. Even at seventy years old, Jim Caywood was a formidable sight, with shoulders wide as hogsheads and fists the size of hams. If Austin could not take down this white man and get away with it, Jim Caywood could. And Mitch knew it. When you come face-to-face with a mountain of hard flesh, you suddenly remember your manners. "I . . . I mean, this colored boy up and picked a fight with me and my partner for no reason." Mitch nodded at Randy.

Randy said, "That's the way it happened."

"Austin rides with me," was the only explanation Mitch was going to get, and he knew it.

Backing up a step, Mitch attempted to repair the damage to his pride. "Well, I don't know how you deal with your coloreds down in Texas, but here we teach them to respect their betters."

"Oh, you do, do you?"

"We do."

Jim glanced at Austin. "Were you disrespectful to these gentleman?"

"I was. And I was about to get a whole lot more disrespectful before you showed up."

Caywood turned back. "Well, let me apologize for my friend's bad manners."

"Apology accepted." Mitch seemed anxious to be out from under Jim's glare.

"Just hold up there," Austin said. "You *boys* still owe this boy a nickel."

A pained look flashed briefly across Jim's face, but Austin could not have stopped from saying it if a hundred wild Comanches had him pinned down and were fixing to lift his hair.

"*Boys!* You can go to hell, nigger—"

Caywood's fist shot out like a steam piston. A short, devastating jab that landed like a pile driver and sent Mitch sailing back, his arms flung wide.

Mitch landed in the muddy puddle. Jim bent for a fistful of the man's vest and picked him out of the mud as if he weighed no more than a kitten. "Reckon now I need to apologize for my bad manners, too," he said, and shoved the stunned man into Randy's startled arms. "Mr. Fandango, shall we go?"

Austin looked at the paper boy and dug a nickel from his own pocket. "Here," he said, flipping it to him. The boy grabbed it out of the air and ran off.

Austin took up the reins of the four horses. "You owe me," he said to Randy as he took the animal past him.

"You best hope we never lay eyes on you around here again, boy," he shot back. "You make sure you never show your black face in Phillips County, Arkansas, not if you know what's good for you, nigger."

A blinding rage momentarily turned Austin's vision to bloodred. Jim's fingers tightened upon his shirtsleeve, tugging him back. Austin heard the old man's softly spoken words bringing him back to his senses. "Just can't let it rest, can you?"

His anger faded and he got control of his fury as they left the crowd behind. "Sometimes my temper does my thinking for me, Mr. Caywood."

"I can see how the likes of those two can get under your hide. But we are not back home, and these folks don't much know how to take a freethinking black man. There are times when it is best to keep your mouth closed and swallow a little pride. And this is one of them. When you feel the bile rise in your throat, that's time to stop and count—"

"To three. I know."

"Then what happened?"

Austin grinned. "I made it all the way to one."

Jim laughed. "Well, that's a start, I reckon."

"And what happened to you?"

"Me?" Jim looked mystified.

"I didn't hear no counting before you keelhauled that man back there."

Jim frowned. "Oh. Well, I just counted to myself, that's all."

"I see. I will remember that. Did you find a boat to book passage on?"

Jim took two tickets from his vest pocket and waved them before him. "First-class staterooms. One for you and one for me, and steerage for the animals. Aboard the *Mollie Walsh*, bound clear down to New Orleans, with a couple ports of call in between."

"Good. I'm mighty anxious to put this year's ride down the Shadow Road behind us."

Jim grinned. "Those two firebrands make you nervous?"

They drew up at a corner where a steady stream of traffic was making its way to and from the wharves, drays filled with cargo bound for steamers and distant ports, or loaded with newly arrived freight and heading for the shops and warehouses.

"Been nervous since we left Texas soil, Mr. Caywood. I can't say why. When does the *Mollie Walsh* leave?"

"Tomorrow morning. Eight o'clock. Come on, let's put the horses up at a livery and find us something to eat and a hotel room for the night."

FOUR

The St. Louis riverfront in the low morning sunlight was a glorious sight. With a hundred riverboats stoking up their boilers and filling the air with their smoke, the rising sunlight turned the river orange and pink for as far as the eye could see. At dawn the river wore a fine shroud of swirling mist, which burned off as the sun rose and heated the air.

The frenetic bustle all along the wharves started early on, and it was in full swing by time Austin and Jim collected their animals from the livery and made their way along the levee to the *Mollie Walsh*'s waiting gangplank. Jim went to talk with the clerk while Austin took the horses up the plank and at a stevedore's direction led them across the wide bow to a deck cleat where he was told to tie them off.

They had brought a bale of hay from the livery and Austin removed it from the saddle where it had been tied up and put it just out of reach of the horses. It would have to last until they made landing again and bought another, and Austin had no idea how far down the river that might be.

Piled all around him were stacks of crates and bundles of merchandise. Farm machinery of various kinds bound for ports along the river filled a quarter of the available deck.

Passengers were boarding, most of them riding steerage, the cheapest passage available. They hurried aboard and immediately searched for a spot of open deck where they could spread a blanket and set a wicker of food for the long trip. The bow filled up fast, latecomers having to settle for what room was left. Usually a perch on one of the crates, or a nook between them.

It was a mixed group, some whites, some blacks. Men, women, children. They all had one thing in common. They were too poor to afford the luxurious accommodations that waited on the next deck up at the top of the wide, polished walnut staircase that curved gracefully from the main deck.

It was upon this sparkling staircase now that a steady stream of folks were making their way up to the promenade, and the main cabin behind the double leaded-glass doors. Most were well dressed. Women carried parasols and men wore tall silk hats and polished boots.

Austin swept his hat from his head and wiped the sweat from its band with his bandanna. The heat was building and it promised to be another scorcher. He wondered how the men who were stoking the furnaces could manage it. Curiosity more than anything else turned his steps to the row of boilers that was located beneath the boiler deck. The fiery mouths of eight furnaces stood open and glaring heat radiated from their iron skins. A crew of burly black firemen, naked from the waist up and already streaked with sweat and grime, chucked three-foot lengths of cordwood into the hellish maws while a white man barked at them to move faster.

"And I thought punching cows was hard work," Austin murmured to himself. As he closed his eyes, his thoughts went back to a time when, like these blacks, he was worked and whipped, and made to kowtow to every white man he met. He had been luckier than most. He'd been a house slave and conditions were marginally better than what field hands had to endure. But as always, his temper had gotten him in a fix with the master of the plantation, which is what had landed him upon the auction block. That was when Big Jim Caywood had come along—over twenty years ago.

Austin shoved the unpleasant memories to the back of his brain, into a locked box where he kept such things hidden away, and watched the blacks working the furnaces. There was no overseer here, and no overseer's whip to spur them on. What they did have was a chief mate, and his sharp words stung just as surely as that old overseer's whip. Austin was familiar enough with riverboats to know that the men who sweated their lives away in the bowels of these ships were generally slaves hired out by their owners. Whatever pay the slave got had to be split with a man maybe a thousand miles away, who had never soiled his hands in honest labor a day in his life.

The notion rankled, but there was nothing any one man could do about it—especially a black man. Frederick Douglass, an ex-slave living in the North, was trying. He was writing diatribes against the institution of slavery and making a lot of noise, but as far as Austin could see, it hadn't made a tinker's damn worth of difference.

"There you are."

Austin turned at the sound of Jim Caywood's voice.

"We're all set." Jim held out a pair of keys with numbered tags. "One for you and one for me. Spoke to the captain, a man named Thomas Greenwood. He says we should be shoving off in fifteen minutes. They will be serving breakfast in the main cabin."

Austin rubbed his stomach. "I could sure go for a stack of griddlecakes and about half a gallon of black coffee."

The staterooms were all located on the second deck, the "boiler deck," as it was called, even though the boilers were in fact located one deck below, on the "main deck." Running around the length of the boat, clear back to the tall paddle boxes that soared overhead, was the promenade, with its gleaming white railing that looked out over the brown swirling river. Above the boiler deck was a third level, the "hurricane deck," and upon this stood the "texas." According to the riverboat lore Austin had once heard in a saloon down in Bayou Sara, the texas was so named because years earlier a boat owner had cleverly given each cabin the name of a state. When he had named them all he discovered he had one state left over. Texas. So he gave its name to the long row of narrow cabins on the next deck up. The texas cabins were where the crew lived, including the captain, whose luxurious suite of rooms perched at the very head of all the others.

Austin didn't know if the story was true or not, but it made for good telling, and he was not opposed to twisting the facts a mite if it added sparkle to a clever yarn.

The *Mollie Walsh*'s steam whistle shrilled three times and the aft gangplank was withdrawn. The chief mate's voice bellowed from below. "Make ready to shove off. Everyone not holding tickets to shore."

At the *Mollie Walsh*'s larboard railing, Jim and Austin craned their necks back toward the paddle box, where the huge wheel had begun to rotate. The boat strained at her hawsers as the last of the visitors hurried down the one remaining gangplank. When the last had disembarked, four blacks hurriedly hauled the gangplank on board while others loosened the mooring lines. With a gentle lurch, the long boat began to move, her stacks belching black smoke from pine knots fed into the furnaces.

With the escape pipes puffing in cadence with the throb of the big steam engines, the big bronze bell clanged and the boat backed away from the St. Louis wharves, into the stream. Once in the river, one of the boat's giant paddles reversed and the *Mollie Walsh* neatly swung about. Then, with both wheels turning in unison, she aimed for the main channel. Starboard and larboard leadsmen jumped to the fenders and cast out their lines. In a moment they began calling out the soundings, their deep, sonorous voices wafting back down the length of the *Mollie Walsh*.

"*Eight and a half!*" came the leadsmen's call.

"Eight-and-a-half!" the word passer picked up, relaying it back to a man at the head of the texas deck, who repeated the sounding for the pilot way up in the pilothouse, perched all of forty or fifty feet overhead.

"*Nine!*"

"Nine!" The word went back in deep-voiced harmony.

"*Nine and a half! . . . Quarter less twain!*"

Austin closed his eyes. The leadsmen's deep voices were

pleasant to the ear, like voices out of his past. His thoughts turned to his father, remembering the deep, rich harmony of the men singing spirituals on the back steps of their cabins in the evening, after the day's tasks had been completed. His father had been a glorious baritone. The air would be filled with the wonderful music of human voices—a sound no instrument of wood and gut could ever match. It was when Austin had been not much more than ten or eleven that the man in the big house began to groom him for the job of house slave. Shortly after this his father had run away. Austin had never heard from him again, but he liked to think that he had made it north. Perhaps on the "railroad." But there was no way of knowing now. His father's fate would always be a blank page in Austin's life, a question impossible to answer now so many years later.

"Maaark twain!"

"Quarter twain! . . . Quarter twain! . . . Half twain! . . . Quarter less three!"

The river was deepening and the boat picking up speed.

"Maaark three! . . . Deep four! . . . Deep four! . . . NO BOTTOM!"

The leadsmen coiled in their lines and left their posts. The boat was in deep water and soundings would not have to be taken again so long as they remained in the channel, or until they put into shore, or if a new shoal had formed, which was nearly as common as rain on this river.

"Hungry?" Jim asked.

Austin pulled his eyes from the wide river, the pleasant memories fading away. The crowd that had gathered along the railing had begun to disperse, some for their staterooms, most toward the doors of the main cabin . . . and breakfast.

His and Jim's appearance must have been striking. Austin noted the not-so-guarded glances cast their way as they strolled for the doorway where the double doors stood open, admitting the throng to the main cabin. Well, their high-heeled boots, trail-weary clothes, and broad Texas hats were not quite the style compared with the men in their five-button broadcloth vests, fitted frock coats, striped gaitered breeches, ruffled shirts, stiff collars, and tall silk hats.

More than at Jim, Austin knew it was at him that they
were staring. And he knew why. Even though they had just
come off a six-week cattle drive, Austin was still dressed
better that most any of the black folk he had yet to see. And
it probably had something to do with the way he carried
himself, the way he held his head, the way he stood beside
Jim as an equal. He was a slave to no man, and he showed
it. He treated every man the same, and when he spoke, he
looked them straight in the eye, be they white, red, black . . .
or *green*! Most white folk in Missouri didn't know how to
take that. It would only get worse the farther south the *Mollie
Walsh* carried him.

Jim just expected Austin to accompany him on these trips
year after year, after the cows were in and the men paid off. He
never refused the man who had given him freedom, a family,
and his friendship. He did not know what compelled Jim Caywood to do the things he did, to ride the Shadow Road each
year, to buy slaves at auction and then give then their freedom
and a job on the JC Connected. He did not even know why Jim
called it the Shadow Road, except for the occasional remark
that "it was dark business he carried on there."

Jim did not talk about it to him. Aside from the scar that
Jim carried above his heart, the tale of Comanches, and that
far-off look he got every time their talks would nudge too
near to that memory, Austin knew as little of Jim's motives
as did the greenest hand on the ranch.

Juanita knew the full story, of course, but like Jim, she
was not talking, and Austin had learned years ago that this
was not an area where prying was appreciated.

The *Mollie Walsh*'s main cabin was an eye-dazzling place.
Its length alone was enough to pop the eyes of a country
boy. Overhead stained-glass skylights ran its length, up one
side and down the other. Beneath the arched ceiling, which
was decorated with enough scrollwork to befuddle the tongue
of an auctioneer, hung a row of crystal chandeliers. The place
was painted bright white and along each wall were doors,
some leading out onto the promenade, others directly into
the more expensive staterooms. There must have been fifty
tables here, at the moment all pushed together in a long line

flanked by cane-back chairs. Colorful carpets covered the floor, and strategically placed along ornate walls that were covered with Italian wallpaper was an army of gleaming brass cuspidors.

"They keep building them fancier and fancier," Austin said, gawking more than he cared to.

"The table is filling up. Let's find us a place to sit." Jim led the way along the aisle behind the chairs. He found two together not yet occupied and pulled them back.

"Ah, suh?" a soft voice said at his elbow. A short Negro server in a black coat and white bow tie was standing there, peering up at Jim.

"You talking to me?" Jim asked.

The black man nodded and said in a low voice so that the other guests could not hear, "No coloreds allowed at dis table, suh. Dey belong down there." He pointed toward the far end of the long room where a separate table had been set up across from the Hamlin Melodeon.

"Oh, is that so? Well, my good fellow, I have paid for—"

Austin cleared his throat. Big Jim Caywood was a man bound up in principles, and doggedly stood by them. "I don't mind, Mr. Caywood," he said. "I'm so hungry they could put me atop one of those tall chimneys and I wouldn't care, just so long as they set a pile of griddlecakes atop the other." He grinned, and saw with a bit of relief that Jim knew what he was doing.

"You sure, Austin?"

"No need to make a fuss over little things. I'll just go join my own kind." Austin turned before Jim could object and strode down to the table reserved for black folk.

"He's a good worker, Mr. Everly. Young, healthy, strong, and comes from good stock."

Franklin Everly stalked around Willis, studying him with a practiced eye. "That so?" He came around in front of Willis and stared hard into the young man's face.

Willis shook in his boots beneath the man's hard gaze. He was so scared he was hardly able even to glance at the freight wagon parked out in the glaring sun, already packed to the gills with black folk. Willis fought back a tear. This was the absolutely second worst thing that could have ever happened to him. Oh, why was he always breaking things and making Master Hill mad at him. It had come down to the worst possible sentence for a slave owned by a good master.

The auction block.

Through his trembling, his eyes slid sideways. There, at the door to his cabin stood his mother, father, and sister. Eyes big and filling, and not a thing they could do to change Thomas Hill's mind. As he stood there fighting back the tears, Willis knew this was the last time he would see the three people he loved most in all the world this side of Glory!

"Open your mouth, boy."

Willis was momentarily confused, watching his parents as he had been. It was a mistake he'd not make a second time. The hard handle of Everly's snake whip drove into his stomach. Willis's breath exploded from him and he buckled, grabbing at his middle.

"I said open your mouth."

Gasping, Willis obeyed the command.

Franklin peered inside a long moment. "Teeth look all right."

"I assure you he is in fine condition, Mr. Everly. Really, he is quite compliant. There is no need to use force with the boy," Hill said, bothered by the man's harsh techniques.

"You don't need to tell me how to handle niggers, Hill. Been hauling stock to auction for almost twenty years." Leaving Willis to stand in the glaring morning sunlight, Everly came back into the shade where Thomas Hill, Peter Deats, and Hobey were waiting.

"Mark it down, Deats," he said, rapping the handle of the blacksnake upon the shingle where Deats kept his written record. "One nigger about five-foot-ten, about one hundred sixty pounds, more or less. Good teeth, good conformation, good breeding."

Deats moistened the tip of his pencil on his tongue and began scribbling.

Everly glanced at Hill. "How old?"

"Eighteen."

"Put that down, Deats. Why are you sending this one to the block?" Everly asked. "He looks to be a good one to keep around. At an age where you'll get the most work out of him."

Hill nodded his head and Willis, sneaking a glance, thought he saw a bit of regret come to his master's face. *Please, Lord,* Willis implored, *don't let Marster Hill send me to the auction block. Oh, Lord, I promise to be good and not break another single thing!*

"He's a good boy, really, except for one thing. He is about as clumsy as a drunken sailor. I can't begin to tell you all the things I have had to replace because of Willis. And I'm sure he doesn't do it on purpose."

"No, probably not. I hear tell these coloreds ain't as developed like us white folks. If you look real close you can see some of the monkey still in 'em. Leastwise, that's what that English fellow says."

"So I have heard," Hill replied noncommittally.

"Well, he won't be damaging your place anymore, Hill. Deats, make a note that this one breaks things."

Deats tasted the lead and scribbled down Everly's words.

"One last detail." Franklin took a piece of paper from his shirt pocket and passed it to Deats. Deats scribbled something on it and gave it over to Hill to sign.

"What's this?"

"Read it."

"Oh, I see."

"That just tells the patrollers, and anyone else who cares, that you have legally transferred ownership of that slave to me. Sign it right there, next to the place where Deats wrote down the boy's name, right there on the bottom of the list."

"Yes, of course." Hill took the shingle and the pencil from Deats and put his name to the paper.

Everly gave the signature a brief glance. "Nice doing business with you, Hill. Deats, pay the man and let's be off. Got two more stops to make before sundown."

Deats dug into his purse and filled Hill's hand with a pile of gold eagles.

"Four hundred dollars," he said.

Hill frowned and he hefted the coins as if to judge their weight. "Willis should bring three times this much at market, maybe more."

"I hope so. If I can't make a fair profit, I don't stay in business. Good day, Hill. And remember me the next time you want to get rid of any more of them." Everly started back to the freighter.

"Come along, boy. Climb aboard and make quick work of it."

Struggling to keep his composure, Willis cast a final glance at his family. He was almost able to hold back his tears, until he saw both his parents openly weeping. It was just too much and he broke down. An elderly, gray-haired slave in the freighter put down a hand and helped Willis over the tailgate.

"It's all right, son. Cry yo'r heart out. I did the first time I was sold off."

Willis scrubbed his eyes and sat on a wood-plank bench built in the side of the wagon. The man who had spoken was old and weary. He had a long, wrinkled face and a thatch of short graying hair, receding sharply at the temples.

"Yo'll get along. We all do."

Willis sniffed and dragged his shirtsleeve across his eyes. He didn't have any words for the old man. All he could think about was the farm where he had grown up—everything that he knew. He caught a glimpse of Samuel watching from the side window, his face showing deep sadness. Willis cast a final look at his mother, father, and sister standing in the doorway of the cabin that he would never see again. His parents held each other, seeming unable to stand on their own as the wagon rumbled out of the yard, forever taking their child away from them.

Then the wagon turned the corner of the house and all that Willis knew and loved was gone. What waited for him ahead, he could only guess. The unknown was a fearful thing, like a burning stake being driven into his heart.

FIVE

Night brought a welcome coolness to the river. Out in the middle of the channel, with the boat booming along under a full head of steam, the breeze off the water was like a reprieve from a hangman's noose. Austin turned his face to the wind, closed his eyes, and inhaled deeply. There is nothing quite like the smell of the Mississippi after a sweltering day. The air was warm and humid, but bearable now, and out here where the nearest land was slipping past a half mile to either side of the *Mollie Walsh*, there was not a blessed mosquito in sight. Not a single one!

Austin leaned back against the bale of hay with his fingers locked behind his head and stretched his long legs out on the deck. Although the bow was crowded with passengers holding only deck-passage tickets and steerage, he could imagine himself all alone, drifting free and easy on this wide placid river—placid at the moment. She was not always this accommodating. The torrential spring rains and the massive spring runoffs were past. The rollicking, untamed Mississippi of only a few weeks before had settled down to a smooth, bankful river.

A real lady! Austin mused.

This was traveling in pure luxury. No dust, no cantankerous horse beneath him, no sea of cows that had to be coddled and urged along and worried over every mile of the way from deep Texas to St. Louis.

Austin grabbed a handful of hay and held it up. He felt the horse's soft muzzle upon his hand and heard the animal's satisfying chomping. The other horses nickered for their portion. "All right, all right." Austin pulled himself from his reverie and gave each horse a handful of hay and a scratch behind the ears.

"Sure beat's walking, don't it?" Austin stroked his horse's strong neck. "Enjoy it while you can. You still have a long walk ahead of you once we leave New Orleans."

"Since when did you start talking to horses?"

Austin turned and grinned at Jim. "Since my compadre up and disappeared on me. Where did you get off to?"

"Found myself sitting in on a card game up in the main cabin. Was only going to watch for a few minutes, but somehow I let a couple of smooth-talking popinjays pull me into the game."

"Lose a lot?"

"Lose? Hell no. I saw what they were up to right from the start." Jim winked. "I played dumb. I figured they'd throw the first two or three hands my way just to oil me up. And they did. I took three hundred dollars off those two gamblers before they discovered I was onto their scheme. I just grinned and told them good night, collected my winnings, and left."

Austin laughed. "Reckon they are hopping mad."

"Reckon they are. I didn't wait around to find out." Jim reached into his shirt pocket and pulled out two cigars. "Here you go. I bought these off of the purser. He guarantees me they are genuine Havana. Charged me two bits each. They better be." He struck a match and Austin poked the end of his cigar into Jim's cupped hands.

A deckhand carrying a torch came through the crowd and the mounds of cargo to set fire to a torch basket mounted on the jack staff. The wick flared and settled down to a dull red, smoky flame that put very little light on the water ahead of the *Mollie Walsh*.

"When do you reckon we will make New Orleans?" Austin asked, blowing a cloud of cigar smoke into the night.

"Captain Greenwood said two days. Says he has got a fast current pushing us along, and his steam engines are pounding to beat the band just to keep ahead of it."

"Good."

"Still unsettled about the trip?"

"Like a centipede with chilblains."

Jim grinned around the fat cigar in his mouth. The red glow of its tip contorted the lines and creases of his weathered face into a demonic mask. "It will be all right. We won't dawdle. Just do our business and go home."

"Home sounds like a pretty good place to be."

Jim peered up at the stars. "Don't see as many of 'em here as you do back in Texas."

"No, but on the other hand, we don't have anything like this grand river back in Texas, either."

Jim thought about that a moment and frowned. "I don't know about that, Austin. I heard tell once of a dryland farmer down below San Antonio who decided he needed to put in an irrigation ditch—"

"Get out of here."

Jim grinned.

The two of them stood there for a long while, listening to the steady splash of the paddle wheels and chuff of the escape pipes as the boat strove to keep ahead of the current. Up and down the length of the river Austin could see the lights of passing steamers, and the lanterns of the barges and rafts taking goods down to New Orleans. The Mississippi was a busy place these days, even after dark, now that it had been somewhat tamed and cleaned up by the famous snag boats that Captain Henry Shreve had devised years ago. Even so, it was a place that still held plenty of dangers. A riverboat pilot had to be constantly on the lookout for sawyers and planters, and the shoal water that sometimes developed around a bend in the river almost overnight, rising like phantoms from the muddy depths where a few weeks before lay deep water.

A riverboat pilot had to know every inch of the river, and

he had to keep it all inside his head. Charts were of little use from year to year on this river that changed its channels as often as some men took baths.

They smoked their cigars on the fenders of the *Mollie Walsh* in quiet companionship. When Jim finished his he flicked the stub far out across the dark water. Its dying tip made a sparking arc of red like a tiny Fourth of July rocket before extinguishing itself in the rolling bow wake. He peered up at the stars again for a long while.

"I don't know about you"—Jim arched his back and stretched—"but I'm just about ready to try out that fancy feather bed in my cabin."

"Me, too." Austin gave one last pull on his smoke and sent it cartwheeling after Jim's.

The two men watered and hayed their four horses, then Austin slung his saddlebags over his shoulder and removed the Sharps from its saddle scabbard. Jim had earlier locked the bags containing the gold from the sale of his cattle in his stateroom. They went up the wide, curving staircase. On the promenade, the doors to the main cabin were open to let a breeze flow through the long room. The night was still young for some men. Austin stood there watching gamblers at the tables, the saloon that was doing a brisk business, and the man sitting behind the melodeon, beating out a lively tune.

"They'll probably keep at it most the night," Jim noted.

"It's a wonder that anyone will get any sleep on this boat before dawn."

The two men started down the promenade toward their staterooms, all the way back near the soaring paddle box. Austin judged that to be a fine location since the steady cadence of the paddle wheel should help mask the melodeon player's spirited music.

One of the side doors to the main cabin opened and spilled a shaft of bright light across the deck just ahead of them. It closed and Captain Greenwood strode out of the shadows. He stood at the railing, watching the dark river, rolling a long cigar thoughtfully between his lips. At the sound of Jim and Austin's footsteps, he turned.

"Ah, good evening, Mr. Caywood. Ah trust you are

having a splendid trip?'' Greenwood was a slender man of about forty and spoke in a soft, easygoing Southern manner. His view settled momentarily upon Austin, then dismissed him entirely and returned to Jim. ''Pleasant night, is it not? Evening and early morning are my favorite times of day.''

''It is pleasant, yes,'' Jim agreed. ''While you are down here, Captain, who is up there steering this fine boat?''

Greenwood glanced toward the ceiling of the promenade as if it were possible to see through it to the hurricane deck, and the pilothouse beyond. He smiled and gave a short laugh. ''Ah see you do not understand the ways of the river, sir.''

''Austin and me, we are drylanders.''

''Texas, ah believe you said.''

''That's right.''

''Well, then let me tell you how it is. Once under steam, the master of a vessel becomes a mere figurehead. Ah have little say in the operations of this vessel, aside from determining where she shall land, and of course most of that has already been determined by the contracts to deliver or pick up cargo, which ah carry. And even that must ultimately be cleared by the pilot. You see, the real authority lies in the hands of the pilot at the helm, and his partner. In fact, once under steam, even the greenest pilot holding only a daylight license would have the say about the operations of this boat.'' Greenwood laughed again and drew on his cigar. ''A mere figurehead, sir. It is the law of the river.'' He shrugged indifferently, accepting his place in the scheme of things with a quiet ease that amazed Austin. He was the *captain,* after all!

''It is only after the *Mollie Walsh* puts into shore,'' Greenwood went on serenely, ''that the roles reverse and ah again become the true master of my boat.''

''I trust the pilot is a good one, then.''

''They are all good, Mr. Caywood . . . well, that is to say, most are. Those that aren't don't last long. They go on to other things. The *Mollie Walsh* has two of the finest pilots on the river. You can sleep confidently on that tonight.''

Jim grinned. ''And sleeping is exactly what we have in mind. We were just on our way to our staterooms now.''

In the faint light of the smoky lamps spaced widely along the deck, Austin saw Greenwood's eyes narrow slightly and shift his way. Austin held the captain in his own unwavering gaze a long moment before the captain's view hitched back to Jim.

"*Both* of you have staterooms?"

"We do."

Greenwood cleared his throat as a pained look came to his face and stole the man's joy. "It appears that we may have a misunderstanding here, sir."

Jim's own smile never faltered, but Austin heard the wary tone move into his voice. "Misunderstanding, Captain Greenwood? What sort of misunderstanding?"

The captain withered beneath Jim's stare, but he stood his ground. "Didn't the clerk tell you?"

"No, I reckon he did not."

Austin knew what was coming next; it hadn't been the first time. He suspected Jim knew it, too—and over the years Jim had lost all patience with such things.

Facing a lesser man than Jim, Austin suspected that Greenwood's position of authority would have held him in better stead. But Jim Caywood's size, if nothing else, was enough to intimidate even the bravest of men. Austin had seen whole crowds cower before Caywood, just like they had back in St. Louis yesterday.

To his credit Greenwood did not back down. "We do not let staterooms to Negroes. Your . . . your boy will have to sleep down on the main deck with the other colored folks."

"Oh, he will, will he?" Caywood's grizzly-bear paws came to rest upon his wide waist and when he leaned forward his belly strained the buttons of his shirt as if a baby buffalo had been caught inside it. The wary tone was gone from his voice now and in its place was a clear note of hostility. Austin knew that when Big Jim Caywood used that tone, whole Comanche war parties would be wise to consider that better part of valor which Shakespeare had spoken of.

Ever since his run-in with the two rowdies yesterday, Austin felt he had stepped barefoot onto a frying pan and slowly a fire was being stoked beneath it. It was only going to get hotter the farther south they traveled, and he had no desire to throw any more fuel onto the blaze than necessary. Austin knew he had to pick his battles wisely, and this just wasn't one worth the fight.

"It's all right, Marster Jim," Austin said, mustering his best slave dialect, "Austin will just go down and sleep wid de horses and his own kind. I be mo' comfortable down der anyway, an' I wo't have to worry 'bout none of my darkie skin color rubbin' off onto de captain's clean white sheets."

It was a game they sometimes played—the master/slave routine. When used in the right circles, it opened more doors than it closed. And Austin figured this might be one of them. It was best to nip this confrontation in the bud. They still had a long road ahead of them to ride.

Jim glanced over. Austin gave him a warning look. Jim drew in a long breath and let it out slowly. "You sure, Austin?"

He nodded. "I already counted to three."

Jim understood.

Austin flashed the captain the widest grin he had, turned, and strode to the staircase, back down to the main deck. There was no accounting for some men's prejudices, and there was certainly no changing them. Anyway, this was not the place to try. He laid his rifle upon the half bale of hay that was left, spread out a couple of saddle blankets, covered it over with his oilcloth and sleeping blanket, and made himself comfortable among all the rest of the slumbering bodies there on the deck.

Austin was sound asleep, enjoying a pleasant dream that had something to do with a tall ship and white billowing sails. The sea around him was so blue it might have been that big chunk of polished turquoise that Juanita Caywood wore sometimes to church services down at Parson Bill Richardson's Presbyterian church. Why a Texan should be dreaming about sailing was a mystery to Austin, one that he did not have time to ponder.

Something nudged his side.

Austin mumbled sleepily and shifted beneath his blanket.

In his half-asleep state, he just figured he'd thrown his blanket down over a stone. Then he was nudged again. He rolled over to discover the toe of a boot, and when he looked up Jim Caywood was standing over him. It was still the dead of night. Austin rubbed the sleep from his eyes and levered himself up onto his elbows.

"What is it?" he asked sleepily, softly so as not to awaken the people around. "Time for my watch?"

"Your watch? This here is a riverboat, remember?"

"Oh . . . oh, yeah." Austin rubbed his eyes. "What's wrong?"

Jim showed him the bottle. "Damn melodeon kept me awake all night. Finally they all went to bed. Barkeep left this setting out."

"He left it out?"

Jim gave him a crooked grin. "Well, not exactly. His liquor chest has a bad lock."

Austin studied the old man. "Bad lock?"

"Oh, don't worry, I left two dollars inside the chest to pay for it."

"Have you been drinking?"

The lopsided grin widened. "They say a man don't have to worry about it until he starts to drinking by himself."

"What time is it?"

Jim looked to the stars. "About four." He motioned for Austin to get up. Still befuddled with sleep, Austin threw off his blanket and followed Jim to a crate. They sat down. Jim put the bottle in Austin's fist.

"What's this all about?"

Jim grimaced. "Greenwood got under my skin. Took about all the willpower I had not to teach him some Texas etiquette."

"Oh, is that what this is about?" Austin tipped the bottle back and let the whiskey course down his throat. His face screwed together with the sharp bite of it and he passed the bottle back. "It do got a stinger."

"I have tasted better."

"Don't let it bother you, Mr. Caywood."

"Seems you got that counting down real good."

"I just didn't figure it was worth making a scene over."

Jim took a sip and handed the bottle over. The second time did not burn like the first. Austin smacked his lips. Except for the constant thrumming of the engines, the chuffing of escaping steam, and splash of the paddle wheels, the boat was dead silent.

"Everyone on board asleep?" Austin asked.

"Mostly. There are some fellows up on the hurricane keeping watch." Jim tasted the whiskey again. "The fact is, I paid good money for that stateroom."

"They'll give it back, if you ask."

"Don't want it back."

Austin shrugged and took the bottle. This time it went down easy. He tried it again . . . just to be sure. "Then what do you want, Mr. Caywood?"

"I want to use the damned room, Mr. Fandango. And why don't you ever call me Shim, anyway?" Caywood slurred.

"Shim?" Austin laughed.

Jim grinned and snatched up the bottle. He dragged the sleeve of his shirt across his chin afterward and stood, stabbing back a foot to steady himself. "Whoa there, hit some rough water."

"Yeah, I think I felt it, too."

"Come on."

"Where are we going?"

"Grab up the rest of that hay."

"The hay?"

"Go on, grab it up."

Austin narrowed an eye at the older man. He took the bottle, tipped its bottom toward the stars, and handed it back. "I guess I don't even want to know what you have in mind, Mr. Caywood."

Jim winked. "Greenwood said no coloreds allowed."

"Yes, he did."

"I paid good money for that room."

"Yes, you did."

"Seems a shame to let it go to waste."

"Yes, it does."

Jim grinned. "Greenwood didn't say nothing about no horses, did he?"

Austin's eyes widened with surprise, and yes, he couldn't help himself, with a bit of impish delight.

"I didn't hear him say anything about horses."

"Well, grabs up the hay, Mr. Fandango."

Jim staggered to the horses and untied two of the four. Carefully leading them around the legs sprawled out on the deck, he started them up the curving staircase. The clatter of their iron shoes upon the polished wood was enough to wake the dead, Austin feared. But the people slept on and no one on the upper deck looked over to see what the noise was.

Maybe no one even heard?

Austin felt the whiskey surge in his brain as he bent and hefted what was left of the bale of hay to his shoulder. He shushed himself, stifled a laugh, and followed the horses up the stairs.

As they clattered along the promenade, Austin waited for lights to be struck in the staterooms they passed. But it never happened. Jim stepped aside to let Austin work the key. The door swung inward.

"Spread that hay on top of the bed," Jim whispered.

Austin broke open the bale and scattered it about.

Jim pulled the horses toward the door. They didn't like the idea and balked. Austin got behind one and put his shoulder to its rump while Jim pulled. Finally both animals clambered into the small quarters. Jim pulled the door shut and fell back against it, exhausted.

"Success, Mr. Fandango."

"Success, *Shim*."

Jim laughed, uncorked the bottle, and they each took another long swig from it.

"To the good Captain Greenwood!" Jim proposed. "May all his staterooms smell as sweet as this one will in the morning."

"To Greenwood!" Austin was beginning to feel tipsy, and he figured they would regret in the light of morning what they had done in the dark of night . . . but what the hell!

They drank to the captain's good health, to the *Mollie Walsh*'s prosperity, and to horses—especially to horses.

SIX

Austin squinted against the glare of the morning sun and wished he were dead. His head pounded like an Apache war drum and his tongue was drier than a prospector's boot—and felt as big as one, too.

Standing beside him, Jim groaned softly, hanging on to the reins of the horses more to support himself than to keep them from trotting away. Austin shaded his eyes against the glinting water. The *Mollie Walsh* was but a white speck out on the wide river. He watched it finally it disappear around a distant bend.

"He sure was mad, wasn't he?" Austin felt vaguely sick at the stomach and was thirsty enough to drink down a watering trough.

Jim slowly shook his head. "In all my seventy years," he croaked, stopping to drag a tongue across his cracked lips, "in all of them, I don't think I have ever heard some of those words."

"It was a lesson my mama wouldn't want me to learn twice. To think that a Southern gentleman could talk like that!"

Jim grinned. "He was no gentleman. But it was worth every minute of it."

Austin moaned and clamped a hand to his head. "Now what do we do?"

Jim pulled his hat down low to protect his eyes. "First thing is find out just where it is Greenwood put us off."

They turned away from the wharf and staggered down the side of the levee. At a place where a road began sat a warehouse. The big building was boarded up and appeared to no longer be used, but there was a faded word painted across its side.

"Laconia," Austin read aloud. The named seemed to stir a memory, but whatever it might be, his brain wasn't cooperating. "Where have I heard that name before?"

Jim said, "Let's find someone who can tell us when the next steamer is due to stop."

They walked the dusty street that led away from the river. A dozen feet or so along it, the street was bisected by a second street called Calhoun, according to a weathered sign. Jim peered up this rutted lane. Drab clapboard buildings lined both sides, and at the far end sat a large livery. Off to one side of the livery, workmen were hammering nails into something that looked like a platform.

"Reckon they are expecting a theater group through here, Mr. Caywood?"

"No telling, Mr. Fandango."

A couple of side streets ran out from Calhoun, away from the river, and a town square sat unpretentiously off to the left, and that was all.

"Not much of a town, is it?" Jim murmured.

"Hope they have a café, or someplace where I can get me some coffee."

"Come on." Jim started off.

Austin held back a moment longer as a spider crawled up his spine. He did not know why, but for some reason he did not like this place. He reached for his saddlebags, thinking to buckle his gun belt on, then stopped himself. *What are you doing? This is a town, for Pete's sakes. There ain't no rattlesnakes, no wild Indians, no highwaymen here.* Austin shook off the uneasy feeling and gathered up his reins again.

"Well, are you coming or not?" Jim called over his shoulder.

"Right on your heels, Mr. Caywood."

It was early and some of the businesses along Calhoun Street were just opening their doors. To the right Austin spotted the sheriff's office, which still appeared to be locked up tight. His view started along the row of buildings . . . then his eyes shifted back to the sheriff's office and the name painted upon the windowpane there.

Roy Calhoun.

Austin wondered if it wasn't but coincidence. Next was a general dry-goods store. A gent with a broom had just opened the door, shooing a billow of dust out onto the sidewalk, into the street. The man eyed Jim and Austin suspiciously as they walked past. A bakery and gun shop followed, and there was a bank just beyond. Glancing across the street, Austin saw a hotel, a barbershop, and a saloon. The saloon's inside doors were still closed tight. Austin stopped to read the name of the place.

BUSTER G. CALHOUN SALOON. SPIRITS AND BEER

"Mr. Caywood?"

"Yes, Mr. Fandango?"

"Have you noticed the names?"

"You mean all the Calhouns? They seem to be a prominent family hereabouts."

"That's what I was thinking."

As they walked up Calhoun Street, the livery at the far end grew larger and the platform across from it where the carpenters were pounding nails came into clearer view. Jim drew up, studying it and the few buildings that trailed off in that direction.

"That don't look like any theater stage I have ever seen," Austin noted.

"It's not."

Austin glanced around the town. "They have a telegraph through here." His eyes followed a line of tall poles out of town. A white handbill tacked to one of the poles caught his attention. He squinted, then walked across the street to read it.

LIST OF
35
NEGROES

*Accustomed to the culture of the lower
Arkansas River
For Sale at Auction,*
—on—
*Tuesday and Wednesday, 26th & 27th of June, 1860
At 11 O'CLOCK, A.M.,*

by
WILLARD P. CALHOUN
Broker
Auctioneer and Commission Agent

Up the street a few paces ahead of him, Jim said, "I've found your café for you."

"Mr. Caywood. Come look at this."

Jim brought the horses over.

Austin spiked the poster with a long, slender forefinger. "Read this."

"Hmm. An auction. Right here in Laconia. Doesn't hardly seem like a big enough place to put one on, does it?"

"It does—if you look again at the auctioneer's name."

Jim gave a short laugh. "The Calhouns seem to have the fingers in most every pie around." Jim dismissed the notice and said, "There is a café ahead, and they appear to be open for business."

But Austin's thoughts were racing far ahead of his aching head and even his hollow stomach. If there was to be a slave auction right here in Laconia, why bother to travel all the way down to New Orleans?

Jim had started away again.

"It's tomorrow, if I got my days right."

"What is?"

"The auction."

Jim looked back at him, waiting for an explanation.

"Mr. Caywood, why not do our business right here in Laconia? If we can find a girl to take Betsy's place, and someone to fill Walter's shoes, there would be no need to catch another steamer on down to New Orleans. We could start back to Texas tomorrow and save ourselves that extra thousand miles."

Jim considered this a moment. "We've never bought slaves this far north," he said, not so much to Austin as to himself.

"There is nothing sacred about New Orleans," Austin noted.

Jim looked at him then laughed, apparently hearing something humorous in his words. Austin reckoned it was because New Orleans was such a "den of iniquity" that Jim had found his statement funny. "You are in a hurry to be on your way home, aren't you?"

"Yes, sir. I've been itching to point my boots back toward Texas ever since we turned that last cow into the pens at St. Louis. I don't know about you, but this trip has got me twitchy like a man staked out on an anthill. This land has become a powder keg, and I for one would like to be far away from it once it blows."

Jim grimaced. "The South had been a powder keg for twenty years or more, Mr. Fandango. I can't hardly remember a time when some popinjay politician or another wasn't talking about secession."

That was true, but this year seemed somehow different. Austin couldn't quite put his finger on why that was. He just figured it took being a man of color to feel it, and Jim was not in full touch with the growing hostility.

"Well, what do you think?"

Jim pursed his lips and his big hat cast a swath of shade across his eyes and nose as he stood there in the morning sunlight thinking it over. "Suppose it wouldn't hurt to spend an extra day here and see what happens," he decided finally. "Who knows, might find two people just right for the jobs."

Austin grinned. "Maybe that Captain Greenwood putting us ashore here was a blessing in disguise."

"We will see." Jim nodded up the street. "How about some breakfast?"

"Breakfast. That is music to this man's ears." For the first time since hitting St. Louis, Austin was feeling the weighty concern lifting from his shoulders. He imagined a pile of eggs, and a mess of fried onions and potatoes, followed by a tower of griddlecakes, all washed down with eight or ten cups of strong black coffee. They tied up at the hitching rail out front of the café and removed the saddlebags. Jim carried the two with the gold while Austin slung the bags holding his and Jim's personal belongings over his shoulder and slid the Sharps from its saddle scabbard.

The café was a long narrow building sandwiched between the bank and a millinery shop. There were eight tables scattered about the floor. A single door with a round window led back to the kitchen beyond. Morning sunlight streamed through the tall streetfront window. Two of the eight tables were occupied. When Jim and Austin stepped inside, a bell above the door tinkled and six faces turned toward them.

"Don't look like they are used to strangers," Austin said softly at Jim's side.

"Riverboats must not stop here regularly."

Not wanting to antagonize anyone unnecessarily, Austin avoided looking at the white men. Jim, on the other hand, seemed to take a particular delight at staring at them, and grinning until the customers reluctantly returned to their breakfasts. As they made their way to a table at the back of the room, heads swiveled and eyes glanced out over the rim of tilted coffee cups.

Jim set the heavy bags on the floor by his chair. Austin leaned his long rifle against the wall and took a chair next to it to watch the room. It had become unnaturally quiet compared with the brisk talk that had greeted them only a few moments ago when they had entered.

"You enjoyed that, didn't you?" Austin said.

"You worry too much."

"Easy for you to say. Try crawling into my skin for a day."

Jim laughed soundlessly.

The door to the kitchen opened. A man in a dingy apron came through carrying a big coffeepot by its bail. He stopped, startled to see Jim and Austin there, then went to the tables and filled the empty cups. He called each man by name and they joked as if they had known each other all their lives—and most likely they had.

One of them said, "Looks like you are going to have extra cleaning-up to do, Orin," and glanced at Austin.

The man in the apron shook his head and cast a quick look back at Jim and Austin himself. "Stick out your cup and close your mouth, Bert."

Orin finished and came on over.

"Morning," Jim said amiably.

But apparently Jim was being optimistic. By the look the man gave him, it was anything but a good morning. "Is this your boy?"

Austin stiffened. Jim let the man's question roll easily past. "Austin and me, we travel together," he replied, grinning. "And we are two hungry men."

"I don't serve coloreds in here."

"I didn't see any signs out front," Austin replied tightly.

Orin shot him a narrow glance. "Probably couldn't have read it if you had."

Austin's fist tightened upon the table's edge. Jim's level voice warned him to do nothing.

One.

"We are strangers here in your town, mister. Don't know too much about your ways, and we certainly don't want to cause any trouble. But we've been traveling a mighty dusty road for most of two months now." As he spoke, Jim casually lifted one of the saddlebags onto the table and began rummaging through it, as if searching for something. He removed the holster belt holding the big Walker Colt and set it on the table with the revolver's muzzle peeking from the bottom of its leather, pointing straight at the man's groin. "Austin and me, we are anxious to get back to Texas. All we want is a little food and to be left alone." He fished around inside the bag some more. "Ah, here it is." Jim removed a leather pouch that held his gold watch and snapped open the cover. "Only eight o'clock? Gets mighty hot early on in this part of the country, doesn't it?"

Orin was staring at the revolver. In spite of his shortcoming in manners, he wasn't dumb. Jim put the watch away and dropped the saddlebags to the floor with a soft thump. But the revolver remained on the table, and Orin's eyes remained riveted upon it.

"Now, I can't speak for my friend here, but for me, four or five eggs scrambled up together, some griddlecakes, and a big cup of black coffee would sure take the edge off of my hunger. I get mighty nervous when I have an empty stomach, you see. And the last time I had anything to eat was yesterday afternoon on the steamer *Mollie Walsh*." Jim grinned. As if by mere accident, and certainly with no forethought, his hand dropped to the table and by chance found the revolver beneath it.

"I . . . I suppose I could make an exception this time, seeing as he is traveling with you." The man managed to drag his eyes from the .44 and turn them at Austin. "What is it you want?"

"Same as Mr. Caywood," Austin answered, "and fry up some potatoes and onions if you got any."

The man slipped through the back door. He returned a minute later with two cups and filled them. "It will be about ten minutes on the food."

"We are in no hurry," Jim assured him. "If you don't mind me asking, where exactly are we?" He grinned. "You see, we had us a disagreement with the captain of the *Mollie Walsh* and he sort of put us off at the first convenient wharf this morning, which just happened to be right here."

"You're in Laconia," the man replied.

Austin noticed that the other customers had gone back to eating and paid them little attention now, except for an occasional glance and a guarded word passed between them.

"So a sign down by the river told us. Where might Laconia be?"

"You are about fifteen miles north of the Arkansas River."

"That's convenient. Can a man catch a boat to Fort Smith anywhere nearby?"

"There is a ferry landing on the Arkansas where a passing steamer will put in at the ferryman's signal. He runs a red flag up to call them ashore. There are no regular stops far as I know."

Jim glanced at Austin. "If we can finish up with our business, maybe we can hop a boat as far as the Indian Territory."

"I'm for that, Mr. Caywood. It would save us days in the saddle."

"You come through Indian Territory?" There was a spark of interest in the man's eyes, and a note of wonder in his voice.

"We did," Jim said.

He wanted to ask more, but a couple of men came in just then and took a table. Orin went over, exchanged pleasantries with these newcomers, and took their orders. Jim and Austin's food arrived ten minutes later—good food and lots of it. They ate, feeling better for it, their hangovers dissipating with the hot coffee, and Orin dutifully kept their cups filled.

The café heated up as the sun mounted higher into the sky and humidity settled heavily upon the town, spilling through the doorway with every man to come in. The tables began to fill with customers, and with each new arrival there followed the inevitable stares and the quick words passed among them. It seemed there were not many places in this country where Austin could go and *not* be noticed.

They pushed their dirty plates aside and Jim said, "We'll rent us a room in the hotel across the way. It should be open for business by now."

"What do you want to wager someone will tell you, 'we don't rent rooms to coloreds'?" Austin said.

Jim Caywood slung his gun belt over his shoulder and patted the scuffed leather holster. "It's an amazing thing how many men change their tunes when deep down inside they know they are wrong."

Austin gave a low chuckle. "You mean when you quietly threaten to blow their manly parts to kingdom come. You know, Mr. Caywood, I can take care of myself. You don't have to keep coming between me and trouble.''

"I know that, Mr. Fandango. After all, I taught you.''

The bell above the door jingled and two men walked in. "Oh, no.''

"What?''

"Remember I said the name of this place struck a chord, but couldn't place where I had heard it?'' Austin nodded at the two men. "Now I remember.''

Jim turned as the two took a table. "Those are the two from St. Louis.''

"Unfortunately.''

"Maybe they won't recognize us.''

"It's too late for that,'' Austin replied. "They are looking our way already.''

Orin wove his way through the crowd and said, "Why, if it ain't Randle Griffith and Mitchel McCory. Haven't seen you two in over a month. Back from your trip up north? Where is all that money you two was planning to make in them Northern steel mills?''

The taller one, the one who had been carrying a cardboard suitcase when Austin last saw him, said, "We tried to get along, but there's just too many of them Republicans about for our liking.''

Orin laughed and glanced at Mitch, the bulldog with the brown beard. "My, my, Mr. McCory, whatever happened to your face?''

Mitchel McCory's hand went to his blue, swollen nose, but stopped just before his fingers touched it. "Had us a run-in up St. Louis way.'' As he spoke, his eyes narrowed across the room on Austin. "It was with a nigger and his white friend, a big man wearing a wide hat. Sort of like those two back there.'' He nudged Randy and stood, kicking back his chair. Raising his voice, Mitch went on. "When is it you started letting niggers eat in your café, Orin? I always thought this was a decent place for a white man to come.''

Austin glanced quickly at Jim. "I got a feeling this day is about to go south on us real quick, Mr. Caywood.''

"Let's try to use our heads instead of our fists," Jim warned. "Remember what I told you."

As Mitch and Randy started back, men scrambled out of their way.

"I know, don't fly off the handle right away and stop and count to three," Austin said to Jim.

Orin was saying, "I don't want no trouble in here, Randle . . . Mitchel. You want to make trouble, you take it outside."

The two men stopped at Jim and Austin's table. Mitch glared at Jim and Randy said to Austin, "Didn't I warn you not to ever show your black face in Phillips County?"

Jim said easily, "Mighty early in the day to be making a fuss, isn't it, boys?"

Mitch ground his knuckles into his fist. "You boys are out of your territory. This time we are on our home turf, and we got lots of friends here. I'm gonna see that you two end up hurting real bad." He looked around the room. "Who wants to beat a nigger today?"

Chairs scuffed back and four men muscled their way across the room.

Austin glanced at Jim, a hard set coming to the big man's face. "We were out of our territory back in St. Louis. You fellows don't want to go busting up Orin's café, do you?" Austin said.

"It's not Orin's place that will be busted up. It's that butt-ugly face of yours that I intend to bust up, nigger. Then I'm gonna run what's left of it into the biggest pile of horseshit Hawthorne has behind his barns. And afterward I'm gonna take a knife to you so that there won't ever be any more butt-ugly niggers running around that look like you."

"Three."

SEVEN

Austin sprang from his chair with the speed of a leopard and the power of a Mexican bull. With knuckles bunched and hard as oak knots, he shot a fist that buckled Mitch in half. Suddenly the entire room was in motion, closing in on him. An upward jab snapped Mitch's head back and laid him out on a table that splintered beneath his weight.

"Come on, boys, let's take him!" Randy shouted, fists whirling as he charged in. The four men who had showed an interest in the fight circled until Austin couldn't keep them all in sight.

Jim Caywood's revolver roared in the crowded room and a cloud of gray smoke unfurled toward the ceiling. "Let's keep it fair, boys," he said. "Only one at a time."

There was not a man there anxious to argue with the big .44 in Jim's paw.

Randy dove in, throwing an uppercut. Austin easily avoided it. A short, quick jab to Randy's chin started the man backpedaling toward the front of the building. The crowd parted as if Moses himself had ordered it so and Austin easily took the advantage, throwing one rapid-fire punch after the other, driving the man across the room. Randy's arms flailed in the air, helpless against Austin's powerful volley. His few futile jabs soon ceased and it took all of the man's strength just to keep his pins under him.

Austin finished the job with a pile-driving blow to Randy's gut that hurled him through the café's plate-glass window. Austin batted away the jagged glass and stepped out right behind him as the men inside scrambled out the door.

Jim Caywood was one of the first outside, the gold-bearing saddlebags over his left shoulder, the revolver still in his right fist.

Randy was sprawled out on the sidewalk and not moving much, except for his steady low groan and his knees slowly drawing tight into his battered midsection.

Austin drew in a huge breath that seared his lungs, and spat into the street. ''Who's next?''

There were no takers.

Men gathered around, mumbling low amongst themselves, keeping a safe distance from the tall, black man with the wide shoulders and ready fists. Austin stood there as if a piece of a mountain had suddenly been planted in the middle of the sidewalk of Laconia.

Although he had easily bested the two troublemakers, and could have taken on any man there, with the possible exception of Jim himself, whose sheer size made up for anything age had stolen from him, he knew that wasn't what stopped them from swarming in and crushing him. It was Jim's revolver keeping the matter orderly—more or less.

''Here, here! What's going on?'' a voice demanded from somewhere beyond the circle of men. ''Who's firing a gun in my town?''

The crowd gave way and a stout fellow of about five-eight with a star pinned to his vest came through. He was hatless. Thick, dark hair was scattered about his head and the tails of his shirt flapped as he walked. In his hand he held a short, double-barreled shotgun. But the hammers were lowered to the caps and the man appeared more flustered at having been suddenly awakened than actually dangerous.

''This here nigger went and beat up Mitchel McCory and Randle Griffith real good, Sheriff,'' one of the men there told him.

"Mitch and Randy?" The sheriff looked down at the man writhing upon the sidewalk and scratched his unshaved chin. "Thought them two was up north someplace."

"They just got back, Roy." Orin appeared to be in a mild state of shock as he peered out past the pieces of shattered glass still clinging to the window frame.

"You did this?" Sheriff Roy Calhoun demanded, glaring at Austin.

"I did."

"Why, you big, arrogant, black sonuvabitch. How dare you lay a hand on a white man. Where were you brought up, anyway, boy?"

Austin started to answer, but Jim cut him off. "He's with me, Sheriff."

"You don't have to speak for me, Mr. Caywood. I can talk for myself."

"Hush your mouth, boy!" Calhoun shifted his view to Jim. "This your boy?"

"They come from Texas," Orin said. "Said they were just passing through."

Calhoun narrowed an eye at the revolver in Jim's hand. "Better put that away, mister, or I'm going to have to take it."

"This?" Jim looked at the weapon as if he had forgotten it was there. "I was just keeping the fight fair, Sheriff. Seems four or five of your young men wanted to tip the odds." He grinned and slipped the revolver back into his holster.

"You know there is a law here against a colored man lifting a hand against a white man?" Calhoun told Jim.

"I didn't know that, Sheriff. Why, down in Texas we generally let men fight anyone who is willing. It don't matter what color they are."

"Well, this here ain't Texas, mister."

And thank you Lord for that! Austin thought.

"What is your name?"

"It's Caywood. And this is Mr. Fandango."

"*Mister* Fandango? He a free man?"

"He is. I gave him his freedom twenty years ago. And

when I did, Austin was so happy he danced a jig. Now, down Texas way, we call that a fandango.''

"I liked the sound of the word," Austin interjected, "and since it was my right to chose any name I wanted, I picked that.''

"Boy, you got to learn to not speak unless spoken to.''

Austin moved toward him. Jim stepped between them. "It's getting mighty hot here in the street. Is there anything else I can do for you, Sheriff?''

"You can stand aside and let me arrest that black buck.''

"On what charges?''

"Hitting a white man and busting up my town. How are them for charges?''

Jim looked surprised. "Austin was only trying to protect me from that fellow on the ground, and the other one inside. I'm getting up in years, Sheriff, and Austin couldn't stand by and watch those two young bucks whoop a feeble old man, now, could he?''

Austin fought to hold back his grin. Jim was about as feeble as an old horseshoe, but he had a way with words that could smooth over a flannel road and charm the rattles off a sidewinder. It completely amazed Austin sometimes the things Jim would say to sidestep trouble.

"That's right, Sheriff. These two were just minding their own business when Randy and Mitch come in," one of the bystanders told Calhoun.

Calhoun combed his fingers through his wild mop and considered. He frowned down at Randy, whom a couple men were helping to sit up. "Damn them two," Calhoun said finally. "Griffith and McCory have been troublemakers since they were knee-high to a colt. Wish they'd have stayed up north." He rapped his open palm with the barrel of the shot-gun two or three times, then said, "All right, you two can go. But I want you out of my town.''

"We were planning to leave in the morning," Jim said.

"Just be sure that by tomorrow evening you are long gone from Laconia, or both of you will be cooling your heels in my jail!''

"What about this window, and the broken tables?" Orin said.

Jim opened one of the saddlebags and took three double eagles from it. "This should cover the cost of a table, some broken dishes, and a new window."

"Err, yes, sir. Thank you!" Orin snatched the coins and grinned at them like a coyote who had just discovered a hole into a chicken coop.

Calhoun eyed the two saddlebags, taking note of the heavy way they pulled at Jim's shoulder. "Carrying a bit of cash with you?"

"Just a little traveling money," Jim allowed.

Inside the café, Jim and Austin gathered up their gear. Mitch had been helped into a chair and was cradling his head, holding a damp cloth against his swollen eye.

Austin grinned. Mitch snarled, the hatred in his battered face an open volume—one that Austin did not care to examine too closely.

Back out on the street, the crowd had broken up. Just the same, Austin felt hidden eyes everywhere, watching him and Jim and his skin crawled like a can full of fishing worms. He levered the Sharps onto his shoulder, grasping its long barrel. "Sure you wouldn't want to start for home today, Mr. Caywood?"

"Let's see about getting us a room." They gathered the reins and angled across the street toward the hotel. "Did you have to lay into that fellow like you did?"

"You heard him, Mr. Caywood."

"Most of that was bold talk."

"Sounded like he meant business to me. Anyway, it was *me* he was planning to make into a steer."

"What happened to one and two?"

Austin grinned. "I counted to myself."

Jim stopped and looked at him. Then he laughed and shook his head. "That temper of yours is going to be the death of me yet."

"It ain't proving to be all that healthy to me, either."

They tied their horses in front of the hotel. It was a musty place with a sun-faded carpet on the floor, a potbelly stove in the corner near the front desk, and a flight of narrow stairs climbing one wall. The man behind the desk watched them from beneath bushy gray brows when they came through the door.

"We need a room, my friend and I," Jim said. "Two beds would be nice, though one of us can sleep on the floor if need be."

"Yes, sir. Got a nice room upstairs. Two beds."

"Your mattresses aren't ticky, are they?" Jim inquired, putting pen to the guest book.

"No, sir. We keep a clean hotel, Mister . . . Mr. Caywood," he finished upon reading the name Jim had penned.

Jim paid and was handed a key. "It's number three. Just up the stairs there and to the left."

"Thank you."

The room was small, hot, and stuffy, and it reeked of stale cigar smoke. But it did have two beds, and the sheets were clean. A window overlooking the Mississippi River offered a pretty view, which was the room's best feature.

Across the broad water a distant line of trees marked the state of Mississippi. Plumes of smoke and the long, rippling wakes from a pair of passing riverboats smudged its otherwise placid surface. Austin worked the window latch and lifted the sash to let the river breeze into the stuffy room.

"Word moves quickly through this town," Jim said, dropping the bags of gold onto one of the beds.

Austin stuck his head out the window and studied the weedy lot behind the hotel that ran down to the river. "He just didn't want the same thing to happen to his hotel."

"Sensible. Surprising how polite some folks can get when their pocketbook might be afflicted." Jim sat at a little table and reloaded the spent cylinder of his revolver.

Austin laughed, left the window, and stretched out on the other bed. "Got me a full belly and nothing to do between now and tomorrow morning, so I reckon I'll just spend the rest of the day right here on this bed, Mr. Caywood. There is not one thing I can think of that would interest me out on the streets of Laconia."

"Come about five o'clock when your stomach starts asking when dinner is coming, you'll think different."

Austin smiled contentedly, locked his fingers behind his head, and closed his eyes. "Unless you smell smoke, don't wake me."

"While you are getting your beauty sleep, one of us needs to take those animals to the livery and get them fed."

Austin opened an eye and stared at him. "Ain't too subtle, are you, Mr. Caywood? All right, I'll give you a hand with the horses. *Then* I'm coming right back here and going to sleep."

Jim paid the stableman while Austin led their animals down the long dusky aisle. He turned each into a stall and removed their saddles and blankets. Carrying them to saddletrees at the end of the barn, Austin replayed the fight in his brain. He had no particular reason to dwell on the matter, but being so recent that his fists still stung and his left side burned where Mitch—or had it been Randy?—had landed a solid punch, Austin found it impossible to put it out of mind. He wondered if Mr. Caywood had been correct. Did he fly off the handle too soon? Could Mitch and Randy have been talked out of their threats, as Jim had suggested? And if they could have, is that what Austin really wanted?

No!

He had taken particular delight in whooping those two and he'd have taken no pleasure at all in turning and walking away—even if that had been possible. Maybe he did carry a temper with a short fuse, but dammit, how much did a man have to take? The Good Book tells to forgive your neighbor "seventy times seven," but that was meant for saints. And he was far from that.

Austin tossed the saddles onto a pair trees and went back for the others. After slinging them over another pair of saddletrees, he stood back wiping his hands and looked at them in the dancing motes in a stream of dusty sunlight through a window high overhead. A sound from a dark corner caused him to whirl around. Instinctively his hand lowered near for the six-gun he had taken to wearing since the morning's row.

The air was hot and humid, and the sharp odor of manure and the mustiness of molding hay filled his nose. He could almost taste them. His ears strained, sorting out the sounds of the horses from the other noises. From the front of the long building, Jim's deep voice wafted down the dim aisle, past the dark stalls.

He heard another voice. It was barely a whisper and had come from the blackness beyond a wall at the end of the stalls. And he heard something else, too . . .

When Austin tried to identify this new sound, all that came to mind was the chains on a doubletree. He stepped quietly along the wall. The stink of manure grew stronger the farther back he went. The wall ended abruptly and emptiness lay beyond. The air hung heavy here, untouched by any breeze from the front door, hotter than a firecracker. He stopped, waiting for his eyes to adjust, breathing shallowly. The overwhelming stench was nearly too much to endure; a solid wall past which he had no desire to go. But curiosity pushed him on once his eyes became accustomed to the faint light seeping past a shuttered window.

He stepped around the corner, feeling the lumps of rotting manure beneath his boots. In the dimness he caught movement along the far wall. There was that sound again and this time he was certain it was a chain rattling softly.

"Who's here?"

Now a half-dozen chains clattered and the whole back wall seemed to move a bit. Austin eased his revolver from the holster, his heart thumping, the stink of ammonia stinging his eyes. He moved to the shuttered window, lifted the crossbar, and swung the panels wide. Daylight poured in, blindingly bright a first, then he saw them.

They were huddled in a corner and strung out across the wall. More than three dozen black folks in the most miserable state of being that Austin could have imagined. Young and old, men and women, some barefoot, chained ankle to ankle and huddled among the aging horse manure, locked up in an airless barn baking in the heat of a hot Arkansas sun.

Some of the slaves shielded their eyes from this sudden

glare, others just sat there with their chins upon their chests, beyond caring. No one said a word. No complaints. Not even the look of hope in a single face.

Austin was no longer aware of the foul, biting air. "My God," he gasped, too stunned to speak more than that. His view swept across the dismal lot. Cattle rounded up in their pens back in Texas lived in better conditions than these people. At first Austin wondered if they were being punished for some crime. Then he realized the truth. These were the slaves destined for the auction block in the morning.

"How . . . how long have you people been here?" Austin asked.

No one spoke at first. Then a young woman's voice said softly, "Three day, I think."

Austin searched among the faces for the speaker. The pair of wide eyes that he found watching him were such a stark contrast to these surroundings that it took his breath away. She was beautiful in spite of her deplorable state, a lily growing up among the rank grass. There was a vitality in those eyes and a determined set to the fine chin that announced to the world that bondage did not mean defeat.

Austin holstered his revolver and took a step in her direction. "Three days?" It was incredible that anyone would leave these people in such a deplorable state for that long.

"Yo' come to bring us water? Some of the young'uns need a drink of water. It has been a long time."

"Water?" Austin was so shocked by what he saw, his thinking had not quite gotten back on track. "Er, no, but I could get you some water—"

Austin heard footsteps behind him. He spun around and discovered a white man standing there. Beside him was a black man carrying a pale and ladle.

"What are you doing here?" He was a slightly rotund man with a thick head of black hair that reminded Austin of someone else. His harsh demand instantly brought Austin out of his trance.

"Are you the one responsible for keeping these people locked up here?"

"Watch your mouth, boy." The man's eyes narrowed. "I

know you. You're that nigger who busted up Orin's café this morning.''

"Austin." Jim Caywood had come around the corner with the stableman at his side. In a glance he seemed to understand what was going on, but all he said was, "I'm going back to the hotel now." He turned and was gone.

There was nothing Austin could do to help these people— nothing anyone could do right now. Jim knew it, and in his own way he had reminded Austin of that. But it was up to Austin to make his own decisions. Casting a look over his shoulder at the pretty girl, he frowned then pushed past the white man and left.

He caught up with Jim on the road and walked alongside him without speaking.

"His name is Willard. Willard Calhoun. He is the auctioneer."

Austin nodded. "I thought he looked familiar. The sheriff's brother?"

"Cousin, least that's what the stableman told me."

They continued on in silence past a couple of buildings. "There has got to be something we can do to help those poor people," Austin said.

"Nothing that is legal. Nothing that won't land us both in Calhoun's jail."

"We could break them out tonight."

Jim stopped and rounded on Austin. There was a hardness in his eyes that rarely showed up. "You know my feelings on that, Austin. We've been over this before and I shouldn't have to explain it again now. But I will. We are in the South, and according to the laws of the land, regardless of how you or I feel about them, slaves are property. Property! That's all. To steal them away is the same as stealing a man's horses or his bank account, and I won't be a party to that." He wheeled away, his heels kicking angrily into the road as he strode toward the hotel, leaving Austin standing there.

Austin grimaced. The sight had gotten to Jim, too.

EIGHT

"Roll out! Time to wake up and get moving!" Everly passed through the sleeping bodies, spurring some awake with a curse and a jab of his boot. Willis was one of those who received his wake-up call in the shape of a boot tip to the spine.

"Owww."

Everly paused and scowled down at the young man. "Didn't like that much?"

Willis rubbed the spot and said nothing. He had learned early on that for this trip at least, a silent tongue was the course of least hurt.

Everly went on his way, waking the other sleeping slaves. It was still dark, but to the east, a faint ribbon of pink was starting to tinge the horizon. Willis sat up, massaging his shoulder to work circulation back into it. He was cold and hungry. Sleeping on the ground with no blanket was a misery in itself. Waking to the likes of Franklin Everly and his two partners made it pure hell.

"I is gettin' too old for dis sorta nonsense," the old man who had given Willis a hand into the wagon the day before said. His name was George and he had been a house slave most of his life, but his master had come onto hard times, and rather than to sell off his younger field hands, who made money for him, he had whittled down the house staff.

Willis gave the oldster a hand up and helped him brush the twigs and dirt from his clothes. "How far is it to this place, Laconia?" Willis asked softly so as not to attract Everly's attention, and his wrath.

"I was der once, long time ago. Oh, seems like it still a long way off. But we ought to be der before nightfall."

"What's it like?"

George looked at him. "What is Laconia like?"

"No, I mean, de auction."

"Oh. Well, dat's easy enough. I tell you exact like it is. De auction man, him just run yo' up onto a plank so all de white folk can see yo'. Den he brags up and down on how smart yo' is, or how strong, or if yo' be a woman, how many chill'ns yo' is gonna bear. He lies somethin' fierce to dem white folks. Den someone calls out a number, and someone else calls out another number, and den the auction man say 'sold!' and yo' go off with yo'r new marster. Easy as snatchin' cherry pie."

"What if my new marster is a hard man?"

George shrugged his bony shoulders and shook his head. "Yo' do yo'r best, son. Dat's all any man can do."

Everly's whip snapped out in the still morning air and cracked three, four times above their heads, bringing the slaves to their feet. "You got five minutes to take care of any business you need to tend to. Then I want you all back aboard the wagon, hear? Do what you need to now. Don't ask to stop later 'cause I won't." The whip sizzled the air again. "Now jump to and hurry up!"

Everly drew the whip into coils and strode over to Peter Deats. "We are behind schedule, Deats. Told Calhoun I'd have this load to his auction in time for the second day. That means we need to get them there this evening."

"I've been pushing the mules as hard as I can. You know how them headstrong creatures can be sometimes. They have only one speed in them when they get a stubborn streak into their thick skulls."

"I don't care how you do it, just make sure we make

Laconia by nightfall.'' Everly went back through the mulling crowd of black people. ''If you're done with your business, climb aboard, and make quick work of it.'' He spied a young girl bent over, rolling up a frayed quilt that she had been given by her former mistress for the journey. Putting a boot to her rump, he sent the girl reeling into the ground. ''No lollygagging, wench!''

Laughing, Everly walked away as two women hurried to help the startled girl to her feet.

''He's a hard man,'' Willis noted softly, stepping behind a tree to urinate.

George did likewise. When they finished, George whispered, ''Him more den hard man. I hear him kilt mor'n ten colored boys. Yo' do best not to get crosswise wid dat man. He is pure devil, dat one.''

Willis swallowed down a lump in his throat, swung a leg over the tailgate of the wagon, and helped George up onto the hard seat after him. The wagon began to fill up. There were fifteen in all and for the most part the children had to sit upon the laps of the older folks. Some even took turns walking behind the wagon. Willis had learned some of their names. There was Adaline, a middle-aged woman who walked with a limp. And Elijah, a lad of twelve who already had a whip-scarred back and wore a belligerent pout. Willis felt fortunate that at his age he had never once been whipped. Josephine was the girl with the quilt. She was maybe fifteen and quite pretty, but she did not smile. No one smiled very much. Willis had heard the names of the others during the long hot ride the day before, but he had forgotten half of them.

Everly stepped up onto the back of the wagon and looked over the tailgate to take a head count. ''They are all here.''

Deats unfurled his whip and cracked it above the lead mule. ''On your way, Fannie!'' he shouted.

The wagon creaked and moved ahead slowly beneath the burden of its human cargo. Willis was hungry, but no mention of a breakfast had been made. Robert, one of the little ones, whimpered in his mother's arms from the ache of an empty belly. Everly ignored it as if black slaves could subsist on air alone.

Willis was heartsick and homesick as the wagon groaned and creaked ahead. He missed his family. He missed the farm. He missed Samuel. And yes, he even missed Master Hill. And he cursed himself for just being who he was. He had no one else to blame for the sorry state he was in now.

A crowd began to gather around the auction stand shortly before eleven o'clock. Expensive carriages lined the street, and stepping from them were nicely dressed women strolling arm in arm with gentlemen in summer jackets, polished boots, and silk hats. Austin knew that he and Jim looked out of place among these wealthy folks. Him particularly, for he was the only black man there not kowtowing at a white man's side. He was the only one wearing a broad Texan hat and a six-gun at his hip. And he was catching his fair share of the stares as he and Jim shouldered their way into the gathering of buyers before the stand.

Austin found his view drawn to the barn across the way, not to the "block." The auction block was a big open platform, empty at the moment, decked out in streamers and colorful paper, and equipped with a set of stairs on one end. But back at the barn they had erected something like a horse stall with a big white sheet drawn across it. From past years at other auctions, Austin knew that this was where the event would begin.

The crowd grew into a sea of tall hats, but Jim and Austin managed to peer over the tops of most of them. Nearby two well-dressed men were chatting about the fine weather and the grand turnout. From their boisterous speech, Austin suspected that they had spent much of the morning over at the saloon.

As the crowd thickened Austin found himself being bumped and shoved about, but so long as he stayed near Jim, no one spoke to him or ordered him aside. It irked him that he still had to hide behind a white man. But here at least, he was willing to play along. To be a black man, and to be bold and stand up for your rights, was a sure ticket to trouble.

He'd already had trouble in Laconia. He didn't need any more. He wanted to be done with this Shadow Road business and get back to the relative safety of the JC Connected outfit.

Texas was a slave state, it was true, but when a black man got his freedom, folks tended to accept it. Perhaps it was because Texas was already a hodgepodge of cultures: Mexicans, Indians, French, and whites, all competing for the same ground. Austin didn't understand it. Maybe it was just that Texas was familiar to him, and Arkansas not. One thing Austin knew for a fact: Down Texas way a man was admired for who he was and what he could do. Color could never be too awfully important in a place where a relentless sun tended to darken all men.

"Here comes the man," Jim said, bringing Austin's thoughts around to the task at hand. It was the same short, round fellow Austin had run into in the barn the day before. Willard P. Calhoun.

Willard climbed the stairs to the platform and beamed at the crowd. Austin saw right off that he was a real showman and was as easy before a large gathering as if these fifty or so folks had been only two or three close friends gathered in his parlor. He raised his hands for silence and the murmuring subsided.

"Morning, morning, morning, ladies and gentlemen. What a beautiful day for an auction! Heh? What do you all say?" Willard clapped his hands and the buyers below responded precisely as he wanted them to.

"Now, before we begin I just want to make a few announcements. First off, for you ladies. If the bidding and buying becomes tedious, Lisa Goodman over at Matley's Millinery has lemonade and sweet cakes all set out. And they are good." He rubbed his ample belly. "I know, already sampled them!"

Willard and the crowd chuckled.

"And we have not forgotten the children either. Now, if you young folks care to gather over in Calhoun Park, my cousin, Buster G., has set up entertainment for you, too. There's a hoop toss, and a seesaw, a marble circle, and for you boys, there will be a shooting match later in the day.

Buster has even donated a keg of sarsaparilla soda and root beer! And they are *goooood*, too. I had to sample them just to make sure.''

The crowd was warming to Willard. It thinned out considerably after the children scampered away and many of the women strolled off in pairs and threes and fours down the street toward the millinery shop. Some of the ladies remained with their husbands. These, Austin reckoned, were the ones who kept a close eye on the purse strings, and how far their husbands opened them.

''Now we are almost ready to begin. You all know how it goes, so I don't have to explain it to you again. But for you who are new to this, a few ground rules. I'll open the bid at a price that I think is fair. It's your job to raise that price.'' Willard winked and grinned, and the crowd took their cue and laughed. ''Now, once we commence to bidding, I'll be raising the call just as fast as they come in, so be aware friends, this is not a good time to go to scratching your head or nose 'cause you just might end up owning a Negro!'' Another pause and another chuckle from the crowd. Willard grinned again.

''There is a man who enjoys his work,'' Austin said.

''It does appear so,'' Jim agreed.

''We are almost ready to start. I have one last announcement. Normally we do an auction like this in one day. However, because of the number of Negroes we are bringing to you this time, the auction will last over two days. At the moment I have about, oh, two-thirds of them over there in Hawthorne's barn.''

The crowd turned their collective heads as if something significant was about to happen at the barn. When nothing did, they looked back at Willard.

''My good friend Mr. Franklin Everly is on the road at this very moment—I hope—with the final lot. He will be arriving this afternoon and that will give us time to get the Negroes cleaned and freshened up for your inspection. Tomorrow, at this same time, we will conclude the auction. All right now. Everybody ready to commence? Good.'' Willard looked out across their heads and raised his voice. "Roy, bring that first buck out here."

Now, when the crowd looked back, the white sheet lifted and Sheriff Roy Calhoun escorted the first of the slaves forward. His leg shackles had been removed, and he came willingly. Austin grimaced. Who wouldn't with a shotgun poking his back? The bidders gathered around the black man for a closer look, prodding and turning him, examining his teeth with their white-gloved fingers. When they were satisfied, Calhoun nudged the slave in the spine with his gun, and he climbed the stairs to the platform. Willard told him to stand in its center.

"This buck is called Joe. He's twenty-seven years old! He's got a strong back and straight spine. Take that shirt off, Joe, and show the folks your back."

The slave obeyed without complaint.

"You good folks take notice here, not hardly a single mark on this buck's back. That tells you he's a good nigger. Never caused his former master any trouble. He's an Arkansas-bred boy from up in Woodruff County. Show the folks how you walk."

Joe trudged across the platform and back.

"See that? Healthy as an ox. How much for this buck? Let's start the bidding at eleven hundred."

"I'll give eleven," someone said.

"I have eleven, how about twelve? Do I hear twelve? Twelve over there. Twelve fifty? Twelve fifty? Do I hear twelve fifty?"

"Twelve fifty."

"I have twelve fifty. How about thirteen, how about thirteen, how about thirteen . . . ?"

"What do you think?" Austin asked.

"If that fellow is twenty-seven I'll eat my saddle. He looks to be nearer to forty than thirty. We'll wait a bit."

The auctioneer's banter kept up at a pace that would turn most men hoarse. But Willard's practiced throat never missed a beat. Joe went for fifteen hundred and right on his heels was a family of three that went all together for twenty-two. They would have brought more if the child had been a boy.

The morning passed with the sheriff escorting each slave from behind the sheet and the crowd gathered around him or her for a closer examination. Austin's attention kept going back to the two men nearby whom he had noticed earlier. As each slave came to the block, they had some comment to make, and none was ever good. Now that Austin had become aware of them, he spied the silver flask that they passed between themselves. That explained part of it, but in Austin's book, drunkenness was no excuse for bad manners.

Jim leaned close at one point and said, ''I'd like to shove something into the mouths of those two crowing popinjays.''

''I have a notion what, and there is plenty over there in that barn.''

Jim laughed. ''That is most appropriate, Mr. Fandango. But I will pass on it for the moment.''

''Ill manners must run in their family,'' Austin noted.

''Oh?''

''They keep calling themselves Cousin Leroy and Cousin Teddy.''

''Do they? Well, neither Cousin Teddy nor Cousin Leroy seems much interested in bidding so far. Just in being annoying.''

The day grew hotter and Austin wondered if Jim was ever going to ''take care of business'' so that they could be out of there. It was vexing enough just to watch his brothers and sisters paraded before them like cattle, but to have to put up with Leroy and Teddy's sometimes lewd and always insulting comments was beginning to grate.

''Now for our next one,'' Willard yelled as an old woman who had just sold for a paltry three hundred dollars made her way down the stairs to clerk's box, where her new owners were paying and collecting a receipt. ''This is a fine wench, a fine one indeed. Roy, bring her forward.''

The curtain parted. Austin instantly recognized the woman who stepped out ahead of the sheriff. In the daylight she was even lovelier than he remembered. She stood straight and tall and walked proudly in spite of her tattered dress and lowly state in life. As she came near there was a lull in the crowd as the men stared. Then they gathered around the woman and went through the usual prodding and examining. Austin was compelled to move with the mass although he could not get close to her.

"Bring her on up, Roy," Willard urged.

The woman's face remained expressionless, but Austin saw that same flash of anger in her eyes that he had noticed in the dusty half-light of the barn.

"There she is, finally."

Austin looked and was surprised to discover that it was Leroy who had spoken.

Finally?

What had the man had meant by that? The auctioneer's voice rang out loudly: "Well, now, gentlemen. Here is a dandy wench. Look at the conformation, the bearing! Don't you gentlemen think she would make a wonderful house slave for the missus?" Willard's wink was almost as suggestive as the remarks Teddy and Leroy were mumbling to themselves. Some of the ladies averted their eyes or hid their embarrassment behind their hand fans.

"Her name is Savilla. Twenty-three years old, already trained in the duties of a household. Say, let's let the gentlemen have a good look at what they will be bidding on. Slip out of that dress."

When Savilla just stood there, Willard's face reddened. I said outta that dress, wench!"

"Do it," Leroy shouted. "I want to see what I will be bidding on!" He and Teddy were on their tiptoes.

"I won't tell you again," Willard said, his voice strained.

"Maybe she needs some prodding, Willard," a man up front said, and handed up his whip.

Willard shook the long blacksnake out and cracked it once in the air in front of Savilla's face. Slowly, she unbuttoned the front of her dress and let it fall in a crumpled blue pile around her bare feet.

"All it took was the proper incentive," Willard told the crowd. "There you have it. Turn around, wench. That's right. All right, men, I think we will have some lively bidding on this one. Let's open it at twelve hundred dollars.''

"Twelve hundred!'' Leroy shouted.

"Twelve fifty,'' another said.

The bidding was brisk. Austin had all he could do to keep his rage from getting the better of him. Counting to three didn't much help, for some reason. When he looked over, Jim's face had gone to stone. His eyes were narrowed and a heavy frown pulled at his face.

"Fourteen hundred,'' someone countered. Leroy came right back with fourteen fifty.

"He means to have her,'' Austin said through clenched teeth. ''And you heard what him and that cousin of his intend to do with her.''

"I heard,'' Jim said flatly.

As the price rose, the electricity in the air energized the crowd. Everyone—even the women—were caught up in the excitement.

"Sixteen fifty!'' Leroy declared. A sigh of wonderment rolled like a wave through the crowd.

"Seventeen,'' a voice called out.

Immediately Leroy was on top of it.

Austin overheard Teddy telling his cousin, ''Whatever it takes, I'll split it with you.'' Austin glanced at Jim, who was contemplating something smoky and unreadable.

"Seventeen fifty to Mr. Leroy Walton,'' Willard shouted. ''Do I hear eighteen? Eighteen. Anyone going to give me eighteen for this handsome wench? The bid rests at seventeen fifty.''

Willard searched the sea of faces. ''Seventeen fifty going once. Seventeen fifty going twice. Sevent—''

"Two thousand dollars!''

A groan of surprise rose from the gathering and every face turned toward Jim Caywood.

Austin was so happy he wanted to cry.

NINE

Up on the platform, Willard Calhoun peered out over the bidders. He cleared his throat and pointed, saying, "I have an offer of two thousand dollars from the tall gentleman from Texas."

They had been in town less than a day and already everyone knew who they were. The low talk among the people ceased after a few seconds. Austin studied Caywood's stern face and eyes. There was usually a twinkle in their depths, but just then they were flint.

Leroy Walton looked at Jim with mild surprise. A slow grin moved across his face. He was a sporting man, and this new challenge was only going add a little spice to the game of trafficking in human flesh. Leroy's confidence had Austin a little concerned. How far was Jim willing to go? There was no reading the cattleman's face.

"The bid stands at two thousand," Willard reminded the people.

Leroy turned back and said with easy confidence, "Two thousand one hundred."

"Twenty-five."

Excited chatter swept the crowd. Jim was the center of attention. Leroy looked over his shoulder again. But Jim might have been the only man in a thousand miles for all the attention he paid them. His view remained smoky, and fixed upon the auctioneer.

"Twenty-five is the bid. Do I hear twenty-seven?" Willard said it to the crowd, but he was looking at Leroy.

Leroy and Teddy conferred briefly. "Twenty-seven," Leroy returned, but his voice no longer held that edge of confidence.

"Three thousand dollars."

Austin had once watched Jim at a high-stakes poker game. He had worn that same stony face throughout the whole night of playing, and when he walked away from the table leaving more than twelve thousand dollars, he did it without a single word, or even a backward glance, and he never once spoke of the loss afterward. If there was one thing Austin knew for certain about his friend, when Big Jim Caywood went up against a man, be it cards, fists, or simply bidding for a slave at auction against a highfalutin "popinjay" dandy, he did it with a single-mindedness of a grizzly bear protecting her cub. It could be frightening to watch at times.

Leroy was getting flustered. He and his cousin put their heads together again. Willard sang out the bid a couple times then slanted an eye at him.

"Do I hear thirty-five?"

When Leroy did not speak up at once, Willard said, "How about it, Mr. Walton? You going to call this gentleman's bid?"

Austin's view shifted to the woman on the platform. Savilla had slipped back into the dress and was buttoning it together in front. Like everyone else, her gaze was upon the tall Texan with open wonderment.

Leroy glanced quickly over his shoulder then back at the auctioneer. "Where is the bid standing?"

"The bid stands at three thousand dollars. I need a reply now."

"Um . . . um . . ." He glanced at his cousin again and got a nod. "Thirty-five hundred dollars."

"Four thousand dollars."

Astonishment silenced the crowd. Even Willard was momentarily taken aback. "Well, well, the gentleman from Texas certainly takes his bidding seriously." Willard had developed a smile that made Austin think of a circus clown holding a pair of chicken eggs in his mouth.

Leroy wheeled around and glared at Jim. "What do you want her for, anyway, old man?"

Jim leveled an eye at him. "That's none of your business, sonny boy. And you can't afford her anyway."

"Four thousand dollars is the bid, Mr. Walton."

Leroy Walton glared back at the auctioneer.

"Do I hear forty-five hundred? Hmm? Forty-five? How about it, Mr. Walton? Maybe four thousand and fifty? Hmm?"

That was a jab and a twist of the knife to the young man's arrogance. It was apparent to everyone that a mere fifty-dollar raise was about as substantial a roadblock to Jim's stampede bidding as a rowboat would be to a plunging barkentine in a gale. In his sarcastic way, Willard was telling Leroy that he was in a race he couldn't win. It was plain that Jim's remark had cut to the heart of the matter. Leroy *couldn't* afford to push the bid much higher.

"Four thousand going once . . . four thousand twice . . . four thousand going three times . . . sold to the gentleman from Texas."

The scattered applause from the crowd told just how some folks felt about Leroy and his cousin Teddy. Leroy glared at them, his face taking on color. He started to say something, then thought better of it, right there with everyone listening.

"Let's go," Jim said, leaving the crowd. "I'll take care of the money. Bring her over."

Austin made his way to the stairs as Savilla was coming down them. He offered his hand. She stopped and looked at it, uncertain of the gesture.

"You going to take it or not?" Austin said. "It doesn't bite."

Savilla looked at him for a long moment, uncertainty softening her hard stare. "Do I know you, suh?"

"Yesterday, in Hawthorne's barn."

Her face brightened briefly as she remembered. "I thought

so. The light was to your back. I could hardly see.'' She placed her hand into his and Austin took her through the crowd to the clerk's booth, where Jim was counting out a stack of gold coins from one of the saddlebags.

''By cracky, that was a good show,'' the clerk chirped. ''That Leroy Walton and his cousin Teddy Marcs have a reputation in these parts, if you know what I mean.'' He winked at Jim. ''It was a pleasure to watch you put them in their place. Don't hardly ever happen.''

''There is no honor in besting a fool, sir,'' Jim said.

The clerk chuckled as he wrote a receipt and stamped the ownership transfer papers. He folded them both into an envelope and handed it to Jim. ''We thank you for your business.''

Jim pushed the envelope into an inside vest pocket, looked at Austin, then Savilla. His stony face finally cracked and he gave her a smile. ''My name is Jim Caywood, and this is my foreman, *Mister* Fandango. I think it will take an act of Congress to convince him to call me Jim. So, I'm careful to always return the favor.''

Savilla stared.

Austin said, ''Don't listen to what he says. It don't take Congress, all it takes is a bottle of whiskey, isn't that right, *Shim*?''

Jim laughed.

''Sorry, suh. I don't understand what you say?''

''Don't worry about it, Savilla. Let's get our horses.''

''We leaving?''

''We are, Mr. Fandango. I have spent enough money in this town.''

The three of them started toward the barn. Although he did not want to appear curious, Austin couldn't help himself. He had to look back. Leroy and Teddy were watching them. That tingling at the back of his neck had warned him they would be. ''Those two are giving us the evil eye.''

Jim kept his view on the wide barn doors. ''Just one more reason to be moving on. We have not made a favorable impression in Laconia. Anyway, I told the sheriff we would leave his friendly town this afternoon.'' He grinned at Austin. "Don't want to give the man an excuse to lock you and me away in his jail, do we?"

Austin shook his head and looked back at Savilla, who was walking a few steps behind them. In the daylight, up close, she was definitely the prettiest thing he had ever laid eyes on.

The barn's cavernous interior funneled a breeze through it, giving some relief from the heat and the glare outside.

"We'll be collecting our horses now, Mr. Hawthorne," Jim told the stableman.

"Yes, sir. Mr. Caywood. They've been hayed and grained, and I even had my boy run a currycomb over them. Will you be coming back this way?"

"Not likely," Jim said. "We'll be making our way south and then west to Texas."

"I ain't ever been to Texas," Hawthorne said. "Hear it's a big place."

"So I have been told. How much do I owe you, Mr. Hawthorne?"

Hawthorne figured the bill. Jim paid it and the stableman brought the horses forward. Jim and Austin saddled the animals, then Jim stood there awhile, frowning.

"Something the matter?" Hawthorne inquired.

"Well, it hadn't occurred to me until just now, but there *is* a problem."

Hawthorne looked apprehensive. Jim studied one of the horses, then considered Savilla. She considered him right back. Jim looked at Hawthorne. "You wouldn't happen to have a saddle around here that was built for a lady to ride, would you?"

"A lady?" He seemed mystified.

"I mean Miss Savilla here, of course. I can't expect her to ride clear to Texas forking a saddle like a man, à la clothespin!"

"Oh! You mean a sidesaddle."

"I'd be willing to trade you a first-class double-cinch Texas saddle and throw in twenty dollars."

After some rummaging around in a storage room, Hawthorne uncovered a dusty sidesaddle. It was old and had not been cared for as it should have been, but it was serviceable, and after it had been wiped off, cinched up tight, and the stirrups adjusted to length, Jim gave his approval and asked Savilla if she could ride sidesaddle.

"I don't know. I never ride a horse before, Marster Caywood."

"Just call me Jim, or Mr. Caywood, as *Mister* Fandango there insists on doing. I am not your master."

Savilla gave him a blank look.

Austin said, "We will explain it to you later."

She glanced from Austin to Jim, her eyes wide and confused.

"This will do, Mr. Hawthorne." Jim put the cow saddle in his hands and added a double eagle. Outside, he and Austin explained the principles of riding sidesaddle to Savilla, helped her atop the horse, and put Laconia behind them . . .

Leroy and Teddy watched them ride out of town. Teddy gave Leroy a small grin. "There goes one handsome Negress. She'd have been some kind of a frolic in the hay, heh, Leroy?"

Leroy glared at him. Teddy had not been the one doing the bidding. He felt the people watching him, thought he heard their guarded chuckles. "I need a drink."

They walked along the carriage-lined street to Buster G. Calhoun's Saloon. Buster was still in the park entertaining the kids, keeping them supplied to their hearts' content with sarsaparilla and root beer.

Teddy called for a beer from Gomer, the barkeep.

Leroy needed something stronger. "Whiskey, and I'll have the bottle, too." He carried it to a table against the wall.

"Don't take it so hard, Cousin Leroy. There will be others."

" 'None of your business, sonny boy. And you can't afford her anyway.' The old fart. Where did that old man come from, anyway?"

"Willard says he was from Texas?"

Leroy tossed back his whiskey and refilled the glass. "Why the hell didn't he stay in Texas?"

Teddy shrugged, sipping his beer. "He was right, you know. You couldn't afford her."

Leroy glared at him.

Teddy grinned. "Did you see those saddlebags he had on his shoulders? They sure looked heavy—gold heavy. And when he paid for the wench he unloaded a pile of double eagles from them. That fellow was toting a mighty big hunk of cash with him. And he meant to keep it, too. Him and that darky with him were both packing six-guns, and they looked the types who knew how to use them."

Leroy refilled his glass and peered long and unhappily at it.

Two men stepped through the batwing doors, glanced around the dark saloon, and came to their table.

Teddy looked up from his beer. "Well, if it isn't Mitchel McCory and Randle Griffith. I haven't seen you two in a while."

"Been traveling," Mitch said.

"Up north," Randy added.

"So we have heard," Leroy commented dryly, contemplating the color of the light through his whiskey glass.

"What the hell happened to your face?" Teddy glanced at Randy. "And yours, too?"

"The same thing that happened to your cousin," Mitch said. "We had us a run-in with that big Texican and his nigger friend—particularly the nigger."

Leroy looked up from the amber glow in his fingers. The whiskey had begun to reach his brain, working on his anger, molding it into a vague notion . . . Given enough time, exactly what that notion was would become clear to him.

"What do you mean?"

"Mind if we join you?"

Leroy kicked back a couple of chairs and called for two more glasses. He'd known both these men for years, though they rarely associated anymore. As small children they had played together, but once Leroy began to understand the distinctions that made them different, the friendship drifted apart. Randle and Mitchel were of the "working class." As adults, there was really very little they had in common.

Gomer brought over the glasses. Leroy filled them.

Randy said, "We saw how that old man whooped you, Leroy. Oh, not like him and his nigger done to us, not with fists. He done it with his money."

"I could have bought her if I had wanted to bad enough," Leroy shot back defensively.

"Sure you could have, but you are smart enough to know that no wench is worth four thousand dollars."

Leroy guzzled more whiskey.

Mitch went on. "The fact of the matter is, he made you look bad in front of all those people. Friends of yours. And him being a stranger in town. Now, that just wasn't right."

"It wasn't right," Leroy agreed, rolling the glass between his palms brooding on that. Mitch wasn't a bad sort, he decided, even if his family never did own any more than forty acres of poor ground.

"Randy and me, we have a score to settle with those two, mainly that buck. And we figure you and Cousin Teddy have one of your own, too."

Leroy stopped rolling the glass and stared at McCory. "What are you driving at?"

Mitch glanced and Randy. "Should I tell him?"

Randy nodded.

"We figure it this way. You and Teddy wanted that girl. Now, I'm not going to ask why." He laughed. "It's pretty plain she was a looker, and if I had to guess, I'd say at least a quarter of the darkies running around this country are mulattoes. I've got nothing against bedding a wench, 'specially a good-looking wench. And if she enjoys it, all the better. But whatever your intentions are, that is your business. Me and Randy, we don't care about the girl. It's that black buck we want to get our hands on." Mitch ground a fist into his hand. "All that interests us is spilling that big nigger's blood, and then that old man. Got scores to settle on both accounts."

"You planning on waylaying them?"

"There is a lot of empty country beyond Laconia. Anything can happen. If you and your cousin want that wench, you're welcome to ride along with us. All we ask is that when push comes to shove, you and Teddy carry your weight."

Leroy glanced at Teddy. "What do you think?"

Teddy shrugged. "It's just that old man and the buck. I judge the four of us can handle them easy enough. And we did want the girl."

Leroy considered the offer. The more he thought about it, the more he liked what Mitch was proposing. That vague notion he had not been able to identify a few minutes earlier was sharpening into focus now. Revenge was what he had wanted to do all along, but it had taken Mitch to put words to the idea.

"Count us in."

"Good. We are wasting time here. Let's do it now, before they reach the river. You have horses?"

"We've a buggy parked around the corner," Teddy said. "That will do."

Outside on the sidewalk, Mitch said, "How about guns?"

Teddy and Leroy looked at each other and shook their heads. "I have half a dozen shotguns, but they are all at home," Teddy said.

Leroy gave essentially the same reply. They both had plenty of guns—all at home.

"We don't have time for you two to go home and get them."

"Why don't we just buy a couple of revolvers?" Teddy suggested.

Everyone thought that a practical solution to the problem, and the four of them crossed the street to the gun shop. Fifteen minutes later Teddy and Leroy had brand-new Colt revolvers tucked under their belts, a flask of powder, caps, balls, and a tin of grease.

They climbed into the carriage while Mitch and Randy swung up onto their horses. It had been almost two hours since Jim, Austin, and Savilla had left, but there were still hours of daylight left, and there was only one road out of town.

TEN

"There is something right pretty about this countryside, isn't there, Mr. Caywood?" Austin drew in the scent of flowers and trees along the road. Far off, at the end of a narrow lane, sat a lonely farmhouse. This stretch of Arkansas, between the Mississippi and the White rivers, was mostly level ground, naturally scant of trees. "Perfect farmland hereabouts, although it appears not many planters have yet taken advantage of it. Smell those flowers."

"You seem to be in particularly fine spirits, Mr. Fandango."

"Leaving Laconia behind has done wonders to my spirits, Mr. Caywood. That place was about a friendly as a nest of scorpions."

Savilla was watching him.

"You from nearby here, Miss Savilla?" Jim asked.

She obviously had not yet decided how to take Austin and Jim. "I come from Jefferson County."

"Where is that?" Jim asked.

"About a day ride in a wagon is all I know, suh. Near the big river. Just across it is Pine Bluffs."

"Where we are going is considerably farther than one day, ma'am. Ever hear of Texas?"

Savilla nodded. "I hear de name once. Don't know where it be."

"Texas is west of here. A good thousand miles to where Mr. Fandango and I live. Different country than what you are used to. Not many trees, but the hills roll on and on like the waves of the sea, and from atop one of them you can see forever." Jim reined in and looked at her. "This will be the last you will see of Arkansas for a long time, ma'am, maybe forever. Is there anyone here you want to see before we leave?"

"See?"

Jim smiled. "You know, a mother or father, maybe a brother . . . a sister? Someone you would like to say good-bye to?"

She shook her head. "I got no one no mo'. My mam died of the ague five year ago. Never know my pap."

"Sorry to hear it. Just thought I'd ask, seeing as you'll be going far away from here."

Savilla stared at Jim for the briefest of moments before averting her eyes. They started moving again. Austin rode beside her.

"You'll like Texas, Miss Savilla. The JC Connected, where you will be staying while you decide, is smack in the middle of a million acres of some of the finest grazing in all the state. The sun rises from the prairie and sets on the prairie. And as far as the eye can see is JC Connected cows. More than two thousand by roundup time next spring."

"Two thousand cows?"

"Yes, ma'am," Austin said.

She looked at him, then cast a wondering glance at Jim. "It must take a powerful lot of slaves to milk all dem cows."

"Milk them?" Austin threw back his head and laughed. "We don't milk 'em. We eat 'em! And what we don't eat we drive to market." He laughed again.

Her startled look cut him short and he said, "It's hard to explain it, I reckon. But you'll see what I mean when we get there. And there are no slaves on the JC Connected."

"No slaves?" Savilla looked from Austin to Jim.

"He is not my master. He is my friend. And he is not your master either."

Jim said, "What were your duties back in Jefferson County, ma'am?"

"I was a house slave, Marster Caywood."

Austin grinned. It was going to take a lot of retraining. It always did when a slave was given freedom. She still didn't understand. That was all right. After twenty years Austin still did not understand what made Jim Caywood do what he did. Someday perhaps the man would tell him—but maybe not.

"Thought that might be so. You have the bearing of a woman schooled in working in a household. I think you and Mrs. Caywood will get along just fine, don't you, Austin?"

Austin had been staring at her wide eyes, the arch of her cheekbones, the way her lips came together in a stern yet somehow soft mouth. "I think Miss Savilla and Mrs. Caywood will get along splendidly."

Jim must have seen Austin staring, for a smirk touched his lips just before he turned away.

Up ahead, the road bent toward a wide river. Where it ended a shack sat at the head of a long pier. A big raft was tied to the pier, near a tarnished signaling bell that sprouted from a pole at its far end. As they drew nearer Austin was able to read the shingle nailed above the door.

HARRIS BERGER'S WHITE RIVER FERRY
Only river crossing for twenty miles!

Jim drew rein at the hitching rail and swung out of his saddle. A man in homespuns and a sweat-stained straw hat stepped out onto the narrow porch and eyed the trio.

"Ferry running?" Jim asked.

The ferryman was a tall, big-bellied fellow with huge shoulders and a grizzled sunburned face that needed a shave. He spat a stream of tobacco juice into the dusty lane. "If you got two bits a head for them horses and another fifty cents for the three of you, it is running."

"I can manage that."

"Then get yourselves aboard. We will leave directly."

Jim motioned Austin to take the horses onto the raft while he paid their fares.

The raft was connected to the near and far banks by a loop of rope and a pair of pulleys. The ferryman drove a long pole into the river and pushed them out into the stream without saying a word except to note that the sky appeared to hold some rain. Other than the observation on forthcoming weather, the burly man shunned conversation and went about his job of poling the raft across the river in silence. In the middle of the crossing the long staff had to plunge deep to find bottom . . . and the White was one of the smaller rivers about, Austin mused. A mere trickle compared with the Mississippi, and not much more than a second-rate stream when placed against the Arkansas. But move it out west and set it down beside the Rio Grande and it would have been an impressive waterway indeed.

Austin watched the far shore draw closer. Upon that muddy bank sat another shack beside another pier with a big bronze signaling bell at the end of the pier, just like the one they had left.

With a thump the raft ground to a halt against the pilings and the ferryman gave it a final powerful shove, bringing it to a stop by a ramp. Jim, Austin, and Savilla led the horses off the ferry.

"How far is it to the Arkansas?" Jim asked.

The ferryman nodded at the road beyond the shack. "It's about five miles ahead. You be wanting to cross over it?"

"If we can find a ferry."

"There is a landing at the end of this road. A steam ferry there will take you to the other side. Be aware that the road forks about three miles yonder. You don't want to find yourself on the right fork. That will take you up along the river and you'll miss the ferry. No, you will want to bear left. That's the road you want."

Jim thanked the man and they started on their way again.

This was mighty peculiar. Austin could see no good reason for having crossed the White River in the first place, not if Jim intended to follow the Shadow Road south, looking for a replacement for Walter. Crossing the Arkansas River made no sense at all unless it was Jim's intention to board a Mississippi-bound steamer. But they could have done that most anywhere along the river.

"Seems like we are going a long way out of our way to New Orleans."

"We aren't going south, Mr. Fandango."

"What have you got in mind?"

"I think it is about time to listen to my instincts, and yours, and head back to Texas."

Austin was delighted at the news, but he was still foreman, and he had the ranch's business to think about. "What about someone to replace Walter?"

"It's not like there are no out-of-work cowboys in Texas, is there?" Jim smiled. "We won't have any trouble finding a wrangler to take Walter's place."

That had been Austin's very argument every year when he and Jim had started down the Shadow Road.

"I know, but . . ." Austin started.

Jim glanced at Savilla. "We found a woman to take Betsy's place. I reckon I have done what I need to."

Austin pondered that a few seconds before asking the obvious question. One he knew Jim was not prepared to answer. He asked anyway.

"Just what is it you *need* to do, Mr. Caywood?"

For a moment Austin thought he might actually get an answer this time. But he didn't. Jim frowned and looked away.

There was something behind this Shadow Road business that Jim kept close to his heart and hidden, something that only he and Juanita shared. Austin respected the secrets husbands and wives kept between themselves, but dadgumit, it was *his* neck on the line every time they crossed the Mason-Dixon Line. *He* was the ex-slave going back to a place where every man with black skin was considered an inferior species, fit only for doing the white man's tasks. Austin knew that it wasn't only whites who owned slaves. There were black slave owners and Indian slave owners in the South, too, but the common denominator in all of it was the black slave.

If Austin had his way about it, he would scrape every last trace of Southern dust from his boots and never set foot there again. And if it wasn't for his freedom, he'd have left Texas years ago. There were plenty of places a man could go. Places like the Kansas Territory, where a big gold strike in the Rocky Mountains was booming and men were far more interested in the color of rocks than the color of skin. Then there was the New Mexico Territory, where folks were generally color-blind, and dark skin was more the norm than the exception anyway. And a man could always head for the Northern territories, where Fugitive Slave Laws essentially did not exist.

Austin thought of his father, who had run away years ago. The master of the plantation had posted a reward and had searched for him for months, but had never found him. Austin liked to think that his father had made it to freedom and was living free and happy in a cabin far across the Rocky Mountains. At least that was what he wanted to believe. There was no way to know now, not after so many years.

They rode on for another mile in silence. Ahead, Austin spied the fork in the road the ferryman had warned them about. Coming off that fork just then was a heavy freighter, overflowing with black people, some walking behind it. Two white men sat upon the driver's box, a third rode horseback alongside.

The freighter creaked to a stop.

"Afternoon, gentlemen," Jim said.

Austin noted the blacksnake whips, the pepperbox pistol thrust into the driver's belt, and the shotgun in the hands of his partner. The horseman had a whip in his left fist and a revolver on his hip.

"Afternoon," the man on horseback replied. He studied Austin and Savilla. His view lingered upon the girl, and when it returned to Jim he said, "See you come from the auction at Laconia."

"I have indeed." Jim glanced at Savilla. "One of yours?"

"Brought her in last week. Dropping these niggers off today for tomorrow's auction."

Austin nudged his horse forward to better see the pile of

humanity crammed inside the wagon box. Young and old, men and women, all packed together like so much freight. And like freight that did not need feeding or tending, these folks looked lean and hungry. Their parched lips all but cried out for water. Unbelievable in a place like Arkansas, where there was so much water to be had. Austin wondered when they had last been given a chance to stretch their legs—or the ones walking a chance to ride.

An old man standing on the road appeared bone weary and only just managing to keep on his feet. A young fellow next to him had given him a shoulder to lean upon.

Austin rode up to the two. "You look mighty weary, Grandpa."

The old man grinned. "Dese old bones have seen a lot of misery, suh. But I will make out all right, Lord willin'."

"When was the last time you had a drink?"

"Ain't had nothing since dis mornin', 'fore we started off."

It was late afternoon and the heat oppressive. Austin bristled at the notion that these people were being herded to market in a condition he and Jim would never permit for their *cattle*! Austin untied the canteen from his saddle and handed it down to the old man.

Like a firecracker going off, the blacksnake lashed out and stung Austin's wrist. With a snap of his wrist, the man on horseback yanked the canteen away.

Austin's fist struck out like a rattler and caught the whip. But the man had a firmer grip on the handle and the braided leather burned as it sang through Austin's fingers.

Instantly the man was out of his saddle and coming at him. "You leave those niggers alone!" he snapped, loathing glaring from his eyes.

Austin flexed his fingers where a red welt began to rise upon his skin. His anger flared. A warning look that Jim gave him forced him to rein it in.

"That's one," he mumbled under his breath.

"You tell your boy not to go poking his nose where it don't belong," the man said to Jim while keeping Austin in his burning glare.

"He's not my boy," Jim replied, warningly shaking his head.

Austin got the message all right. They were in the South and they had already had one run-in with the law. They did not need another. He got it, but he didn't like it. Biting his tongue, Austin dismounted.

The slaver gave him room to bend for the canteen. Suddenly his boot came up and drove hard into Austin's spine, sprawling him at the feet of the old man.

The driver and shotgun rider laughed.

Austin lurched around cat quick.

The slaver glared at him. "I see you don't like being told what to do, do you, nigger?"

Past the slaver's shoulder Austin read the look of alarm in Jim's face, and the silent signal he was giving him.

That's two.

"Let's go, Austin," Jim said, his voice stretched tight. "We are not out to have trouble here."

But oh, how he longed for trouble. It was all he could do to stop himself. Every fiber in his being cried out to spring at the slaver's throat. To shake him insensible like a dog shakes a rabbit and then tosses it aside. Austin's fists ached to feel bone break, his knuckles thirsted for blood. But he gathered in his anger. Jim was right. They didn't need any more trouble. Not here.

Austin stood, snatched up the canteen, and glared at the white man as he moved for the reins of his horse.

"I don't like what I'm seeing in your eyes, nigger. Ain't no one ever taught you never to look a white man direct like that? Where is your upbringing, boy?"

The man was taunting him, eager for a fight.

Austin stiffened. Every instinct demanded that he teach the rowdy a lesson on manners. No man ought to be allowed to speak to another man that way. If this had been Texas instead of Arkansas . . .

Austin took what little pleasure he could in that thought.

The slaver laughed as Austin turned away and stepped into the stirrup.

"Gutless pile of dog shit."

Anger flared white-hot and exploded in his brain, blinding Austin to the peril of what he was about to do. He spun on the other man like a top and in a heartbeat his fists flew out. Startling fast, Austin plowed into the slaver. Pent-up anger raged through his fists as the man shrank beneath his quick and powerful blows. Austin buckled him with a low jab and followed it with a bone-shattering uppercut that snapped his head back. Teeth jarred together, blood flowed, and the slaver dropped.

Out the corner of his eye Austin saw Jim sawing at the reins of his startled horse.

Up on the wagon seat the driver grabbed for the pepperbox in his belt.

"Look out!" Austin shouted.

Jim's hand stabbed for the Walker. It cleared leather and boomed. The driver jerked back against the wagon bed then lurched forward into the team of mules.

Shocked, the man riding shotgun stared at his partner, flailing down among the traces and skittish mules. Then he came to his senses and his thumbs stroked back the hammers of the shotgun.

"Don't do it!" Austin warned, but it was too late to stop him.

Jim's revolver barked again. The .44 ball kicked the shotgunner off the seat, dropping him in the dirt beside the wagon.

With a haze of gunsmoke in the air and the roar of the shots still ringing in his ears, Austin's view leaped around the scene, quickly checking that no one was moving.

Jim Caywood's craggy face was heavy as lead as he swung to the ground and went around to the far side of the wagon where the second man had fallen. Austin grabbed the driver by the belt and dragged him from beneath the nervous mules. Their hooves had made a mess of the man's face. The fellow was beyond such mortal cares anymore.

"Austin!" Savilla's voice shrilled.

Instinctively he realized his mistake. He leaped aside, hand slapping the grip of the Navy Colt as he rolled. The draw and the crack of his revolver came together. The man on the ground jerked once and his head split wide. The revolver in his fist discharged harmlessly into the road.

Jim burst around the back of the wagon, gun ready. He drew up, staring at the bloody mess at his feet. It was really all over now.

"These two are dead," Austin said, his voice pitched higher than usual. Not something he was able to control. He stood and his whole body tingled from the rush of blood that beat against his ears.

"This one, too," Jim said soberly.

The slaves had dived for cover when the shooting had started. Now one by one their heads peeked over the wagon, eyes like goose eggs. The ones who had been afoot slowly crept from the brambles alongside the road. Savilla sat petrified upon her horse, staring at the blood seeping slowly into the dirt.

Austin drew in a long breath and said, "That is three."

Jim shook his head. "Damn."

"They had it coming."

Jim looked worried. "Maybe. But did it have to be us who gave it to them?"

"What did you expect me to do?"

"Whatever happened to counting to three?"

"I just did."

Jim snorted and shook his head, looking at the bodies.

"You heard all that stuff he was saying."

"I heard."

Austin slowly returned his revolver to its holster. "What would you have done?"

Jim shook his head. "I don't know. I was hoping you'd keep your head 'bout it."

Jim was right. They were in a real pickle barrel now, and it was because he had lost his temper—again. "What do we do now?"

"This is a fine time to be thinking about closing the barn door."

"All right! I lost my head, dammit! I let that lowlife push me into a fight. So what's our next move?"

Jim glanced up and down the road. No one was on it and

hopefully no one had heard the gunshots. "It's a sure thing we can't stay here," he said finally. "What's done is done. Nobody is going to believe that we killed them in self-defense. I say we get ourselves across the river before these men are found. Try to lose ourselves in the backwoods. Texas is southeast of here about five hundred miles, if that's any consolation."

"We have witnesses."

"A wagonload of slaves? Who in this part of the country will believe them."

"All right, so we run with our tail between our legs."

"I am open to suggestions, Mr. Fandango. You have a better idea?"

"No." Austin searched the man he had shot and found a paper folded up inside his vest pocket. It was a list of the names of the slaves he was transporting. Franklin Everly was the man's name. Austin shoved the paper into his own pocket.

Jim mounted up, looking at Savilla. "You all right?"

Her eyes were still saucers. She slowly shook her head. "No, suh, Marster Caywood. I is skeared."

"Don't call me 'Master'!" His abruptness startled her and she shrank beneath his stare. Jim grimaced and said, "I'm sorry. This isn't your fault. I don't need to blow up at you too. Come along."

He started away, but Austin remained there looking at the wagonload of black people. Jim reined around. "Well, Mr. Fandango? You coming or do you intend to stand there and wait for the law to show up?"

"What are we going to do about these people?"

"Someone will come along and know what to do."

"They'll see three dead white men. What do you think they will do to them?"

"What are you driving at?"

"We just can't leave them. We will have to take them with us."

"Take them with us?" Jim rode back. "They don't belong

to us. Not only will the law be after us for killing those three, but they'll hunt us for stealing slaves, too.''

Austin knew what would happen to these helpless people left alone, and he couldn't allow it. He *wouldn't* allow it. "I'm sorry, Mr. Caywood. I've never gone against you on anything, but I have to this time. If we don't take them with us, then I'm staying too.''

ELEVEN

"Do you know what you're doing, Mr. Fandango?"
Austin shook his head. "Not exactly, Mr. Caywood. I only know we can't leave these folks behind."

"Someone will come along and see that they are returned to their owners."

The young fellow who was helping the old man spoke up. "Maybe, maybe not. Likely they will shoot us dead just 'cause we is here."

Jim glanced at him. "What's your name, son?"

"It's Willis, suh."

"You think that could happen here, Willis?"

"I hears it happen all de time. Hear it through de grapevine telegraph. De pattyrollers find a runaway slave, and if dey have a mind to, dey just shot him for de fun of it and drop him body in de bayou."

"Pattyrollers?" Jim asked.

"Patrollers," Austin said. "They look for runaway slaves."

Jim considered the crowd of black faces watching him. He frowned and glanced back at Austin. "This is crazy, you know. How can we expect to get all these people clear to

Texas without being found out? And even if we did, we'd be *stealing* them.''

''Not if they came of their own free will,'' Austin countered. ''Then they would be runaways. You would not oppose helping a runaway, would you?''

''No, of course not.'' Jim was torn.

Austin said, ''And we wouldn't have to take them to Texas. In fact, taking them back to Texas would be a bad idea, since the authorities would just take them back. All we have to do is escort them as far as the Indian Territory. There they would be beyond the reach of the law and free to go where they want.''

''Beyond the reach of the law, but not of the Comanches,'' Jim pointed out.

''I'd face a hundred wild Comanches to be free,'' Willis declared. ''How 'bout the rest of yo'? Yo' want freedom?''

Almost everyone there said they did.

One little girl holding her mother's hand said, ''I don't want no wild Comanche to eat me.''

Willis hunkered down by her. ''I'll protect yo' against dem Comanches, Amy.''

Austin looked at Jim. ''Well?''

''This is crazy,'' Jim said again, but with a reluctant nod of his head he relented. ''All right. We only have one extra horse, so you folks are going to have to walk and it's going to be a mighty long way to Indian Territory—if we ever make it at all,'' he added under his breath.

The wagon instantly disgorged itself of its human cargo. Austin made a head count. There were fifteen. Fifteen slaves officially running away. Fifteen men, women, and children wanted by the law—not counting himself and Jim.

And it was all Austin's fault.

The ferry landing on the Arkansas River was a larger, more elaborate affair than the simple raft crossing they had made at the White River.

Austin watched the wide, slow river swirl past. Here near its mouth where it emptied into the Mississippi, it was perhaps a quarter mile across, maybe more. The Arkansas River had its beginning far to the west in the Rocky Mountains, more than fifteen hundred miles away. For most of the river's course, steep walls contained its water in a narrow channel, but once past Fort Smith, the flat alluvial plains of Arkansas allowed the river to seek some elbow room. At some places along its course the Arkansas River spread to ten miles or more.

"No one is here," Jim said, emerging from the building and looking out across the river. The landing office was built on pilings that reached out over the water. A wide pier stretched more than a hundred feet into the river and off to one side was a covered repair shed where the ferry could be moored and worked on out of the weather.

"Damn!" Austin turned and looked up the lane where they had just come from. They had left the wagon and the three bodies about a mile back and so far had met no one else on the road. But that kind of luck was not likely to hold. He glanced at the shed. It had no walls, only a low, pitched roof. Through the open timbers that supported the roof he saw workbenches and tools, but no ferryman, and no ferryboat.

Jim and Austin followed the boardwalk out to the pier and shaded their eyes across the water. The lowering sun glinted painfully off the vast moving surface before them. Austin spied something and pointed.

"There, about halfway out. See that?"

Jim squinted to bring his old eyes into focus. "Can't make it out."

"It's a smudge of smoke and it looks to be coming this way."

The smudge grew larger and soon they could make out the shape of a large raft with a steam engine in the middle, a paddle wheel behind, and a man leaning hard onto a long rudder such as used to be used on old-time keelboats.

The ferry docked a few minutes later and a spry young man grinning behind a wind-tangled brown beard leaped onto the pier and spun a hawser about a mooring post.

"Afternoon, been waiting long?"

"About twenty minutes."

The ferryman glanced from Jim to Austin, then to the crowd of folks standing with the horses. ''All of them belong to you?''

''They are with us,'' Jim said.

''You want over, I reckon.''

''We are in kind of a hurry,'' Jim answered.

The man glanced at the sky and nodded. ''I can see why. It will be dark in another hour.'' He sniffed the air. ''Smells like rain.''

Austin wondered if all ferrymen were required to forecast the weather to their customers.

''All right. How many?''

''Eighteen and four horses.''

''That a bunch of people, mister. Where you taking them?''

''Across the river.''

''Hmm.'' He looked at the sky again. ''It's is getting mighty late. Will be dark by the time I get back here.'' He looked over and grinned. ''Reckon I will need a dollar a head to take you over now. If you want to wait until the morning . . .''

Jim flipped him twenty dollars gold. The ferryman caught it, fumbled, and almost lost it between the cracks in the pier. ''You can keep the change if you get us across before the sun hits the top of those trees.''

''Yes, sir. Get yourself aboard and just give me a few minutes to carry on some more wood.''

''I'll help you,'' Austin said, signaling for Willis to follow. Jim herded the people and animals onto the ferry while they went to the woodpile. In two trips there was enough fuel on board for the crossing.

Nervously, Austin kept glancing at the road, but their luck was holding and no one showed up to ask hard-to-answer questions about three bodies found on the road. The ferryman lowered a gate, tossed four lengths of wood into the small furnace, and threw the engine into reverse. With a hiss and a puff of gray, the paddle started turning, backing them into the river. A hundred yards out, he pulled back on a lever. The paddle slowed to a stop then began beating the water, driving the ferry into a sweeping turn, its blunt nose aiming for the open river and the far shore beyond.

Austin let go of a long breath. Jim was still frowning, staring back at the receding dock and road.

So far so good, Austin thought. But they were a long way from safety. The more he thought about it, the more impossible the trek ahead seemed to be. But Austin resolved not to worry about what might happen next month, next week, or even tomorrow.

One day at a time with steady nerves and a watchful eye. That's what it is going to take to get us through.

And even that might not be enough!

Mitchel McCory dismounted and knocked on the door.

"He's not here," he said when he got no answer.

"Looks like Berger is on the other side," Teddy said from the seat of the carriage.

McCory strode out onto the pier and clanged the big bronze bell three or four times. It was answered from across the river. The ferry left the distant landing, slowly working its way across the river.

When the raft made landing, the ferryman waved and said, "If it ain't the cousins Leroy and Teddy."

"Evening, Mr. Berger," Leroy said. "We need to get across."

"Sure, still enough daylight for that."

They boarded the raft and it shoved off.

Once under way, Mitch said, "There didn't happen to be a white man and two niggers come through here a while back?"

Propelling the raft across the current, Berger kept one eye on the river and the other on the reach of the pole as the muddy bottom dropped away. "In fact, I took a party like that across about two hours ago. The white man was a good head to a head and a half taller than you and wore one of them big hats. Him and his boy both carried guns. Don't see many like them in these parts. I reckoned they must be foreigners, so I just kept my mouth shut. You trying to catch up with them three?"

"He's a friend of ours," Teddy piped in. "We heard he was in Laconia, but he pulled out before we could find him. We just want to say howdy before he left Arkansas. They are foreigners. Come from Texas."

"Thought they might be." Berger added a stream of tobacco juice to the flow of the White River.

"They didn't happen to say where they were heading, did they?" Mitch asked.

"Not exactly, but they did ask about making a crossing at the Arkansas. I told them how to get to the landing. Probably already there. If you hurry, you might catch them before the ferry shoves off."

The last thing Leroy wanted was to catch them at the ferry. That would be too public a place. A long, lonely stretch of road without witnesses would do much better. But it was beginning to look like they had lost their chance at Austin and Jim.

When they had disembarked and were on their way again, Leroy glanced at Randy and said, "If they have already crossed over to the other side, I'm turning around. I've better things to do than chase those three clear to Texas."

Teddy agreed and wondered if they might not have time for a couple of beers back at Calhoun's Saloon if they turned around now.

Mitch and Randy's bitterness ran deeper than the cousins', but even they saw that their scheme could be pushed only so far before it became unprofitable.

"Maybe you are right," Randy said. "If they have already crossed over the river, it will be another day before we can catch up with them, and I'm not prepared to sleep out on the ground tonight."

Mitch grumbled about letting the men from Texas get off free as jaybirds.

Leroy was getting hungry, and Teddy's comment about the beers sounded inviting. "Consider it an adventure, Mitch. One that never got off the ground." He grinned at the bearded man. "If we turn around now, we might be able to catch the ferry before Berger shuts it down. In another hour we could be back in town having a beer at Calhoun's."

They came around a bend in the road and a small stand of trees. Up ahead was a freight wagon off to one side, its team cropping the grass.

Leroy gave a laugh and said, "That looks like Franklin Everly's freighter." But after a moment's study his smile vanished and concern came to his face. He pulled the buggy to a halt and narrowed his eyes. "Something is wrong here."

Ahead, one of the mules glanced up at them then went back to its feeding. Teddy said, "Isn't Everly supposed to be bringing another load of slaves to Laconia for the auction tomorrow?"

"That's what Willard said this morning."

Mitch leaned forward in his saddle, peering hard. "Don't see no slaves, nor anyone else."

"What is that on the ground?" Randy rode a few dozen feet farther and came suddenly to a stop. When he craned his head over his shoulder at them, his face had paled and his eyes were huge. "I think those are bodies up there!"

They hurried ahead. Leroy and Teddy hopped out of the buggy and bent over the first man, then the second. When they came to the third Mitch was already there, shaking his head. "It's Franklin, and it ain't pretty."

A dead silence fell over them.

Leroy said, "Someone went and blew his brains out."

"That's about as plain as daylight!" Mitch came back sarcastically.

"Who would have done that?" Teddy wondered.

"And where are all the slaves he was supposed to be hauling?" Randy added.

Mitch hunkered down over something in the road. "By these tracks, I'd say the darkies left the wagon and started off in that direction, toward the river."

"They run off?" Randy asked

"Sort of looks that way."

"But who killed Franklin, and his men?"

Mitch was studying something in the road. "Give you one guess?" He pointed at a track among the barefoot prints. "Tell me how many men you know wear shoes with that kind of narrow heel?"

Leroy frowned. "It was that Texan!"

"I'd bet fifty dollars on it! You saw those guns they were wearing."

"What should we do?" Teddy asked.

"I think someone ought to go and fetch Sheriff Calhoun," Leroy said.

Mitch nodded. "You and your cousin go on back to Laconia and bring the sheriff out. Meanwhile me and Randy will head for the ferry and try to keep it from leaving if it hasn't already. If it has, we will wait there for you and the sheriff. In any case, it looks like we have us a couple murderers and a passel of runaway slaves to go after." Mitch grinned. "Things are looking up, boys. Looks like we might have us a real chase on our hands. And think of the reward for bringing all them runaways back."

"What about these bodies? We can't just leave them laying here."

Mitch shrugged. "You can stay and sit with them if you want, Teddy. But they ain't going nowhere—leastwise not under their own steam they ain't."

"It's crazy to try and cross over now," Berger said. "You know what would happen if a sawyer comes down that river and slams into the raft? It could kill us all! And besides, it's nearly midnight!"

"This is official business, Mr. Berger," Sheriff Calhoun replied, his tone leaving no room for argument. "I will take responsibility for whatever happens. Now unmoor that raft and get us across this river."

"Taking responsibility ain't going to bring you, me, or these men back from a watery grave, Sheriff. If we have an accident, we will all end up in the Mississippi!"

"Eventually we are all going to end up somewhere, Mr. Berger," Calhoun replied philosophically.

The ferryman shook his head in dismay, but he saw that the sheriff meant business, and he had two deputies along to back him up. In the lamplight his eyes seemed to plead with Leroy and Teddy. "I thought you two, at least, had more sense. Say, weren't you boys driving a buggy last time?"

In town, Leroy and Teddy had exchanged the buggy for horses at Hawthorne's Livery, thinking that if this affair turned into a real chase, they might require a more maneuverable means of transportation.

Leroy said, "The spring floods are behind us, Mr. Berger. You know the likelihood of a tree coming down the river and capsizing the raft is small."

Defeated, Berger could only stand there and look at them. The sheriff did not intend to relent. Finally the ferryman shook his head. "All right, have it your way. I can see that you intend to cross regardless of any warning I can give. Go take yourselves aboard while I finish getting dressed."

Berger carried his lantern back inside the shack, where its light flickered behind the dingy windowpane. One of Calhoun's deputies, Matt Kelso, a half-breed Cherokee and professional tracker, lifted the gate by the pier. Leroy and Teddy led their horses onto the dark ferry. Calhoun and the other deputy, Harold Klemper, took the horses aboard. A minute later Berger stepped out onto the dock, set the lantern at the head of the raft, and taking up the long pole from its deck, started the company of men across the White River.

They made it to the other side with no dire consequences and Sheriff Calhoun told Berger to wait. "I might want to come back across," he explained briefly before riding away into the night.

Twenty minutes later they reached the place where the slavers' bodies lay. They had not been moved. This road was not heavily traveled and Calhoun was not surprised as he walked among the dark shapes, examining the scene in the moonlight. The freighter and four had moved several hundred feet away as the mules leisurely cropped the grass as best they could still hitched in the traces.

"Klemper. Fetch Mr. Everly's wagon back here," Calhoun told the deputy.

When Klemper strode off for the vehicle, Calhoun said, "Looks like we got a case of murder on our hands. Plain and simple."

"Wonder what brought it on?" Teddy mused aloud.

"It was that big Texan," Leroy said.

Calhoun shook his head. "If I had to make a guess, I'd say it was that black buck traveling with him. He seemed to have a hairtrigger temper. He likely saw all the slaves Everly was hauling and blew his top."

They loaded the bodies into the back of Everly's freighter. Calhoun told Klemper to drive the bodies back to Laconia while he and the others made for the Arkansas ferry landing.

Mitch and Randy's horses were tied at the rail out front of the landing. Inside the long, low building a lantern burned. The ferry was moored to the pier.

At the sound of the sheriff's arrival, Mitch stepped outside. Leroy couldn't see the man's face for the darkness, but he heard the disgust in his voice. "They had already crossed over to the other side by time we got here. Eighteen in all, says the ferryman. Seventeen of them niggers."

"Was it the Texan?" Calhoun asked.

"Yep. Paid for them all, and some extra to get them across before nightfall. We won't be able to cross before daylight."

Calhoun went inside, questioned the ferryman, then scribbled out a message on a piece of paper and shoved it into Kelso's hand. "Get on your horse and see that Klemper gets this before he makes the river crossing. Tell him that as soon as he gets back to Laconia, he is to wake up Arnold Hingle and have him send this telegraph to Sheriff Graff over in Napoleon. My guess is that Texan will head for thick timber and take one of the forest roads straight for Indian Territory. He's got a jump on us, especially if he presses on all night, but traveling with all those people afoot is gonna slow him to a crawl. If we can squeeze him between us and a posse from the south, we can have them by nightfall."

Kelso shoved the telegraph message into his pocket, swung back onto his horse, and kicked it into motion. In a moment the darkness had swallowed him up.

"What's stopping you from taking us across now?" Calhoun asked the ferryman.

"It's late and I need sleep."

"Not good enough."

"It's dark and there is a lot of traffic on this reach of the river."

"So?"

"So we can be run down by a big packet heading down to the Mississippi."

Calhoun frowned, not convinced. Leroy considered it a genuine concern, unlike Berger's lame excuse about being hit by a passing tree.

"You got a running light, don't you?"

"I got a light," the ferryman allowed. "But I still ain't going until morning." He stretched out on a bed against the wall and in a couple of minutes was snoring softly.

TWELVE

Austin's eyes strained up the dark road ahead while his ears, set like a spring trap, sifted through the sounds coming from the black wall of trees on either side. The hour was late, well after midnight, and no one was out and about—no one that is, but himself, Jim Caywood, and more than a dozen runaway slaves. They were passing through a sparsely settled countryside, hardly a house or a fence anywhere in sight. There had been a small settlement along the Arkansas River where they crossed over, but those houses had petered out after the first mile. From there on, the forest had shouldered up alongside the road, where it remained, solid, black, impenetrable.

This road was making Austin nervous, this single thoroughfare. It was the only obvious way to go this side of the river, and the first place anyone would search for a band of runaway slaves, and for two men being hunted for murder.

Savilla walked ahead, alongside Jim, leading her horse. The little girl named Amy straddled Jim's cow saddle while Adaline, the woman with the limp, roosted upon Savilla's sidesaddle. George, the old man, sat upon the horse carrying Jim's gold, and two others, Rebecca and John, rode Austin's animal. The rest of the people had to walk. Most were barefoot. All were hungry, tired, and scared. Especially scared . . . even Austin. When Jim grew quiet and thoughtful, it was usually because he was worrying over something. And Jim had not said but five words since leaving the ferry behind them.

Austin was marching at the rear of the column. *Riding drag again,* he mused, thinking of the long trail drive to St. Louis. He would have been well on his way back home to Texas if Jim had not insisted on riding the Shadow Road this year. And they wouldn't be fleeing the country now if he had held his temper in check. Austin frowned.

They tramped on through the night without a word of complaint from the slaves. They would sometimes ask how far ahead Texas was, and when Austin told them, silence was their only response. How could someone who had never traveled more than fifteen or twenty miles all his life even begin to comprehend walking a thousand or more. Austin might as well have told them they were marching to the moon, or to Glory!

When the sky began to brighten to the east, Austin went to the head of the column and said, ''We better be looking for someplace to hunker down.''

Jim nodded without comment.

''I'm going to shoot the next deer I see. These people haven't eaten for hours. The children are suffering.''

With concern in his eyes, but a reassuring calmness in his voice, Jim said, ''One shot. Don't want to draw attention to ourselves.''

With the dawn, they took a trail off the road and followed it back about a quarter of a mile to a grassy hollow where a spring flowed cool and sweet from the layered, moss-covered ledges. The people lowered themselves wearily to the ground, groaning softly in the luxury of a few moments of respite from the night's long march.

Austin pulled the long Sharps from its saddle boot and thumbed the hammer and checked that the cap was firmly over the nipple.

''I'll be back in a little while.''

"Be careful, Mr. Fandango," Jim warned, collecting wood for a fire. "I'll keep an eye on things here."

"Want me to come with yo'?" Willis asked. "I can help with de butchering and toting all dat meat back."

"Can you move quietly?"

"Yes, suh, Mr. Fandango. I can be quiet as a church mouse."

"You can come along."

Austin led the way, studying the lay of land and fixing it in his brain so that he could find his way back. Deep and eerily quiet, the forest grew hot beneath the morning sun. Dank humidity hung heavily all around them. Occasionally a bird would chirp in the branches overhead. Beneath their feet the thick carpet of leaves crunched softly with each step. From long habit Austin placed his feet carefully, but Willis tromped barefoot along as if the local deer population was deaf.

The young man was full of questions about the West and the Indians. Had Austin ever seen a real Comanche? He asked about freedom, too, and couldn't quite grasp the notion that Austin was not Big Jim's slave, but his friend and employee. Austin briefly tried to explain it to him. Willis understood friendship all right. It was the part about a black man working for money, free to up and leave his employer if he so chose to, that confused him. The young man was brimming with questions.

Finally Austin had to stop him. "Willis."

"Yes?"

"You ever hunt deer before?"

"No, suh. Never done so in my life. I catch a rabbit once in a snare and bring him back to my mam and pappy. Have us a real feast dat night! Just like de man in de big house have every night."

"Well, let me explain it to you. See, there is a whole passel of deer out here, but they don't much cotton to the idea of becoming roast venison. The trick is we need to sneak up on them, at least close enough for Old Reliable here to bring one down. But the way you go on and on, boy, you're scaring every last one of them deer clear to Indian Territory!''

''Oh.'' Willis closed his mouth.

''The plain truth is, if we are ever to find one of them critters, you have got to keep quiet and walk softly. Not a word unless you happen to spy one out yonder there. And then a nudge will do. Got that?''

''Yes, suh. I got it.''

''Mouth shut and eyes open.''

Willis nodded.

Austin found a place among some rocks and settled down to wait. Willis fidgeted, wanting to be moving around. He wanted to talk, too, but a sharp look from Austin reminded him why they were there. Austin considered stalking the area, but he worried that he might not find his way back to the others, so he hunkered down and waited.

Half an hour passed, then an hour.

Then fifty yards or so through the trees, something moved. Austin tapped Willis's shoulder and pointed.

The young man searched the dense timber a moment, then he spied it, too.

It moved again back among the shadows where it was too dark to see clearly, even though the sun was high, not yet straight overhead.

''Deer?'' Willis mouthed.

Austin shook his head and formed the word ''bear.''

Willis's eyes grew large. Apparently bears were a thing he wanted nothing to do with.

Austin put the rifle to his shoulder and narrowed an eye along the barrel. The bear was rooting for berries, moving around behind the cover of a fallen tree. The intervening branches and brambles made for a tricky shot. Austin held back the rifle's trigger as he cocked the hammer so as not to make any noise.

Willis crawled to a better vantage point. His foot pushed a sapling, shaking it. The bear stopped feeding and lifted its head, weak eyes straining while its keen nose sampled the air. Suddenly it turned and bolted.

Austin cursed beneath his breath. He was determined not to let their breakfast escape so easily.

Leaping to his feet, he swung the rifle to his shoulder. The bear was bounding behind a tree. Austin caught a glimpse of black fur in his sights and squeezed the trigger.

Lester Graff felt it welling up deep inside him again, starting at the bottom of his chest and clawing its way up his lungs. He tried to resist, to hold it back, but the cough burst out just the same: racking, aching, exhausting. When it ended, Lester straightened in the saddle and dragged a sleeve across his mouth.

"You gonna be all right, Sheriff?" Boyd Hendricks asked, riding up alongside the man.

Lester blew his nose and shoved the handkerchief back into a pocket. "I'll be all right. Should have stayed in bed. Hell of a time for a bunch of slaves to get it in their head to run away." He glanced at the three other men riding with him and added, "I'm sure we all have something better to do this morning."

The telegrapher's messenger had awoken Lester before dawn. Wally Dobbs had apologized for having done so when the sleepy-eyed lawman had stumbled to the dark door, sniffling into a rag. A persistent cold had lagged on for weeks now, keeping Lester Graff away from the office.

"This just came through," Wally said, regret in his voice for being the bearer of unpleasant news. "I was told to get it to you right away. Sorry."

"That's all right." Lester coughed into his fist, opened the envelope, and turned the message toward a candle he had brought with him. After reading it, he thanked Wally and went back to tell his wife he had to leave.

Lester was distantly related to Sheriff Calhoun. They had met two or three times at family gatherings as they shared a distant aunt through marriage, along with forty or fifty other folks on this side of Arkansas.

Before daylight arrived, Lester had roused Boyd Hendricks, John Meader, and Homer Goshen, all part-time deputies. Coffee and leftover biscuits served for a quick breakfast. With the dawn still pink and fresh in the sky, they had ridden out of Napoleon, heading west for the river road, where Calhoun's telegram had said the runaways had been put ashore by the ferry the night before. It had warned Lester of the two armed men with them—men wanted for murder as well as slave stealing.

Lester's plan was to follow a forest trail west to a point where it crossed the road near the tortured course of a river called Bayou Bartholomew. If the slaves *had* taken the road, Lester reasoned they should be somewhere between the Arkansas and Bayou Bartholomew right now. By cutting across country, he hoped to jump ahead of them, then backtrack and squeeze them between his men and Calhoun's men, who by that time should have made the ferry crossing and be heading south.

A racking cough caught the sheriff off guard. When it passed he glanced at his companions and said, "Don't give me that look. I ain't gonna die—not yet at least." He cleared his throat and spied the break in the trees ahead. "There it is, boys. The river road. Now keep your eyes peeled so we can catch them runaways and get back home. If they hear us coming, they will jump to the trees for cover. Watch the forest. Remember, some of them are armed. They left three dead men behind them."

The deputies checked their guns. Hendricks appeared calm enough, but Meader and Goshen looked nervous. Neither of them had faced killers before. Their dealing in their official role of deputies had been mostly with drunks and riverboat gamblers. Killers were a different matter entirely. Lester grimaced and wondered if he had made a mistake by bringing them as he checked the caps on his shotgun.

They emerged from the trail onto the wider road. Wider only because instead of a single rut, this trace was two ruts wide. Still, it wasn't much more that a weedy track through the forest.

To the south a rickety bridge crossed over the Bayou Bartholomew at one of its narrower bends. To the north, thirty miles or so, flowed the Arkansas River. And in between lay a wild, tangled land of mostly uninhabited forests. Lester and his men turned north and started back toward the Arkansas. Up ahead Sheriff Calhoun and his deputies would be coming south. And somewhere between them would be the runaways.

Lester coughed into his fist. He did not want to be here. What he wanted most was to make short work of this job and put the matter back into Sheriff Calhoun's hands. He wanted to go home.

Two women tended to the skewers of roasting bear meat over a little fire while others napped in the warm morning, dappled with sunlight through the tall leafy ceiling above their heads. Still others talked excitedly about freedom while two or three fretted over what would happen once the "patty-rollers" caught up with them.

"Patrollers aren't going to catch up with you," Austin told them. "Not if we stay low and keep moving . . . and keep off of main roads."

"Mr. Fandango."

Austin came about. Jim gave him a small nod then walked off a few dozen paces, out of earshot of the people there.

"We need to talk about this," Jim said quietly.

Austin had seen the worry on the old man's face all that morning. It wasn't surprising. Austin was worried, too. They had killed three men. It mattered little that they had only done so in self-defense. This was the South, and these were runaway slaves. In the eyes of any judge, they would be found guilty as sin—that is, if they ever made it before a judge. Likely anyone on their trail would be inclined to end it short and quick. Who would question the death of killers and slave stealers in these parts?

"We've been dealt from a stacked deck, Mr. Fandango."

"So long as I've known you, Mr. Caywood, you've always played them as they've fallen."

"This time it is different, my friend." Jim glanced at the peopled gathered in the hollow. "Everything we are doing now cuts across my grain."

"I know how you feel about slaves, and the laws of the land, but how could we have done different?"

"We could have left them."

"We already covered this ground."

Jim frowned. "Whatever was I thinking to go along with your lame idea. Damn! If you had just kept your temper back there."

Austin bristled, but he drew back on his anger. This was Jim Caywood. His friend. Jim didn't make accusations lightly. And deep down inside, Austin knew it had been a half-baked notion to begin with. One colored by the heat of passion in a moment of muddled thinking. Muddled for both of them.

"All right. It was a lame idea. What is done is done."

Jim ran fingers through his thinning hair and tugged his hat down over his eyes. "I know. I've been thinking about rounding back and maybe trying to find a steamer going west." He glanced at the runaways again. "It's a sure thing these people aren't going to be able to walk a thousand miles barefoot. Look how they are suffering already."

"Could we do it?"

Jim frowned. "I don't know. Not very likely—not now. Maybe last night. By now they have already found those three bodies. They are hunting us. Word has gone up the river to keep an eye out for you, me, and fifteen runaways."

"I agree."

"It's almost solid wilderness between the Saline River and Indian Territory. A couple of scattered settlements along the way, Corea Fabre and La Grange, and maybe one or two others." Jim was thinking out loud. "The question is, how far is it to the Saline?" He peered off into the west as if to judge the miles, even though the only thing visible in that direction was trees and more trees.

He gave a sudden and definite shake of his head. "No, it's a wish, that's all."

"It's possible," Austin countered.

"And pigs fly, Mr. Fandango!"

The people below looked over at the sound of Jim's sudden outburst. He lowered his voice again and said, "Face it, we have got only one chance to make it out of Arkansas with our skins still intact, and that is to leave these people here.

They'll be found, and they'll be returned to their owners. That's just the way it has got to be.''

"Don't they have some say-so in this?''

"No. Not now. Not this time.''

Austin's spine stiffened. "You'd send them back to slaving when it's freedom they want?''

"And what do you want, Mr. Fandango?'' His voice was rising again. "You want to keep *your* freedom, or swing from one of these trees? If we get caught with those runaways, think anyone will go easy on you just because you are riding with me? You are a black man who has just killed a white. Think because I bought you out of slavery twenty years ago it is going to make any difference here? They will put a rope around your neck and leave you hanging for buzzard bait!''

"I don't need you to stand between me and trouble, Mr. Caywood.''

Jim was about to say something, then stopped himself.

"What?''

"Nothing.'' Jim wheeled away and strode into the forest.

Austin watched the trees close behind the tall man, then he became aware of someone standing behind him. When he turned, Savilla was there, looking up, her wide brown eyes probing his face, a worried set to her pretty mouth.

"Where did he go?''

Austin was angry and sad all at the same time. He and Jim never argued, and now he wondered why. Was it because he respected the old man? Or was it because he figured he owed him?

"He has a lot on his mind, ma'am. It's Mr. Caywood's way to go off by himself when he is troubled.''

"Is it because of us?''

"'Us'? No. It's them.'' He nodded at the group of fifteen.

The people were silent now, watching. The two women by the fire had stopped turning the spits of meat. Everyone had heard their heated words. They looked confused that a black man could argue with a white and get away with it. They had a lot to learn about freedom, Austin mused. And he wondered if they would ever get the chance.

Savilla's gaze seemed to cut clear through him. It made him uneasy and he looked away. "We are in a bad way here, ma'am. Mr. Caywood, and you, and me, with the horses we have could make Texas in a week. But them. Afoot like they are and not but half of them owning shoes—well, it puts us all in a tight place. Mr. Caywood thinks we should leave them to be picked up and returned to their owners."

"Dey will be bucked and whipped if dey go back."

"I know that. They might very well die if they go on."

"Some things are worth dying for, Mr. Fandango."

"You mean freedom?"

"Maybe Mr. Caywood, him should ask de people what dey want, Mr. Fandango."

"Maybe you are right, ma'am."

Suddenly Jim Caywood was standing there again and Austin wondered if he had heard. Jim glanced briefly at Austin, then Savilla. He strode past them toward the people and said, "You people probably know this already, but if you don't, let me put it to you straight. Yesterday Mr. Fandango and I killed three men. We are wanted men here in Arkansas. And you are runaway slaves. That makes you wanted, too. But as far as I know, they don't execute slaves for running away. They only haul you away and put a whip to your back.

"I know every man, woman, and child here wants freedom. Wants it bad enough to taste it, to do crazy things to get it. But the time has come for some hard thinking about what you are starting out on. If you stop here and go back of your own accord, there is a good chance nothing will come of it. Tell them we took you against your will, if you like. It might make it go easier for yourselves if you do. But if you decide to push on with us, be aware that we have little food and no horses for you to ride. And a posse is likely sniffing out our trail right now. Go on and we all might end up dead."

Willis said, "I want to go. I will take my chances."

Another man stood and said, "I do't know 'bout no one else, but I'd take dying over going back!"

Most agreed. Rebecca was cradling John in her arms. She said, "I do't want my darlin' t'die."

The man who stood asked her, "Yo' want him to grow up to the sting of a whip and a life of misery?"

Someone else said, "We is running away from what we know. But we do't know what we is running to. What is dis place yo' talk of, dis Indian Territory?"

Jim said, "It's not a state and there is no slavery there. But there is danger. The Cherokee live there, and the Comanche and Arapaho roam the country, too. Some are friendly. Some will lift your scalp as soon as look at you. But they won't be doing it because you are black. In fact, being black might be an advantage. It is white men most Indians don't like."

"What would we do if we go to dis Indian place?" the middle-aged woman named Adaline asked.

"Nothing in the territory," Jim said. "But from there you can go to other places."

"What other places?"

Austin had an answer to that. "You can go to the mountains. Right now there is a big gold strike in the Kansas Territory at a place called Cherry Creek. Most of you could get jobs in the gold camps. Maybe even prospect for gold on your own. Then there is New Mexico Territory to the south. A man of color can live free in Santa Fe or Taos. Or you can go to the Northwest, to Oregon. Or to the Dakotas. There is a whole wide country open to you."

Willis said, "Mr. Fandango, how can we find dis place, de gold camps?"

"That's easy enough. You just find the Arkansas River and go west. It ends at the Rocky Mountains. Turn north and about a hundred miles or so you are in the gold camps."

The old man said, "I been bound to a white man all my life. Just a chance to be free is a breath of fresh air to dis old body. I want to go with yo'. I want freedom!"

The voices were unanimous. Austin knew they would be, and he suspected that Jim had known it, too.

Jim nodded his head, his face weighed down with concern. "All right. We will probably all die trying. Mr. Fandango, think these people can fashion moccasins from bearskin?"

"I think these people could do anything they want to."

Jim frowned. "Eat up and then let's get moving. I don't want to linger in one place too long." He glanced at the sky, which had begun to cloud over. "Looks like the weather is going to change, Mr. Fandango."

"So the ferryman warned." Austin hesitated. "I'm, sorry we had words, Mr. Caywood."

Jim said, "We don't often, do we? I should have listened to you from the start." He looked at the people, than back at Austin. "This will not be a cakewalk, Mr. Fandango. I only wish there could be some other way."

By the time they had finished eating, a fine drizzle had begun to fall. Jim asked if anyone knew where they were. A woman named Violet said she once belonged to a man who lived near here, in a place called Hatten's Creek. She remembered taking this trail once, but all she could recall was that it came to an end at the Bayou Bartholomew. But the river was shallow and weedy at that place and she thought another trail picked up on the other side. Her master told her so. Said he used to hunt ducks there when he was younger.

Jim wanted to avoid the main road at all cost. This trail wound its way more or less in the direction he wanted to go and he assumed that most trails went somewhere.

Having an idea where they would end up, Jim started the company moving again.

THIRTEEN

"Wonderful weather. Just what I need." Sheriff Graff scowled at the graying skies. His deputies were already shaking out their oilcloth cloaks and pulling them on. Lester coughed, cleared his throat, spat, and reached behind his saddle for the mackintosh tied there.

Hendricks and Meader were riding a little ahead, eyes searching the sides of the road. Homer Goshen came up alongside him and complained that his hands were acting up again, and that this weather was murder on his finger joints.

What a fine state of health we are in. Lester coughed again and said to Hendricks, "How far ahead do you reckon the river is?"

"I say we are about twenty miles, Lester."

"That's about how I figure it, too. Calhoun should be coming along soon."

"Do you know this man ... this Sheriff Calhoun?" Meader asked.

"Oh, we've met a few times. But I can't say as I know him well."

Meader shook his head. "Why should the sheriff of Phillips County bother crossing over into our county to chase down a bunch of runaways?''

"Some men were murdered. Maybe they were friends of his.'' Lester huddled deeper into his raincoat and fought down another coughing spasm.

"We'll be coming to the Bartholomew Trace shortly,'' Goshen said.

"That don't go nowhere but down to the river,'' Hendricks pointed out.

Lester said, "That's true. But a pack of runaways might not know that.'' A light drizzle began to spatter Lester's mackintosh.

In a few minutes the road became muddy and began to cling to their horses' hooves. When they came to the trace, Meader slid off his horse and studied the ground. "Looks like maybe a lot of people turned off here, Lester.''

The sheriff dismounted, handed his reins to Goshen, and hunkered down beside Meader. "Hmm. I'd say you are right. Most of them look to be barefoot.''

"That would fit a runaway.''

Lester gave a grin and a short laugh. "Barefoot would fit about half the folks in this neck of the woods, Homer, be they white or black.'' He considered a moment, working his lips into a knot. "Reckon we best check it out.''

Shoving a boot into the stirrup, Lester swung back onto his horse. "Boyd, you wait here for Sheriff Calhoun and his men to come by. Me, Goshen, and Meader will check this out. If we find them runaways, we'll haul them out and Calhoun can take them back home with him. In any event, it is only about six or seven miles to the river. If they aren't up this trace, we should be back here in a few hours.''

"Be careful, Lester. Remember, they already killed a couple of men.''

"We'll watch ourselves.'' Lester and his deputies turned their horses up the trace.

Austin and Jim slipped into their ponchos. Unfortunately they had not brought along any extras for the slaves to wear, or for Savilla. The slaves did not seem to mind the drizzle.

They were a people used to hardships. A little moisture was the least of their worries. They walked on, not complaining.

Austin found that he could not help but look at Savilla. The rain streaked her face and flattened her hair to her neck. Mud worked its way between her toes. Even so, he was held by Savilla's beauty. He forced his eyes off her, giving himself a stern reprimand. He wasn't looking for a woman. He had said so to Mrs. Caywood more than once. A man in love was about as useful as a barrel of shucks. No, he was a bachelor, and he liked life that way. It was less complicated.

"There it is," Jim said, bringing the company to a halt. "The end of the line."

Austin stood there watching the wide river meander past. The people wandered down to the sluggish water's edge and peered through the rain at the far side. The Bayou Bartholomew was maybe two hundred yards across, its surface mottled with the rank growth of water grasses. Dead trees stood out a little ways along the bank and an army of cattails marched far out from the shore.

"It do't look deep," Savilla said.

"No, it doesn't," Jim agreed. "But we will likely sink to our knees in the mud."

Austin said, "According to what Violet told us, there is a trail on the other side."

In spite of the rain, the mosquitoes were thick, swarming about their heads. Austin slapped his neck and said, "One thing is certain. If we stay here long enough, these pesky critters will eat us alive."

Jim gave a short laugh, eyeing the languid river suspiciously, as any confirmed drylander might. "Cross that and the catfish will do the same."

"Our only other choice is to go back," Savilla said.

Jim pondered the matter.

Austin did not like that idea. The law was that way! Yet no one knew for sure what lay ahead either. If indeed there was another trail on the far side, as Violet thought there might be, who knew where it led to.

Past the patter of gently falling rain Austin heard something. He looked over his shoulder at the trail that tunneled back through the trees, ears tuning out the rainfall. He heard it again. Now he was sure. It was a muffled sound, as if someone was stifling a cough. And it was not that far off.

"Mr. Caywood!" The urgency in his voice brought Jim and Savilla's heads around. "Someone is coming!"

Jim stepped past the horses, and at the same time down the trail the first man appeared.

"Damn," he swore softly, giving Austin a worried glance. "Let me do the talking." He turned to Savilla. "Go tell those people to act as if nothing is going on here. Let's see how good I can bluff them. Mr. Fandango."

"What?"

"Maybe the law, maybe not. Keep back and blend in with the others."

"I can do that."

The riders drew closer. Austin counted only three.

Jim spoke out of the side of his mouth, keeping his voice low. "If they go for their guns, you take the one in the lead. I'll go for the two behind him."

The riders came forward and spread apart. A man who appeared to be the leader drew to a halt in front of them and swung a shotgun from beneath his raincoat, resting it across his thigh. A swarm of butterflies took flight somewhere behind Austin's belt buckle as the man silently considered the huddled slaves by the river and the four horses.

Jim managed an easy smile. How he could do so was beyond Austin's ken.

"Kinda off the beaten path, aren't you, mister?"

Jim gave a short laugh and let his gaze linger a moment on the black slaves along the weedy riverbank. "Am I glad you fellows come along. It looks like I went and got myself good and lost."

Austin grimaced. Jim was the sort of man who generally spoke the truth straight and damn the consequences. But now he was thinking of the safety of the slaves. He would do what he could to protect them.

"Is that a fact?"

"Yes, it is."

"These people belong to you?"

"I'd be able to answer that a whole lot better if I knew who was doing the asking."

Austin's view shifted toward one of the riders. He was fidgeting under his rain gear and Austin caught a glimpse of the distinctive shape of a gun beneath the man's oilcloth. Looking quickly across the way, Austin saw that the other man had drawn his revolver, too, and was trying to keep it hidden beneath his dripping cloak.

"Lester Graff. Sheriff of Desha County."

"Desha? Well, in that case you are a godsend, friend. No, they don't belong to me. I'm only moving them for Mr. Samuel Packwood of Baton Rouge. He just bought these slaves at auction, over at Hatten's Creek."

Samuel Packwood? Hatten's Creek? Austin was sweating.

"Hatten's Creek? Now, what was a buyer from Baton Rouge doing way up here?"

"Just passing through. He got a real good price, I heard. Hired me to take them to Napoleon and put them aboard a steamer for him."

"Napoleon is east of the main road. You boys are on the wrong side—if you are headed for Napoleon." The sheriff suddenly fell into a fit of coughing. He hacked so hard that Austin practically felt it in his own chest. The coughing passed in a few moments.

Jim laughed and shook his head. He glanced at the cloudy sky and said, "Well, it has happened before, Sheriff. I have trouble telling east from west even when the sun *is* shining. I heard there was a cutoff somewhere around here, but I reckon I must have taken the wrong one. Where am I now?"

"Reckon you did. You turned east." Lester was showing no sign that he was buying Jim's story. "I don't suppose you have papers to prove your story?"

"Papers?" Jim's voice faltered.

Austin winced. The sheriff had caught his stumble, too. So had his deputies.

"Err, well I had something that Mr. Packwood gave me." Jim felt his vest beneath the poncho. "I think I put it in one of these pockets—"

"Where are they?"

The tension turned electric. One of Graff's deputies had gone stiff as a flagpole, his mouth hardening into a frozen gash tight across his face. Austin had seen that look before. Seen it on the faces of men who were scared—real scared.

Jim hemmed and hawed, suddenly at a loss for words. In another moment the charade would be over. He was scrambling for a believable line to give the sheriff.

Austin had to think of something fast. "Hoo! Marster Franklin!"

Austin's voice startled them.

The deputy swung over and the muzzle of his revolver briefly poked from beneath the oilcloth.

Austin's breath caught. He forced both his hands to remain in sight in spite of the gun following him. He fixed a wide, innocent smile upon his face and sauntered toward the men, particularly careful that his poncho remained in place, covering his revolver. The last thing he wanted was to give that skittish deputy a reason to reach for the trigger.

"Am deses dem papers yo' is looking for?" he asked. With his left hand he carefully removed the papers he had taken off of Franklin Everly's body. "Here dey be, safe and dry. Just like yo' tell me I should keep 'em, Marster *Franklin*."

"Oh, yes, that is where they went," Jim said, recovering his composure.

"Yo' done gibe dem to me, Marster *Franklin*, 'member?"

Jim passed the papers up to Lester Graff.

Graff peered hard at Jim. "You say these slaves were purchased in Hatten's Creek?"

Jim nodded, glancing at the men on either side of Lester. They were hanging by a hairtrigger. Every cattleman who had ridden the Shawnee Trail had seen that same look hundreds of time before—in the eyes of frightened cows a heartbeat away from stampeding. These men had obviously been told of the bodies left behind and they were smart to be cautions. But Austin sensed something more here. These weren't hardened lawmen. They were too nervous. They were shopkeepers or farmers. Upholding the law was only something they did part-time. These were men thinking about the wives and children they had left behind, and they were scared.

As Lester unfolded the papers he spoke to one of his deputies. "Homer. Your sister lives in Hatten's Creek, doesn't she?"

"Mary lives on a farm about five miles outside Hatten's Creek," he said stiffly, his wide eyes not straying off of Jim. So far no one had paid much attention to Austin. Black men with guns and the know-how to use them just weren't a concern in this part of the country. Like Randy had said back in St. Louis, *Is it legal for a nigger to carry a gun?*

"You ever hear of a slave auction taking place thereabouts?"

"None that I recollect, Lester."

"Hmm?" Lester studied the papers. "And you are Mr. Franklin Everly?"

"That's right."

Austin chanced a glance at the runaways. Every one of them was stiff as a door and staring at Lester and his men as if they were spirits from the afterworld. Austin tried to be relaxed, but he was tight as a fiddle string, too—like Lester Graff's deputies.

"Hmm. Says here you own these slaves."

"That is just the way Mr. Packwood put it down." Now that the crisis over ownership papers was past, Jim was beginning to roll easily with his yarn. "He said it would be easier to book passage for them if it looked like I was the owner."

A horde of mosquitoes had settled over them all, but no one made a move to shoo them. Lester refolded the paper, considered a moment, then handed it back to Jim. "I'm going to have to ask you to come with me to Napoleon for a bit more questioning, Mr. Everly." He grinned. "But since you were supposed to be headed there anyway, I don't suppose you would mind." Lester put a fist to his mouth and coughed until he almost gagged himself. He wiped his mouth on the sleeve of his mackintosh and said, "Come along now. I'm sure Sheriff Calhoun has some questions for you, too."

Jim tried not to look alarmed. "Why don't you just point

us in the right direction, Sheriff? We travel real slow afoot like these people are. I'll come around to visit you at your office as soon as we get in.''

Homer said, ''You know, Sheriff, come to think of it, I'm pretty sure there has never been a slave auction in Hatten's Creek. That little place can hardly support one saloon and a blacksmith. No one living there has any money to buy slaves.''

''I'm thinking the same thing, Homer. And I'm thinking these are the runaways Calhoun is searching for, and this big fellow here must be the one who murdered them three back there in Phillips County.'' Lester thumbed the hammers on his gun. ''No more talk. Let's go.''

''Now, Sheriff, let's be reasonable about this.'' Jim reached beneath his poncho to put the papers away.

''He's got a gun!'' the other deputy shrilled.

Startled, Lester jerked his shotgun around.

Homer yanked his revolver from under his raincoat, cocking it as he swung toward Jim.

''Mr. Caywood!'' Austin threw himself into the big man. A revolver cracked. Austin felt a tug on the poncho. He rolled across the muddy ground. His Colt cleared leather and barked once. Then his ears were filled with the roar of Lester's shotgun. Something like a fist punched his left shoulder. Another gun barked. Austin wheeled upon the ground and fired twice more.

Jim's Walker roared.

Austin rolled again and leveled his gun at the first deputy, but all he found was the man's horse sidestepping nervously. The saddle was empty. He swung toward the sheriff and again found only an empty saddle. The third man was down, too.

It had happened so fast Austin had had no time to think, and now suddenly it was over. The haze of gun smoke hung in the damp air and the acrid odor of black powder stung in his nostrils. Austin swung back toward the first man's horse. The deputy was on the ground, facedown in the mud, not moving. Unsteady, Austin stood, his revolver leaping to each of the three bodies. None moved.

"I . . . I think they are all dead, Mr. Caywood." Austin drew in a long, deep breath. It did not calm him. His brain felt light, his thinking vaguely muddled.

He kicked the shotgun from Lester's lifeless hand and peered down at the wide, vacant eyes looking up at him. Austin crossed the muddy ground to the one called Homer and turned him over. He was becoming aware of a stinging that was slowly engulfing his left shoulder.

Homer had taken Austin's bullet through the neck. There was a huge artery there, but hardly any blood showed. He had died instantly. The third man was dead, too.

Austin slowly shook his head. "They are all dead," he said in dismay. "Damnation, Mr. Caywood. We just killed us three more white men!" Austin sat down in the mud staring at the dead man at his feet, the shock of what had just happened slowly registering. His shoulder was beginning to ache.

He was aware of a hand touching it examiningly. Austin looked over.

Savilla said, "Yo' is hurt."

Austin rotated it. "It was the shotgun. I must have caught the edge of the pattern. It's not bad." When he stood, his legs were shaky. "We better make tracks, Mr. Caywood."

Jim didn't answer.

"Mr. Caywood?"

Savilla's hand tightened upon his arm.

Austin turned back. Jim was sprawled at their horses' hooves, the side of his poncho ripped to shreds, the right side of his vest drenched in blood.

"Mr. Caywood!" Austin shoved the revolver into its holster and went to his knees beside the big man. "Jim!"

Slowly Jim Caywood's eyes opened. They stared right through Austin at first, then he blinked and his focus sharpened. A faint smile touched his lips. "Jim? Finally, after all these years, you said it. I knew you'd come around one of these days, Mr. Fandango."

"Don't talk." Austin tore opened Jim's vest. The wound was worse than he had imagined.

A sudden spasm ripped the faint grin away. "I . . . I don't have much time, Austin."

"Oh, Lord! What do I do?"

Jim weakly grasped his wrist. "Nothing you can do . . . not now."

"I'll try to stop the bleeding!" Austin was letting emotions get the better of him. He fought to get them under control. Jim was right. There was nothing he could do now. Nothing anyone could do. Jim was dying.

"Listen . . . got to tell you . . ." Jim's words trailed off.

"What?"

"Tell . . . tell Juanita I will miss her. Tell her I am sorry . . . tell her I love her."

"I will." Austin was choking up.

Jim nodded. "See that she gets the money."

"Of course."

"I know you will. Got to be careful now. This . . . this is enemy territory for you."

Austin swallowed hard. His heart climbed right back up into his throat. His eyes were misting.

"Something else . . ." Jim's voice was growing weak.

Austin leaned closer to hear.

"I need to tell you . . . it's about the Shadow Road."

"What about the Shadow Road?"

"Why I ride it . . . every year."

"The promise?"

"Yes. Listen." Jim tapped his breast. "This scar. Comanche give it to me. Left me for dead."

Austin nodded. He knew that much of the story. But only that much.

"A man . . . he came along and found me. A good man. But he was on the run. Law chasing him. Had nothing but the shirt on his back, but he gave it to me. Stayed with me for over a week. Kept me alive. He was a poor man, he owned nothing, asked for nothing. Afterward took me home."

Jim coughed up blood.

Austin lifted Jim's head onto his knees. "Go on."

"Man stayed with us for a while, but he needed to go. On

the run. I gave him a horse and he took it—but that was all he would take. Told me about his son. The boy needed help. Asked only one thing from me . . . only that I help his son if I could. I . . . I promised him I would . . ."

Jim lapsed. An odd sensation began filling Austin. Suddenly he had to know the end of it. "Yes? What is the rest, Jim?"

The old man's eyes parted. He was hardly breathing. Just barely holding on. "I went and brought the boy back."

"Who . . . who was the man, this man on the run?"

Jim's grip tightened upon Austin's wrist, then the finger's parted and slipped off. He struggled for one last breath. "The man who helped me . . . he . . . he . . . he was your father, Austin."

FOURTEEN

"Where? Where did my father go to?" Austin pleaded. Jim shuddered, and closed his eyes, and quietly let go of life.

Austin cradled the old man in his arms, his tears mingling with the drizzle, emotion ripping him like a raging grizzly bear. Paralyzed by Jim's death, he did not move for a long time. He had loved this man like the father he hardly remembered. It was still beyond his grasp to accept that it had been his father who had saved Jim's life all those many years ago.

Austin had no idea how long he knelt there in the mud and rain. He realized that Savilla was beside him. She didn't speak, just sat there with him, as if telling him she was just there to share his pain with him if he chose to.

Austin lowered Jim's head back onto the wet ground. Rain streamed over the old man's face, dripped from the corners of his closed eyes, the edge of his lips, gathered in the creases and folds of his tired face.

"What will we do now, Austin?"

Savilla's question hit him like a hammer blow. It staggered him back from his daze to the present—back to reality.

This is enemy territory for you.

He stood. In the dripping clearing alongside the dark, sluggish river, the people were watching him. They were turning to him in the same way, Austin realized with a shock, they had turned to Jim, for leadership.

Savilla's wide dark eyes searched his face. "Where do we go?"

For over half a lifetime Austin had been looking toward Jim Caywood to answer that same question. Now Jim had no more answers. But the question would not go away. Austin had no time for his grief—not yet at least. Sixteen people depended upon him to get them away from there and to freedom. Juanita was waiting in Texas for them to return, and if Austin did not make it back, how would she ever know how Jim died?

There was nothing Austin could do for Jim. The living needed Austin now. "Gather the horses. We are going across that river."

Austin looked down at his friend one last time, then turned to the people. "Move quickly," he ordered. "We've got to be long gone from here before these men are discovered."

He would have liked to take Jim back for a proper burial in the family plot behind the house, near his son, and someday Juanita. But that was impossible. He didn't even have time to bury his friend, even if he could have found a shovel to dig a hole with.

They gathered on the river's bank, sixteen miserably wet and frightened people and Austin, whose misery was felt deepest on the inside. Before leaving, Austin took Jim's heavy revolver. The Walker was a huge gun, but it had always seemed just the right size for Jim's big paw. Looping the holster belt over the saddle horn of Jim's horse, Austin waded out into the water.

He would have welcomed a parting of the river just then—or even a lessening of the rain. But he was no Moses, and if the Deity was planning on lending him a hand, it wasn't going to be in such a spectacular way. The water deepened to his waist, then his chest. The muddy bottom sucked at his boots, trying to pull them off with every step. He held his revolver and rifle above the water. A fire burned inside his shoulder, but Austin ignored it, fighting a more fierce battle with his emotions. He glanced over his shoulders, but the rain obscured the bodies he had left behind.

Resolutely, Austin turned his eyes ahead.

A snake skimmed past, and a snapping turtle the size of his hat plunged into the water from a rotting log. Frogs splashed from half a dozen places among the mats of floating vegetation. The band of fugitives slogged on, feeling for the bottom, which kept dropping away. Austin was neck-deep and holding the firearms at arm's length when most of the people and the horses had taken to swimming. He was expecting to have to do this, too, but then the river bottom began to angle upward and soon the company of runaway slaves dragged themselves up the muddy embankment.

The forest pressed close. If there was a trail, it was not here. Austin walked the slippery bank first in one direction and then another, looking for a passageway into the forest . . .

Willis called out, "I found de trail, Mr. Fandango."

It was overgrown near the riverbank, but once past the rank grasses and bramble, the trace opened up. It was not well traveled anymore but appeared to have been at one time, an old Indian trail, Austin suspected. He gathered the people around him, dripping like half-drowned kittens. They looked at him as if they expected him to say something encouraging. Something that would give them hope. He had no good news for them. He was scared, just as they were. Scared, lost, and heartbroken.

Savilla was watching him differently than the others. She seemed to be attempting to penetrate to his soul, to determine the character of this man who all of a sudden had become the sole protector and savior of these people. Austin grimaced at that thought. Being a savior was not a job he was cut out for. Her eyes made him uneasy and he looked away.

"Anybody know where we are?"

No one spoke. Some wagged their heads. Others just stared.

"Violet. You said you had a master who spoke of this trail. Did he ever say where it went?"

"No, suh, Mr. Fandango. Him just say it was here. Dat's all."

"Great."

George said, "Reckon the only way to know then is to follow it."

Austin put the old man, Amy, Rebecca, and John atop the horses and started along the trail. The rain was growing heavier; cold and miserable, it matched Austin's mood perfectly.

Boyd Hendricks was in the lead and he reined to a stop, staring. "My God."

Roy Calhoun, Leroy Walton, Teddy Marcs, Mitch and Randy, and Matt Kelso came to a halt in a half circle around the bodies. Leroy had seen Hendricks go stiff in his saddle, and now he understood why. His view swept over the four bodies, stopping finally upon the big Texan who had made a fool of him at the auction. Leroy allowed a faint grin to pass over his face. *Can't say as you didn't have it coming, old man.*

Hendricks stepped down from his saddle and bent over Lester Graff's body. Frowning, he examined Homer Goshen and John Meader. Calhoun stood over Jim Caywood, shaking his head.

Leroy and Teddy remained by their horses, watching, as Calhoun's deputy stalked around the clearing, peering at the ground, trying to make some sense out of the jumble of footprints in the mud.

Mitch McCory peered down at Jim Caywood and nudged the body a couple times with the toe of his boot, just to be sure the Texan wasn't faking it. "Rather it had been me to put you down, mister," he said to himself.

Leroy grinned.

Randy joined Kelso, trying to decipher the trail. Hendricks said to Calhoun, "Looks like they put up a helluva fight. I should have heard the shots and come to help."

"It would not have made any difference if you had. We must be five, maybe six miles off the cutoff where you met us. There is no way sound would travel that far through this forest."

Hendricks just shook his head. "They were family men, every one. Lester has two sons. John left five children, none older than fourteen. Homer's kids are mostly grown, but he still has one at home. Damn!"

Calhoun drew in a long, sobering breath and let it out slowly. "This happened hours ago. They are already cold and starting to stiffen. Nothing you could have done to prevent it."

Leroy considered the old man lying there. Jim had paid a huge sum for the girl and Leroy wondered if some of that money might not still be on him someplace. Casually he began rummaging through his pockets. He discovered some papers that meant nothing to him. But the envelope he withdrew next brought a grin to his face. Swiftly he hid the envelope in his own pocket and dutifully handed the other papers over to Calhoun."

"Ah, these belonged to Everly." Calhoun studied the soggy paper. The penciled names were still clear. "Now we know the names of the runaways and who their owners were. Willard will be pleased."

Leroy strolled back to his horse.

"What are you smirking about?" Teddy asked.

He showed him the envelope. At first Teddy scowled, then understanding illuminated his face and he beamed ear to ear.

"All we have got to do now is catch up with them," Leroy whispered. In spite of the gloomy weather and four more dead men, the day was looking bright to him.

"Sheriff Calhoun," Kelso called from the riverbank. "Come take a look at this."

They gathered around with the rain spilling from the brims of their hats. Kelso said, "By the look of these tracks, I say they all crossed the river at this place. Horses and people." He peered through the gray shroud at the far side and pointed. "Probably left the water about there."

"Anything over on that side?" Calhoun asked.

Hendricks shook his head. "Not as far as I know. Least I have not heard of anything. It's almost solid forest. Nearly impossible to travel through."

"Unless there is a trail," McCory said.

Hendricks shrugged his shoulders. "Like I said, I don't know."

Calhoun frowned. "This I do know, a bunch of runaway slaves could easily lose themselves in that. They have a head start on us of several hours. If we ever intend to find them, we best get a move on now." He glanced at he overcast sky. "It's getting on in the day. Will be dark soon."

Hendricks said, "You can go after them if you want, Sheriff. I intend to return to Napoleon and bring a wagon back for these men. Their families would want it so."

"I understand." Calhoun looked at Lester Graff. "We were related—through my wife's second cousin or something." Then he looked at the others. "Me and Kelso have to go on, but none of the rest of you is obligated to do so."

Randy and Mitch exchanged glances. "There is still that nigger," Mitch said, his fingers instinctively going to his battered face. "He had a hand in this as well as that white man. I want to see to him personally."

Calhoun nodded. "Don't blame you."

Ten minutes earlier Leroy would have been happy to go home, put on dry clothes, and spend some time with a bottle of his father's sipping whiskey, but now he had reasons to continue on. "I believe my cousin and I will ride along with you, Sheriff. After all, we all want to see that murdering buck brought to justice."

"Most admirable of you, Mr. Walton," Calhoun said. "All right, let's get ourselves across that river and hope we can get the job finished soon. I didn't bring coffee or a blanket, and I'm getting mighty hungry."

"Good luck to you, Sheriff," Boyd put in. "I will be waiting word on that other man. He is wanted in two counties now."

Calhoun gathered up his reins. "I'll wire you soon as I get back to Laconia, Mr. Hendricks." He considered the bodies and added, "Give my condolences to their families."

"I will."

"Tell them we will find that murderer for them. Bring him back alive if we can manage it. But I don't intend to be gentle with the criminal. One way or the other, that black buck will pay for what he and his friend have done here today.''

They were leaving tracks even a baby could follow, and there was nothing Austin could do to prevent it. Even alone it would have been difficult for him not to have left a trace in this mud—one that a good Indian tracker could have followed. Austin was certain they were being followed now. The trail he and Jim had left behind had been too bloody not to have attracted the attention of the law.

Well, it couldn't be helped. Austin pushed the fugitives on through the cold rain all that day. As the evening stretched across the sky, the rain became a drizzle, and then it stopped and the clouds parted. The sun peeked through, fading on the horizon. Before they completely lost its light, Austin turned off the trail and led the weary group about a quarter mile through the thick timber to a wide ravine where a small stream cut through the forest.

He told the people to scrounge for dry wood. They spread out, turning over deadfalls and clawing at the flaking wood inside rotting logs. Soon Austin had a small fire going and piled wet logs nearby it to dry. The people gathered around, warming themselves until their soaked clothes began to steam upon their backs. Austin unsaddled the horses, tied them down by the water where they could feed on its grassy banks, and hung their blankets up to dry.

As night fell across their camp, Austin watched the stars past the tattered remains of the fleeing clouds. He longed for Texas. It wasn't the first time, but tonight the yearning was full of pain. Jim would not be there. It was to be his burdensome task now to tell Juanita how her husband had died.

Austin knew it was best to fill his mind with other thoughts. He turned to his collection of damp guns. He disassembled the Colts first, dried them, reloaded them with dry gunpowder, and thumbed fresh caps on the nipples.

At the fire, women were combing each other's hair while men with glowing brands removed ticks from those who had acquired the unwanted company.

Savilla left the fire ring and sat beside him on the wet log.

For a long moment she peered at the firelight in silence. Finally she said, "I watched my uncle die when I was ten. It was a hard thing to see."

Austin concentrated on the Sharps, which he was reloading. "How did he die?"

"Him and some others was putting shingles to a barn roof. Him fall through a hole and break his back."

"Bad way to go."

"Him suffered three day before the Good Lord take him home. But now him got freedom."

Austin winced. Freedom was so important to people that even death was a welcome doorway to it.

"Mr. Caywood, him was good to you?"

Austin looked over, holding back his emotions. "He was like a father to me."

She shook her head. "I don't understand dat. But I believe you."

Austin pinched a percussion cap from the tin, pressed it onto the rifle's nipple, carefully lowered the hammer, then drew it back to its safety notch. Savilla fidgeted upon the log as he set it aside. There was something on her mind, but she seemed not to know how to go about saying it.

Fireflies flashed golden light above the stream, a rising moon casting chalky light upon its rippling surface. For such a miserable day, the night was becoming pleasant. It was warm, and so humid Austin was certain their clothes would still be wet come morning. It was going to take a good dose of sunlight to finish the job.

"Why did Mr. Caywood buy me?" Savilla blurted suddenly.

So that was it. "He bought you to help his wife with the housework. Cooking, cleaning, you know, domestic things."

"In Texas?"

"Yes. That's where we live."

"Him spend a lot of money?"

Austin smiled. "Yes, him spend a *lot* of money."

"Why?"

"Why? Well, I reckon it was because he wanted you. But on the other hand, those dandies wanted you, too. Mr. Cay-

wood would have called them 'popinjay dandies.' " Austin
grinned. "Popinjay. That was one of his favorite words.
Frankly, Mr. Caywood did not like what they had in mind—
if you know what I mean. I suppose at some point it became
a game to him, and Mr. Caywood had enough money to play
high stakes."

Savilla fell into a thoughtful silence.

Concern for tomorrow, and the next day, and the one after
that, and for the welfare of these people crowded Savilla's
questions from Austin's thoughts. Bringing these people
safely to Indian Territory was going to be a formidable job,
one he could not do all alone. He was going to need help.
But who among all these runaway slaves could he call on?
Likely not a one of them had ever lifted a hand against another man, white or black. To do so would have brought on
a whipping. They had been taught from birth to be docile
and it was going to take more than just words to change that.

Austin remembered how it was when Jim had brought him
out of slavery. He'd been a young, timid man, unsure of
himself, frightened by a world he knew little of. But he had
gumption, as Jim Caywood had more than once declared.

Austin looked at the wet, frightened people huddled
around the fire. *Gumption,* he thought to himself. *Who has
gumption?* His view settled on Willis. Somehow the young
man reminded Austin of himself . . . the way he had been
back all those years ago. Willis was an awkward lad, but he
showed potential.

"Well, you work with what you got," Austin said to himself.

Savilla looked questioningly at him.

Austin said, "Willis."

At the fire the young man looked over. "Yes?"

"Come here."

Timidly, he stood and stepped in front of Austin. "What
did I do?"

"You didn't do anything."

"I am sorry I scared dat bear dis morning."

"Forget it. You ever shoot a gun?"

"Shot a gun? No, suh."

"Didn't think so. We need food. Tomorrow morning early you and me will see what we can scare up. I'll show you how to load my rifle and revolver. I'll give you a lesson on aiming and shooting them. What do you think of that?"

Willis obviously thought considerable of that, if his sudden grin was any indication.

It was still dark when Austin woke the boy. He inclined his head at the dark forest. "Let's go," he whispered.

Willis uncurled himself and sat up, groaning and rubbing his spine. Austin was already striding off. Willis scrambled to catch up. They followed the stream until daylight streaked the sky. They had come to a wide valley and Austin stopped at one end of it.

"How far you judge it to be to the other side, Willis?"

"I do't know, Mr. Fandango."

"First thing you need to do is learn to judge distance. I'd say it is two hundred yards across."

"Two hundred. I will remember dat."

Austin gave him the rifle and explained the rudiments of adjusting for elevation. Windage would have to wait for another time. This was, after all, a crash course. He explained how the rifle was loaded, but that would become clear to the young man once he tried it for himself. Austin set up three rocks the size of pumpkins on a log and paced off the valley. Two hundred and three yards. Willis whistled out his respect for Austin's judgment.

"This is how it is done. Pay attention." Austin shoved the rifle into his shoulder, explaining what he was doing as he narrowed an eye along the barrel. When he squeezed the trigger, the boom filled the valley and Willis flinched. At its far end one of the rocks gave off a spray of dust and disappeared behind the log.

Willis smiled and clapped his hands. Austin shoved the Sharps into them. "Show me how to load it."

Willis looked blank as his eyes lowered to the heavy rifle in his hands. Austin took him through it, step-by-step, then stood him up, adjusted the rifle to the young man's shoulder, and told him to take his best shot.

A second boom rocked the valley. Willis yelped and rubbed his shoulder. Across the way a tree branch sagged and dropped to the ground.

"A mite high." Austin frowned. This was worse than he had expected. "All right, let's try it again." He worked with Willis another hour with the rifle, moving next to Jim's revolver. It was a heavy, awkward thing, but after shooting their way through three cylinders, Willis was beginning to put the bullets more or less where they needed to go. They were making progress.

After reloading the Walker, Austin went right to the heart of what concerned him.

"If that was a man standing there, could you shoot him?" They had moved to within ten paces of an oak tree that was man size in breadth.

Willis lifted the revolver with both hands, aimed, and fired. A chunk of bark sprayed from the oak.

"That's good, but it's not what I meant. I meant up here." Austin tapped the young man's head. "If it was a man standing there, could you pull the trigger, knowing when you did, that man would die?"

Willis thought it over and said, "I don't know."

"Fair enough. No one ever knows until the time comes. What if the man you were aiming at was white?"

Willis shook his head, perplexed.

"What if it was your master? What if he had just whipped you? Then could you?"

"Oh, Marster Hill never whipped none of his niggers," Willis said. "Him a good man."

This wasn't going where Austin had intended. "All right, how about that slaver, Franklin Everly. If it was him, could you pull the trigger?"

Willis's face took on a hard set. "I don't know for sure, Mr. Fandango. But of any white man I ever did knowed, dat Franklin come closest to a mean and ornery dog, and I could shoot a mean and ornery dog."

"At least we are moving in the right direction." Austin told Willis to empty the revolver into the oak tree then reload. They started back. On the way Austin shot two rabbits and a squirrel. Mean fodder for so many mouths, but it was all they could manage, and he did not have all day to spend hunting bigger game.

FIFTEEN

He did not like waiting, but the people needed to eat. *He* needed to eat. Austin frowned and stared into the forest. The air was filled with the odor of roasting rabbit and that made him nervous, too.

"What's you looking at, Mr. Fandango?" He turned and saw that it was Amy. Amy was seven years old, one of two children who were to be sold with their mothers.

He smiled at the child and said, "I'm looking at the men who are following us."

Her eyes expanded. "Can you see them?" she whispered.

Austin took her up into his arms and pointed. "They are over that way."

Amy stared. "I don't see nothing."

"I'm not surprised. I can't see them with my eyes either."

"You can't?" She looked at him and blinked.

He laughed. "I see them inside my head. They are following that muddy trail we left behind us yesterday right now, and if I haven't missed my guess, they are not more than seven or eight miles away." Austin lowered his voice to a whisper. "Just like I can see what is happening right now behind my back."

Austin wheeled around with a suddenness that brought Savilla to a startled halt.

Amy giggled. "You really can see behind your head!"

"What is this all about?" Savilla asked.

Austin was struck by the way the morning sunlight glinted off Savilla's eyes. It brought out specks of gold that he had not noticed before. She was bedraggled, like the others, but her smile made Austin take notice. For a moment he could not speak, drinking in Savilla's beauty. Then he took back control and said, "We were looking for bad men on our trail."

"And what did yo' find?"

"Mr. Fandango says he can see them coming inside his head," Amy said.

"Oh, is dat so?"

Austin set the child on the ground. "Looks like those rabbits are just about done. Go get your share, chile."

Amy ran off. Savilla said, "You really think they are still following us?"

"They won't give up, not with so many bodies to bury."

"What are we to do, then?"

Austin shook his head. "I don't have a good answer for that. One thing I do know, we better not go back to the trail. We'd be sitting ducks for them if we did. This stream runs south and the land hereabouts looks wild and mostly unsettled. So long as we keep heading in the right direction, then we will get to where we are going eventually."

"It makes for hard travel," Savilla pointed out. "Hard on de feet."

"How are the moccasins coming from that bearskin?"

"We started cutting dem out, but we got no needle, no awl, and no thread to stitch with."

"I know it's not easy. We have to do the best we can."

After breakfast the company of fugitives continued on. Austin led them into the stream and told them to stick to the middle. Their progress in the water was slow and unsteady, but about a mile along he spied a place where a gravelly shoal lay. They left the water here, hopping from boulder to boulder. Austin brought the horses one by one then went back to obscure their tracks as best he could.

It was a simple attempt to throw off the men following them, and it just might work. But Austin wasn't ready to count on it. He would still be doing a lot of looking over his shoulder. They covered another half mile tramping through the timber before he brought them back to the stream, where the trees were less crowded together and the grass easier on their feet.

They passed a farmhouse, its acreage already thick in corn. Austin swung wide of the place and by chance hit upon another trail . . . or was it the same one they had left the day before? He had no way of knowing for sure, but the sun had dried it and there were no fresh tracks to indicate anyone had recently tramped its sun-dappled course.

Savilla walked at Austin's side most of the way. Austin liked that. He liked the way she laughed, and he was even getting used to the way her eyes would sometimes narrow down and peer deep into his soul. He doubted she could have seen very much there, but then Amy had doubted that undefinable sixth sense of his that told him that somewhere, not too far away, men where coming after them.

Willis had taken to wearing Jim's revolver, carrying Austin's rifle, and standing a little taller as he roamed ahead of the party, scouting the trail and keeping an eye out for trouble. It was late in the afternoon when suddenly he came running back toward the group.

"Der is another farmhouse up ahead, Mr. Fandango," he said, breathless. "Maybe we should move de people into the trees when we pass it by."

"How far off the trail?"

Willis thought a moment, then said confidently, " 'Bout two hundred yards."

Austin grinned. "Well, let's see." He told the people to move into the forest and wait until they got back.

The farmer had cleared a large patch of forest—maybe two acres' worth. At the far end of it sat his crude log cabin. Austin briefly studied the farmstead and was about to leave when a wagon parked under a lean-to barn caught his eye.

"Let's have a closer look." It was easy to work his way toward the farmhouse through the thick timber, but Willis crashed through the undergrowth like a cow looking for forage. Finally Austin stopped. "You wait here. And for heaven's sake, keep quiet!"

Willis hunkered down behind a tree, gripping Austin's Sharps in both hands.

Moving like a wisp of smoke, Austin made his way through the forest. At the back of the barn he lingered a moment, searching for the occupants of this place. When no one appeared he slipped into the barn and crawled alongside the wagon. It would be big enough to hold most of the fugitives, he decided. This wagon, along with their horses, should accommodate all of them. All the tack and traces were there. Only the animals to pull it were missing.

Austin slipped back into the forest and worked his way around the property until he found a two-rut lane leading down a hill, away from the cabin. The afternoon was drawing to a close. Austin cast about for the inhabitants of this place. At first he saw no one, then a noise drew his attention. Down the lane a young man not too many years older than Willis was leading a pair of heavy draft horses. Austin hid behind a raspberry bramble as the man passed by.

"You girls did your fair share of work today," the farmer was telling the horses. "We nearly got that new patch of ground cleared of all them stumps. Some hay and an extra pail of oats for you two tonight. Heh, Patty? . . . Paula? What do you think of that?"

The farmer took the animals to the barn and fed them. A pretty woman wearing a green-and-yellow gingham apron over her swollen belly came from the cabin and began tugging a currycomb through the horses' coats. Afterward they returned to the house. Austin quietly went back to the place where he had left Willis.

"I think we have found a way to get all our people out of here. There is a road yonder. Don't know where it leads, but if everything works out, we should be miles away from

here come morning. Far enough that no one will come looking.''

   ''Yo' gonna steal dat wagon?''

   ''Steal it? 'Course not. I'm not a thief. I'm gonna buy it
from them.''

   ''What if dey don't want to sell it to yo'?''

   ''I'm not going to ask them. Come on, Willis, let's get
back before the people commence to worrying.''

   After dark Austin led the runaways through the forest to
the little lane he had found. About a mile farther it connected
with a slightly wider road that appeared to run west to east.
West was the way Austin wanted to go . . . more or less. He
hid the people among the trees while he and Willis went back
to the farmhouse to wait.

   The cabin had no glass in its window frames, only shutters
to close out the summer rains or the winter winds. Tonight
they stood open to a cool summer night's breeze. Lamplight
spilled from them into the darkness. The occasional flicker
of a shadow told Austin that the occupants were still awake.
Austin left Willis alone in the forest and made his way in
for a closer look. The open window tempted him, but he
resisted the urge to sneak a peek. He'd know soon enough
when the couple went to bed—once the lights went out.

   The door opened. Austin flattened himself in the deeper
shadows of the cabin as footsteps crossed the porch. In a
moment he heard the soft rhythmic creaking of a rocking
chair. The couple spoke of the day past, of plans for the new
field that the husband was clearing, of the baby on its way.
His name was Windy, at least that's what his wife called
him. Windy just called her ''dear.'' Austin peeked around
the corner. Windy and Dear's backs were to him. Windy's
chair leg tapped the porch gently in time with Dear's rocking.
The sweet aroma of a pipeful of tobacco filled the night air
and made Austin wonder why he'd never taken up smoking
a pipe. Cigarettes were his usual, or a cigar whenever he
could lay hands on one. Dear was mending clothes in the
light from the window at her elbow. Her wicker sewing basket was on the porch next to her rocking chair.

   Slowly and oh so carefully, Austin reached up and over.

His hand slid along the rough boards until the basket was beneath it. Carefully, gently, he hooked a finger over its edge and inched the basket toward him. Then he had it on the ground beside him. Austin quickly rummaged through the contents in the dark. He searched by feel more than sight, grabbing out a spool of thread and an awl. He nearly let out a yelp when he discovered the heavy needle and sucked his fingertip, tasting blood. He dropped a coin into the basket that would have reimbursed its owner for the entire contents ten times over and returned it to the porch, beside the rocker. Shoving his booty into a pocket, Austin crept back around the cabin. Hunched over low, he followed a line of trees back to the forest where Willis was still waiting.

An hour later the lights went out. Austin waited for more time to pass. He wanted the couple to be sleeping the sleep of the dead before he attempted to take the wagon. Willis was fidgeting, scratching and yawning. Soon soft, even breathing came from his direction. Looking over, Austin gave a small grin.

Another hour passed. Coyotes were prowling nearby. At a noise, he turned to discover a greenish-gold eyeshine watching him from a safe distance. The moon moved across the sky. Finally Austin gently shook Willis awake.

"What!"

"Shush! Keep your voice down."

"Oh . . . yes, suh." Willis suddenly remembered where he was and why he was there.

"We have plenty of time. We don't have to work fast, but we got to do it quietly."

Willis nodded his head.

"First thing is take the horses down the road, around the bend, and out of sight of the cabin."

Willis nodded again.

"Then we will come back for the wagon. Remember, not a sound, and watch what you do with your feet this time, all right?"

"Yes, suh, Mr. Fandango. I be quiet like a church mouse."

Austin frowned. He recalled hearing that before.

They crept to the barn and Austin took great pains to look the wagon and the barn over carefully, feeling in the dark for anything that might lie in its way or happen to be leaning against it. When the time came to move the vehicle, he didn't want to run over a tin can, or have an overlooked rake clatter down along its side.

The horses were in stalls a little beyond where the wagon had been parked. When Austin approached their gate, Patty and Paula became nervous. Austin calmed the ladies with gentle words and a handful of hay. He started to open the gate, but it let out with an awful squall. He ceased immediately and they both stared to the cabin. No lights came on, no one stepped out the door. Austin started to breathe again. He slowly moved the gate, this time taking up some of its weight in his arms. That seemed to solve the problem.

Slipping on bridles, they brought the animals out into the corral and took them down the road a couple hundred yards.

Back in the barn he and Willis muscled a plow aside to give them more room. Austin took five gold coins from his pocket and stacked then upon the top of the gatepost in payment for the rig, then grabbed hold of the wagon tongue. Slowly it rolled clear of the barn. Austin complimented the farmer for taking good care of the wagon. Obviously the hubs had recently been greased, for there was not a sound from them as they pulled the heavy vehicle onto the road and slowly passed the cabin. Where the road started down Austin had to dig in his heels to hold it back. He whispered to Willis to climb up on the seat and work the brake.

The strain was getting to Willis and he seemed in a hurry to be out of there. "Let's go," he said, stabbing at the brake with his foot.

Austin eased out of his crouch and the wagon began to move. It came slowly at first, but as the road steepened the vehicle began to pick up speed.

"More brake."

Austin started to jog, holding the wagon tongue off the ground. "More brake!" he whispered, not daring to shout so close to the cabin. Austin glanced up at the wagon seat.

The young man was stabbing frantically in the dark with his foot, searching for the brake.

"Willis!"

Just then Austin tripped on something in the road, dropped the tongue, and fell on his face as the heavy wagon rumbled on. Flattening himself on the road and covering his head, he felt the iron-rimmed wheels roll past, only inches away, picking up speed. As the wagon swept on past him, Austin lifted his head just as Willis leaped from the seat. The lad was soaring through the air. A moment later the heavy wagon slammed into a tree. With the groan of splintering wood, it upended itself and crashed onto its side, its upturned wheels spinning wildly as a fine cloud of dust rose in the moonlight.

The sound of the crash brought the flickering light of a match to the cabin window and a face appeared there.

"Willis! Get the hell out of here!" Austin grabbed the stunned boy's arm and tugged him up off the ground, shoving him toward a rail fence along the lane.

"I is sorry, Mr. Fandango—"

"Shut up!" Austin pushed him through the rails.

At the window the man shouted, "Hey, what's going on out there?" He disappeared from the window, diving out onto the porch in his longhandles, holding a shotgun in his fists.

"Make for the trees!" Austin shouted, no longer worrying that he might be overheard. Behind him the night exploded and a flash of light pushed his shadow far out in front of him. Bark sprayed from a tree to his left, stinging his face and hands. Then the forest closed in to protect their rear. The shotgun roared again. Austin ducked. He did not look back to see if the man was following but plunged on into the forest, hearing painful oohs and aaahs and ouches from Willis, who was barreling on ahead of him, barefoot.

They raced on through the blackness, not daring to stop until the farmhouse was far behind them. Only then did Austin draw to a halt, bent over and gulping for air.

Willis fell against a tree.

"You did it again!" Austin managed to say between breaths.

"I didn't mean to."

"We almost had it! Now we are back where we started!"

"I do't know what is wrong with me, Mr. Fandango. I always do something stupid. Dat is de reason Marster Hill sold me to de auction block."

"I don't want to hear it. Dammit, Willis, I don't want to hear any excuses!" Austin whirled away and stomped off in the direction of the road. Willis started off after him, trying to keep up. Austin did not slow for him in spite of the young man's groans and yelps as his feet came down on pointed sticks and sharp rocks. Anger had lifted its head again, and for Austin this was a better solution than turning his wrath on Willis.

He had stomped his anger out by the time he reached the road and aimed his steps west. Willis was still behind him, wisely keeping his distance. Moonlight powdered the road beneath his feet, turning it into a pale slash cut through the dark forest.

Austin judged Arkansas to be about the most wooded state in the entire Union. Wooded and ticky, and he longed for the dry, wide Texas prairies, where a man could see forever. When he thought of home a searing pain squeezed his heart and forced him to consider other matters—matters like getting out of Arkansas with his skin intact, and getting the runaway slaves in his care safely off to freedom.

Ahead, a dark form stepped out of the shadows, silhouetted against the chalky moonlight. Austin broke stride and his hand reached for the revolver at his side. Then he stopped. The shape standing there watching him was vaguely familiar. As he drew closer he knew a sudden excitement that he could not explain, nor did he care to ponder it very closely right then.

"Savilla," he said when he was but a few paces away. He was surprised and delighted.

"I was worried about yo', Mr. Fandango."

He smiled at her. "Call me Austin, please."

"Where is de wagon?" Her eyes searched his face in the moonlight, wide and full of concern.

Austin hooked a thumb over his shoulder at Willis, who

was cautiously drawing up behind him. "We almost had it, but *he* got in a hurry. Almost got us both a load of birdshot in the seat of our britches. It cost us one hundred dollars of Mrs. Caywood's gold." He shot an accusing look at the young man.

"I said I was sorry." Willis looked pleadingly at Savilla. "What more can I do? My foot slip offa de brake and I let de wagon get away from us."

She smiled faintly. "I think Mister—Austin will get over it. Least you two didn't get shot."

"I'm over it. Although it took a good long walk to work it out of my system. Anyway, we are no worse off than we were a few hours ago . . ." Austin remembered the thread and needle. "In fact, Savilla, we are a mite better off than we were before." He put them in her hand. "I did manage to get these. We can start making moccasins for the people right away. And the first pair goes to Willis. I walked him through some pretty rough country, mostly on purpose."

"I can get by till de women and children have ders first," Willis replied.

Savilla smiled at him and turned toward the forest. "The others are waiting," she said, starting back, Austin walking at her side. "We was getting worried."

It would have been easy to allow Savilla's handsome looks, her caring ways, and that smile that seemed somehow special whenever directed toward him, to captivate him . . .

But Austin reminded himself again that a man with a woman on his mind wasn't worth a barrel of dry shucks, and he couldn't afford to let his guard down now, for an instant.

He let the distance between Savilla and himself widen. If she noticed, she gave no indication of it.

Calhoun remained astride his horse, listening as the man told his story. When he finished, the woman standing at his side nodded her head and said, "That is how it happened, Sheriff. Just like Windy says. Now the wagon is all busted up." She pointed at the heap that Windy had towed back into the barn.

"You say you did not get a good look at these thieves?"

"Like I told you. It was dark, and I was still half-asleep."

"Could they have been colored?"

"Colored?" Windy shrugged. "I can't say."

Mitch said, "You saw only two?"

"Two is all I saw, mister."

Leroy glanced at his cousin. "I'll wager it was them. Who else could it be? Stealing a wagon only makes sense."

Teddy nodded.

Kelso and Randy were walking a pattern near the edge of the forest, heads bent down.

Calhoun said, "Is there anything else you can remember?"

Windy thought. "No. Nothing. Except I don't think they were thieves—well, not the way most folks think of it."

"Oh, and what makes you say that?"

Windy grinned. "Because these *thieves* left a hundred dollars sitting on the gatepost. Reckon if they really intended to *steal* my horses and wagon, they wouldn't go through the trouble of paying more than they were worth. Fact is, considering they got away with nothing, I wonder who is really the thief."

"They wrecked your wagon," Calhoun pointed out.

"It can be fixed, Sheriff."

Calhoun gave him a tight smile. "If the money is troubling you, I'd be glad to see that them runaways get that hundred dollars back once I catch their worthless hides."

Windy shook his head. "I reckon I can live with my conscience."

"Thought that might be the case."

"You still don't know for certain that these two are the same men you are looking for. Tell me about the runaways, Sheriff. How many were there? Have their owners posted a reward?"

Calhoun was about to answer when Kelso called him. "Come and look at this, Roy." He was bent over something near the forest's edge.

Calhoun climbed off his horse and strolled over.

Kelso pointed at the track. "It was made by a boot, one of them high-heeled boots like those Texans were wearing."

"So it was."

Leroy and Teddy stuck their head in for a look.

"And here." Kelso pointed at a second print. "Barefoot, just like we've been following for two days now. It was them all right. No doubt."

Calhoun glanced at Windy. "I would say it is certain." To Kelso he added, "Think you'll have trouble following those tracks?"

"Not a bit, Roy. Those two lit out of here in a big hurry."

"Darn right they did," Windy proclaimed. "They were only one jump ahead of my scattergun, Sheriff. They skedaddled outta here like scared jackrabbits. You'll likely never catch up with them."

"We will see about that." Calhoun gathered up the reins. "All right, boys, let's see where these tracks take us."

Leroy was growing weary of the chase, but when he reminded himself of the pleasurable prize waiting at its end, it didn't seem so tedious. He figured that Mitch and Randy were thinking the same thing, only they intended to take their pleasure in an entirely different manner. Leroy discovered he was grinning as he considered what was in store for that black man once they caught up with him.

Leading their horses, Kelso took the point, his nose to the trail as the posse continued their relentless pursuit.

SIXTEEN

All the next day Austin pushed the people on. They were hungry, tired, and hurting, and as yet only a few wore the crude moccasins that the women who rode the horses were stitching together. No time to linger in the shade of the forest and rest, no time to wait for the posse to catch up with them. No time even to eat the roots some had dug up along the way. Hunger was a constant companion, but their bellies would have to wait. Baby John was crying while Rebecca sang softly, soothingly to him.

Twice during the morning riders had appeared. Each time Austin or Willis spied them at a distance and each time the runaways scattered off the side of the road, into the dense woods, before the riders rode past. Austin always tried to get a glimpse of their faces, even though the only faces he might have recognized would have been one or two from Laconia. And there was no telling how many men were out and about searching for them now.

Hundreds, he imagined.

This is enemy territory for you.

Whenever the fugitives came upon a farm, Austin would steer them into the forest to pass by it unseen. He took no chances. He did not like using the road, but forest travel was too slow and hard on the people. And the few trails across this virgin timberland went the wrong way. This road at least was heading west.

"Austin."

Savilla came up alongside him, leading her horse and its busy rider. Violet was working at punching holes in a scrap _of bearskin. As she finished it, someone on foot would take it to the next woman, who would begin stitching the moccasin together. A third woman was cutting blanks from the ragged remains of the bearskin with Austin's shaving razor.

"Austin."

He looked over, annoyed that she had interrupted his thoughts. "What?"

"De people need rest. You need to find dem some food and make a fire to cook it over."

"No fire!"

His brusque answer shocked her. "What do yo' mean?"

"I mean we make no fire. The smoke will give away our position."

She considered this as they marched on. "Well, how long can dey keep this up—without resting?"

"Until we reach Indian Territory—if they want to get away from here."

"Austin."

His didn't need this distraction. He had more important matters to worry about. His eyes bored straight ahead, searching for riders. Overhead the sky had begun to cloud up again. *Not more rain!* Austin was not thinking of the discomfort of slogging through a dripping forest again, but of the clear trail their footprints would leave behind in muddy ground.

"Austin!" Savilla grabbed his arm and yanked him around. The ragtag company behind him drew to a halt.

"What?"

"We can't go on like this. De people need rest." Her dark eyes flashed, her face was hard as obsidian. It was still a lovely face, one that managed to steal Austin's breath every time he peered into it, but it was a demanding face, too, one to be reckoned with. Savilla had had about all she was going to take of this. "De young'uns are tired and suffering and everyone is hungry. What do yo' think we are? Yo'r Texas cattle to be driven to market?"

That stunned him. *Was* he driving them like *cattle*? Could he, a slave once himself, have forgotten the bitterness he had known at being pushed to his limits by an unfeeling overseer? Was he treating these people the same way? Was it because somehow, somewhere, buried deep within himself, there was sprouting a seed of superiority because of his freedom?

Austin could not accept that. Here, without Jim to stand between him and the white world, he was no better than any one of these slaves. Worse because he had killed men. No one in Arkansas would care that it had been in self-defense.

The people were all watching him, wondering what he would say. They were relying on him to bring them through safely. It was a daunting responsibility, one Austin had never asked for and one he did not want.

"We can't afford to stop now, Savilla. Not yet."

"You do't even know that we are being followed."

That wasn't true. He did know it. But how do you explain a gut feeling? "Look, even if we aren't being followed, there are just too many folks living in these parts for us to take a chance being spotted. We got to get our people out of this part of Arkansas, and the sooner the better. What would folks think if they saw all us black people here, together, alone? First thing they will think is where is their master? And what they will decide is that we are all are runaways. No, we can't stop, not yet at least."

"If you push us too hard, Austin, we will be too lame to run if someone does find us."

"Austin!" Willis's shout brought the debate to a stop. The young man had been traveling several hundred yards behind the main party, as a rear guard, and now he was sprinting up the road like a man with a tiger on his tail. He ground to a stop, breathless. "Der is riders coming!" he said, gulping for air.

"Off the road!"

This was not the first time they had had to flee for cover.

The fugitives were becoming seasoned in the fine art of scattering and hiding. Within seconds not a trace of them could be seen anywhere around. As had become their practice, the runaways fled deep into the woods while Austin found cover near the road where he could see who was coming.

Glancing over his shoulder, he could see nothing of the fifteen runaways or the horses. Turning back, Austin caught a glimpse of a man coming over the rise in the road. Right behind him came others. Seven men in all.

He lay perfectly still in the undergrowth as the riders drew nearer.

"Calhoun," Austin whispered to himself. He recognized the two dandies and the pair of thugs he and Jim had run into on the wharves at St. Louis. There was only one man among them that Austin did not recognize.

The posse rode past without even a glance in his direction. When they had moved on, Austin let out a held breath. In spite of his dislike of using roads, they had one advantage. With so many tracks it was easy to overlook theirs. Austin waited until the posse had disappeared up the road, and hurried into the woods. Suddenly from out of nowhere he was surrounded by inquiring faces.

"It was them."

"Them?" Willis asked.

"The posse I knew was tailing us."

"The people yo' could see inside yo' head, Mr. Fandango?" Amy asked.

"The very ones, honey. The sheriff from Laconia, along with some local boys."

Austin's eyes went to Savilla, saw her worry. He didn't mention the two dandies. He saw no reason to alarm her any more than she already was.

Worried chatter filled the deep forest where they had come back together. Amy was confused. She sensed the grownups' fear and said that she was scared.

George looked at the matter with a pragmatism that comes only with old age. "If dey is der and we am here, den it is a safe bet we can't go back to de road no more."

"I don't suppose anyone here knows where we are?" Austin had already asked that question and gotten only shaken heads and blank stares in return, and it was no different now. "Violet, you said you lived in these parts once."

"Dat am a long time ago, Mr. Fandango. And clear to de udder side of dat muddy riber. I do't know nothin' 'bout dis side. Except I hear of another riber somewhere."

A skinny woman in her forties or fifties named Fannie said, "I hear dat, too. Dat riber, him called Saline. Him wind him way somewhere west to de Bat'omew Bayou. Dat all I knows."

The Saline River lay west of them, and beyond it stretched a forest and land as yet virtually untouched by white men. It was wild country except for a few places like Corea Fabre, Washington, La Grange, and one or two other names Austin recalled reading upon a map once. These were places easy to hide in. To the north and east of them was where the population was largest. But where he was headed, few people had yet to settle.

"If dey went ahead now, maybe dey wo't come back dis way to look for us," Willis suggested.

"I wouldn't count on it. You can bet that they will tell everyone they meet about us. There might even be a reward." Austin looked at the old man and made a wry smile. "What George says is right. We can't use the road anymore."

"Then we make our own way, through de forest," Savilla said.

Austin agreed that the forest was the only safe way still open to them.

"But first we finish making shoes for the people," Savilla said.

"No, first we put some distance between us and the road. *Then* we stop."

Savilla scowled at him.

Austin's heart nearly melted and his resolve wavered. He turned away from her just in time. With Calhoun closing in, he had to be strong, and that meant he couldn't allow the feelings that were beginning to grow inside him toward Savilla to interfere with his thinking—not now.

A man with a woman on his mind ain't worth a barrel of dry shucks!

A glimpse of sunlight through the gathering clouds gave Austin his bearings. He pointed the weary runaways toward the west and pushed on.

The sky began to weep again and soon they were soaked to the skin, but Austin kept on. Savilla had stopped walking beside him, and whenever he happened to catch a glimpse of her face, he was rewarded with a pointed scowl and smoldering eyes. She tromped through the dense undergrowth, carrying herself with a confrontational bearing that spoke of a woman just looking for an excuse to unleash her tongue.

And Austin was determined not to give her one. He simply ignored her, or at least he tried.

They hit upon a game trail that made traveling marginally easier. After a while the trace angled down and dropped onto a wide, heavily timbered terrace, littered with old growth and downed timber. It was ripe for a wildfire . . . if it ever dried out, and judging by the last few days, Austin was becoming doubtful that it ever did.

They descended to a lower terrace where the trail leveled off alongside a river whose steep banks dropped nearly straight down to the swift water twenty feet below them.

The company halted and looked across the wide, deep river. There would be no wading across this one. Swimming was out of the question, too.

"Dat am de Saline Riber," Violet declared. "It got to be."

"How are we gonna get across it, Mr. Fandango?" Willis asked.

The fugitives sat upon the wet ground, contemplating this new problem while Austin prowled the bank, thinking. He hadn't brought these people this far only to be stopped by a wild river. Beyond the Saline, unsettled land stretched clear to the Red River, and the Red was their ticket into Indian Territory! Getting across the Saline was all that lay in their way now. Bridges most likely spanned this waterway somewhere, but Austin did not know where they might be. A bridge road would be a heavily traveled place and he could not hope to bring this company of runaways across it without drawing a lot of attention.

He briefly considered the underground railroad. Though mainly operating farther to the east, on the other side of the Mississippi River, some conductors did secretly take runaways north into Canada through Arkansas as well. But how did someone catch a ride on that train? Austin did not know and he could not rely on the "railroad." No, the task still rested heavily upon his shoulders.

As he stood there pondering possibilities, his thoughts turned back to the story Jim had told, and Austin found himself grinning in spite of their circumstances. It had been *his* father who had saved Jim's life! He *had* made it out of the South and to freedom! Where had he gone? Where was he now? Austin wondered if Mrs. Caywood knew where his father had gone after leaving them. Was he still alive? That had been over twenty years ago. Austin was shocked to realize that he did not even know how old his father had been when he ran off. He could now be fifty—or eighty, for all Austin knew. But more importantly, he *could* still be alive and living free somewhere!

"Mr. Fandango." George's soft voice pulled Austin from his reverie.

"Yes?"

"I got a idea about crossing ober dis riber."

"What idea?"

"We can build a raft," the old man said.

Austin had briefly considered that as well. "With what tools?"

"Tools? Shoot, son, we don't need no more than what de Good Lord gib us. We got our hands." George swept an arm toward the forest that crowded the steep banks of the Saline. "And we got 'nough downed timber to make a pretty good one, an' more than 'nough strong backs here to do de work."

George's idea had merit.

"You ever build a raft before?"

"Shoot, build dem all de time when I was a young'un. Me and de little marster sailed dem on de high seas like pirate ships—well, it was only de Mississip we floated down, but we pretended.''

Austin nodded. ''All right by me.'' He figured it was as good a plan as any. ''You're in charge, George. There are a couple ropes on the saddles you can use, too.''

Downriver a few hundred feet they found a little cove below the steep bank where a raft could be constructed. Immediately the men fanned out and began dragging timbers to the edge and dropping them to the building site down below. The women not making moccasins also lent a hand.

The enterprise seemed to invigorate the old man. George scrambled spryly about, directing the younger men.

Savilla took her place beside them, working shoulder to shoulder, hauling deadfalls to the bank, where they were dropped to the muddy building site. The heavier logs were tied to the horses and dragged to the drop-off place.

Seeing that the project was in good hands, Austin left it for George to run and swung up onto his horse.

''Where you going?'' Willis asked.

''Take a ride up our back trail a piece. Hand me up my rifle.''

Willis passed the long Sharps to him. ''To scout dem men who am following us?''

Austin shoved the rifle into its saddle boot. ''I want to make sure they didn't pick up our trail. And I'll be keeping my eyes open for food, too. These people need to eat.''

Willis nodded and patted Jim's revolver, which dwarfed his narrow hips. ''I'll take care of things here while you am gone. Don't yo' worry 'bout us.''

Even if Willis was about as graceful as two buffalo at the bottom of a wallow, the lad had spunk and determination, both qualities that Austin admired. Not for the first time, Willis reminded him of himself when he was fresh out of slavery and tasting freedom for the first time.

But they were a far cry from freedom at the moment. ''You keep an eye peeled, Willis. I'll be back in a little while.''

Austin turned his animal away from them and rode back the way they had come.

• • •

Calhoun snarled up at the dripping sky as if threatening it would do any good. Then he drew rein and came about. In the middle of the road, Matt, Leroy, Teddy, Randy, and Mitch circled in until their horses' muzzles nearly came together.

Leroy looked at each man there and gave a wry grin. He figured he must look about as miserable as all the rest of them, huddled there beneath their rain slickers, water streaming off the brims of their hats. The sheriff was frowning. Maybe he was going to call an end to this chase and tell everyone to go home.

Leroy, for one, was ready to turn back in spite of the envelope he carried. Maybe with the papers he had taken off of Jim's body he could make a valid claim on the wench. But wenches were easy to come by—much easier than this! Was she worth the misery of the last few days? Leroy didn't think so . . . not anymore he didn't.

"They must have given us the slip," Calhoun said, looking at each of them. "No way all them runaways afoot could have come this far."

"They must have left the road someplace back there," Mitch figured, hooking a thumb over his shoulder.

"Looks like we lost them." Leroy tried to sound glum about it, hoping Calhoun might give up.

Teddy shook his head, disappointed.

Calhoun glanced at Walker. "What do you think our chances are of picking up their trail again, Matt?"

The deputy shrugged. "I can still find it, so long as we don't sit here jawing about it while the rain washes their tracks away."

Mitch wanted to keep on trying. Leroy knew the man took his grudges seriously.

Randy kept his thought to himself, but judging from his frown, Leroy figured the man was ready to throw in the towel, too.

"All right. We will go back and take another look. Be sharp now, boys. They had to have left some sign where they strayed off the road. If we miss them this time, we might as well forget about getting them runaways back, and that murdering nigger leading them.'' Calhoun turned his horse from the others and started back. The men fell in alongside him or behind, eyes to the side of the road, scouring the ground for any sign that might have been missed.

The young doe came cautiously toward the clearing then stopped and stood as if rooted there in the forest. Her nose twitched, her ears swiveled around searching for warning sounds. When she heard none she stepped into the clearing, stopped again, and looked around.

Austin squeezed the trigger. The big Sharps boomed in the still forest. He rose from his hiding place and went to the animal. Quickly he dressed out the carcass, propped the body cavity open with a couple sticks so that it would cool, then tied the deer across his saddle and started back.

He had already ridden several miles up their back trail without seeing Calhoun or his men. Austin hoped they had finally given the sheriff the slip. Even so, he rode another mile north to do his hunting . . . just in case Calhoun was still somewhere within earshot.

Austin had been gone five or six hours by the time he found his way back to the place where the fugitives were building their raft. The rain had stopped and the sun was leaning low in the sky when he untied the deer and let it fall to the ground. Instantly the women took over, skinning it and slicing into the joints to separate the limbs.

''We are going to feast tonight,'' he declared, grinning as he strolled to the edge of the steep bank to see what progress had been made. The raft was taking shape, and for the first time he had a good feeling. They just might make it to Indian Territory after all.

''How soon?'' Austin called down to them.

''It be ready to go tonight,'' George shouted back.

With all the damp wood about, building a fire was not an easy task, but fuel was plentiful, considering all the timber people had hauled in for the raft. Much more than George needed. Some of it was rotted, some containing dry pulp. Though the fire smoked badly, Austin figured they were far enough off the beaten path not to be noticed. The women dug up wild onions, set them near the fire to cook slowly, and angled thick, skewered roasts over the flames.

Later the men clawed their way back up the steep bank. They were tired, but each had a wide pleased look upon his face. This work had been *their* work. Not done for some overseer or white master in the "big house." As Austin peered down at the finished product, he decided that they had done a first-class job of it.

Savilla came to him. Not too near, as had been her custom. This time she kept her distance, watching him, not speaking until he finally looked over at her.

"Food is all done cookin'," she said.

Austin looked back at the raft. George's creation was a hodgepodge of different-size sticks and logs, all expertly woven together with grapevine and good hemp. It was most of fourteen feet square and stout enough to float high in the water. There would be plenty of room for all the people and the four horses.

"They did an admirable job."

"Dey wanted you to be pleased."

"Me?"

Savilla gave him a wan smile. "You are giving them freedom. De raft was all they had to give back."

"They don't have to please me."

"Dey know that. It is not what dey have to do. It is what dey want to do."

He had never considered that the runaways might hold him in any esteem. He was only doing what he had to.

Savilla took a step closer. "I'm sorry for this afternoon. I was only thinking about how de people were feeling. I forgot to think about what dey really needed."

"Are the moccasins all finished?"

Savilla nodded. "Now everyone have shoes."

"That will make the rest of the trip easier on them."

Austin remained aloof. He was drawn to her in a way he did not understand, a way no other woman had ever affected him, and he suspected that she felt the same way toward him. But he had too many battles to fight now, too many fronts to keep an eye on. He didn't need one more getting in the way. Weren't the needs of these people more important than the needs of one man's heart?

She came another step and suddenly Austin longed to hold her in his arms. Instead he looked away and felt more than saw her stiffen. "We will have trouble getting the horses down this embankment to the raft," he said flatly.

The silence was thick as morning fog on the Mississippi River. It was almost more than Austin could bear. Savilla turned to leave. Austin wanted to stop her. But he didn't. Then one of the horses whinnied. The sound was nearly lost in the confusion that had suddenly filled his head.

Almost, but not quite.

Living and working with these animals most his life, Austin knew when a horse sensed another nearby.

The horse whinnied again and this time it was answered from someplace out in the still-dripping forest.

Someone was coming!

SEVENTEEN

"Willis!"

The young man looked over.

"We got visitors." Austin pointed at the rifle leaning against the tree.

Willis grabbed up the Sharps, looking warily all around him.

"Everybody to the woods!"

Dismayed by the suddenness of it all and not seeing any immediate danger, the fugitives gathered themselves up in no hurry, looking around the campsite, confused.

"Now!" Austin barked, reaching for his revolver.

Suddenly riders appeared on the trail.

The fugitives understood this and scattered for the cover of the trees, grabbing up children into their arms in their haste.

One of the men shouted, "Get them, boys!" and riders broke in all directions. Austin saw Willis scrambling toward the higher ground that lay opposite the river. Horses thundered past and he wheeled to make his own escape, but the butt of a shotgun came out of nowhere, clubbing him alongside the head. Lights exploded in his brain and his revolver sailed into the undergrowth as he plowed into the ground.

Three men leaped from their horses and surrounded him. Austin pushed himself to his knees and shook the haze from his eyes. It was the sheriff from Laconia he saw first, then the two thugs from St. Louis . . . what were their names again? He couldn't recall just then.

"Looks like we finally got the nigger," the man behind the brown beard said. Then Austin remembered. Mitch was what his friend had called him. And Randy was the other's name. Austin's view shifted between the three of them. The hate he saw in their faces made his blood run cold. In the distance he heard the horses and the shouts of terrified people. His heart sank. After all his effort, it had come down to this.

"I got first claims on this buck," Mitch said, throwing a vicious kick into Austin's side.

Sheriff Calhoun scowled. "Looks like I'm just going to have to turn a blind eye to whatever happens here, boys. After all the dead men this nigger left behind, he will get his justice here and now."

Randy was grinning foolishly.

Mitch was seething with hate. He lashed out with another kick. Austin had been expecting that and snagged the boot in mid-flight, giving a wrenching twist that sent Mitch sprawling into the wet ground.

But before Austin could scramble to his feet, Calhoun and Randy dove for his arms, pinned them to his back, and hoisted him off the ground.

Mitch stood, cursing Austin with every foul word he had ever heard. Calhoun and Randy held him there while Mitch squared off and threw a fist into Austin's gut.

Austin grunted and buckled.

Mitch gave him a thin, loathsome grin and said, "I've been itching to do this since St. Louis." He swung out, clipping Austin on the chin.

The blow rattled his teeth. Austin's fingers bunched at his back, making hard fists, but he couldn't break loose. All he could do was stand there and take whatever it was Mitch was going to dish out.

Mitch lurched forward, bringing up his knee. Austin saw

it coming and managed to swivel a hip at the last moment, taking take the blow full on the thigh. Fire coursed up his leg into his hip. He would have collapsed if it hadn't been for Calhoun and Randy holding him up. With unabated fury, Mitch drove in raining blows to Austin's face and chest and side. His gut ached and knotted until he could hardly breathe, and still Mitch laid into him with no sign that his revenge was ever going to lessen. His intentions were clear. He was going to beat Austin to death with his fists, and no one there intended to put a stop to it.

Fleeing before the riders, Willis ran blindly into the forest, not caring where his feet were carrying him, just so long as it was away from these white men. Whippy branches slapped his face and hidden vines grabbed at his feet. He almost lost his new bearskin moccasins, and he probably would have never noticed if he had.

The sounds of pursuit diminished as the riders and fugitives scattered throughout the forest. The land was climbing and Willis spied a ledge of rock that looked as if some animal had burrowed beneath it. Heedless of the possibility that the animal who had dug it might still be at home, Willis dove for the small burrow and squeezed himself as deeply into it as the rock would permit. He lay there not able to hear above the pounding of his heart and his deep, ragged breathing. Minutes passed. His hearing returned. Slowly it dawned on him that no one was on his tail. He had made a clean escape!

Willis knew a brief moment of rejoicing. He squeezed his eyes and said a prayer . . . then he remembered Austin. The last that he recalled, Austin had not fled before the riders. He had remained behind, almost as if to give the others a head start. Concern began to replace elation, becoming a deep, burdensome worry. Wiggling his way out of the den, Willis hunched low and cautiously made his way back, his fist wrapped so tightly about the rifle that his knuckle began to pinken. He crawled behind a mossy rock and peered over it.

Below him he could see the beating they were giving Austin. With each punch that bull-shouldered man threw, Willis flinched. He watched them a minute, not knowing what to do. He had to think of something!

Then he remembered the rifle.

Quickly he slid it over the rock. It seemed weightless in his hands, but when he peered over the long barrel and put the bearded man in his sights, his trigger finger suddenly became infinitely heavy.

Willis glanced away, trying to recall all that Austin had taught him about the Sharps; how to aim it, how to shoot it. He held a vision of those big rocks Austin had set up and how they exploded into a cloud of gray dust when he had fired at them.

But when Willis tried again, he couldn't pull the trigger. He pressed the rifle into his shoulder just the way Austin had showed him. He concentrated on the bearded man, trying to think of him as nothing more than a rock, and pulling the trigger nothing more than target shooting.

But Willis could not pull the trigger. All he could do was sit there watching the man beyond his sights throw one brutal punch after the other while Austin went limp in the arms of the men holding him.

Fear held Willis captive—fear and upbringing—just as surely as any iron shackles could. And he hated himself for both as tears of despair flooded his eyes and streaked down his cheeks.

Consciousness blurred, his vision faded, and he had begun to gag on his own blood. Oddly now the pain of the beating seemed somehow remote, as if it was happening to someone else, not to himself. Austin was losing his grip on reality. Death looked certain and he almost welcomed it.

Almost.

Drawing from an inner well of strength, Austin steadfastly refused to give in to his body's aching cries. He refused to let it end like this. Marshaling his resolve, he lifted his right leg and with all his remaining strength drove the narrow heel of his boot down hard into Calhoun's foot.

Calhoun yelped and let go, hopping in a circle as he cradled his foot in both hands. Austin drove a fist over his

shoulder and caught Randy in the nose. A fountain of blood
erupted and suddenly Austin was free of their hands. Calhoun cursed and did a one-legged dance by himself while
Randy sputtered and cupped his nose in his hands, trying to
stem the flow.

Austin toppled to the ground without their support. Mitch
aimed a boot at his face. Austin just managed to crane his
head aside. As he did, he grabbed for the boot and held on
for dear life. In his clouded thinking, this was a wild cayuse,
and he intended to ride it to the end.

This caught Mitch off guard. Austin could do little more
than hold on, but that was all it took for Mitch's momentum
to catapult the bearded man onto his back.

Feeling like he'd been run over by a train, Austin pushed
himself to his knees, got a leg under him, and stood like a
wobbly newborn colt. His view still drifted in and out of
focus, and he could not straighten up. His ribs ached fiercely,
and one or two felt cracked or worse.

Mitch was back on his feet as if he had been wearing
bedsprings. Calhoun stopped dancing and reached for his pistol. Randy had backed up against a tree, his head tilted up,
nose pinched.

"Damn you, nigger. I'm gonna bust your head wide
open!" Mitch grabbed up a length of firewood, cocked it
over his shoulder, and batted out at Austin.

It whistled past his nose. Austin staggered back a step.
Mitch rushed forward and took another swipe. This time
Austin managed to throw up an arm to block the weapon.
White-hot pain exploded anew. The force of the blow sent
Austin spinning away. Then the ground gave out beneath his
feet. He tipped over the precipice, flailed the air with his
arms, and went over the side. A bramble rushed up and
grabbed at him, ripping his skin with its thorns. A rock
smashed his shoulder, another cracked him on the side of his
head. Then he hit the river below. Its cold water swirled
around him, pulling him beneath the surface and dragging
him along the rocky bottom . . .

Up on the bank Calhoun and Mitch rushed over and
looked down at the river. Calhoun cocked the pistol and

fired. Mitch emptied his revolver into the water at the place where Austin had disappeared. They stood there waiting, but the body did not resurface.

"That done him," Mitch said, jamming the revolver into his holster.

Calhoun watched the swift, swirling water and slowly shook his head. "He was a tough bastard."

"Not tough enough." Mitch flexed his fingers and massaged his bloodied knuckles.

"Well, you satisfied now?"

"Too bad it didn't go on awhile longer." Mitch worked his fingers. "Don't know how much more my hand could have taken it, though."

Calhoun looked him in the eye. "Not a word of this to anyone, understand?"

"Sure, Sheriff. No one but us will know."

Calhoun glanced at Randy. "You hear?"

Randy was too busy nursing his nose to hear anything. Mitch told Calhoun that Randy would never tell how justice had been carried out in this isolated spot along the Saline River—not that it would have mattered to most folks thereabouts.

Calhoun walked to the horses and eyed the pair of saddlebags. He opened one and grinned at the sight there. "I suspect this is stolen money, boys, and by the authority invested me as sheriff, I'm confiscating it until I can find its rightful owners."

Just then the first of the runaways began to arrive back at camp. One by one the fugitives were caught. Calhoun got their names as they were brought in and checked them off against the list Leroy had taken from Jim.

They came into camp in twos and threes, and before long thirteen runaway slaves had been recovered. Then Leroy returned after going out again. He was grinning ear to ear as Savilla walked in front of his horse, fighting him each step, and each time Leroy would walk his horse into her, threatening to run her over if she didn't march of her own free will to where the others were already lined up.

"Look what I found," he announced. "My runaway."

"*Your* runaway?" Calhoun eyed him narrowly.

"She belongs to me."

"Since when do you own this wench?"

"Since she was sold at your cousin's auction." Leroy produced the envelope and drew out the papers.

Calhoun looked at Savilla, then at the paper, then at Leroy. "You didn't buy her. Everyone knows it was that Texan."

"But I have the papers on her."

"That's right," Teddy said. "She belongs to him . . . and me." He grinned and lowered his voice. "You don't say nothing about this, Sheriff, and me and Leroy won't ask whether or not you ever find the owner of all that gold."

Calhoun narrowed his eyes at the young man's brashness. He glanced toward Mitch and Randy to see if they had heard. They hadn't. Calhoun looked back at Savilla and said, "What's your name, wench?"

With white-hot defiance, she stared him in the eye.

Calhoun backhanded her. The crack of the blow resounded in the forest and snapped her head back. "I asked you a question, wench!"

Savilla wiped a trickle of blood from the corner of her mouth. "It's Savilla."

"That's the name on the paper." He passed the receipt back to Leroy. "Don't know how you connived this, Leroy, but I ain't going to argue it with you." He studied the line of slaves. "Well, that's all of them, all but one buck, according to the list."

"Want us to keep looking?" Mitch asked.

Calhoun frowned up at the darkening sky. "It will be night soon. That nigger is likely clear up into the next county by now. He won't get far, not without a pass. First patrollers he comes across will know he's a runaway."

Calhoun led the horse carrying the saddlebags of gold to his own and mounted up. "All right, let's get these niggers someplace safe until I can have a prison wagon sent out to pick them up."

EIGHTEEN

Willis crept back into camp dragging the rifle behind him.

A real man would have strode in upright, carrying the rifle. But Willis wasn't such a man. He had run away when danger reared its head, had failed Austin, had failed them all. He had been failing people all his life. It was because of all his failures that Marster Hill had sold him to the slavers in the first place.

"Dat is what got me into dis mess!"

Oh, how he wished he was back home with his parents, back on Marster Hill's farm, where he was safe and happy. Whatever did get into his head thinking he could find freedom? What good is freedom when you are all alone?

In the twilight he plucked Austin's broad black hat from the ground and ran a finger along the deeply creased crown. He wanted to cry all over again, but managed to hold it in. He started for the riverbank and in the gathering gloam his toe bumped something hard. Bending, Willis came up with Austin's revolver. The Navy Colt was considerably lighter than the Walker he was wearing. It seemed a more elegant firearm and fit his hand better than the Walker ever did. He set the hat, rifle, and revolver on the ground and peered over at the darkly swirling waters.

He'd seen Austin fall, watched the two men fire shot after shot into the river afterward. No man could survive that. It was almost too dark to see and the moon was yet to mount the sky. It was hopeless, but just the same Willis called out Austin's name.

His plea was answered by silence, and the gurgling flow of the passing river below. A screech swept past his ear and he ducked as a darting goatsucker dove for insects.

Willis walked along the bank. If nothing else, he hoped to find Austin's body and pull it from the water. He came to the place where the raft he and the others had worked so hard on was moored.

"Mr. Fandango?"

Willis had never realized how quiet the deep woods could be when one was alone in them. The raft was nearly lost in the darkness now. The others were beyond his help, but maybe he could negotiate this fast stream and maneuver the raft to the other side of the river. Austin had said more than once that once across the Saline, they were practically home free. Oh, it was still a long walk to Indian Territory, Austin had said, but there were hardly any settlements between here and there, and a man could make it easy.

Willis clambered down the slope and walked out onto the raft. Two ropes held it in place against the current. George had even devised a crude rudder so that once in the main flow, with enough muscle, the raft could be steered across to the other side. He stood there listening to the river whispering to him when he heard another sound. Willis wheeled, eyes probing the deep shadows.

"Who there?"

It might have been a bear, or a badger, or nothing at all. His imagination was running wild, playing tricks on him. Then he heard it again. This time he was certain it had been a soft groan. Cautiously Willis stepped across the raft to where it stuck out into the water. Something appeared to be stuck between the chinks in the logs. Willis did not recognize it at first and prodded it with the tip of a stick as one might prod a dead snake one had happened upon.

Willis leaped back when it moved.

Another soft moan came from the water, from just beyond the raft.

"Mr. Fandango?" Willis crawled to the edge and looked into the water. All he could see was a head and a shoulder, and an arm reaching up through the logs, clinging there. "Mr. Fandango! Yo' am alive!"

"I . . . I wish I wasn't."

"I thought yo' was dead! I see dem shoot a powerful lot of bullets."

"Bullets don't go very far through water."

Willis untangled him from the raft and pulled him around it and up onto the muddy shore. Austin moaned with the effort and seemed to be desperately fighting off unconsciousness.

"Yo' look awful."

"That good?"

"Oh, Mr. Fandango. Do't joke about it. Yo' am bad hurt."

"The others. What about the others?"

"Dey am all gone. Dem white men round dem up and take dem away."

"Savilla?"

"She, too."

Austin tried to sit.

"Don't do dat. Just lay quiet!"

"Don't have time. Help me up, Willis."

Willis lifted Austin to his feet and then walked him around the muddy ledge a bit to get his legs moving. Each step was a torment. It tore Willis up inside to hear Austin try to stifle his groans.

"Help me up that embankment."

Willis started up, pulling Austin as he went. He felt the other man's agony with each step, and with each muffled moan. Finally Willis reached the riverbank. Leaning over it, he dragged the battered man onto the trampled grass. Austin lay there a moment, exhausted. With Willis's help he stood and hobbled to a log near the fire pit.

The flames had gone out but living embers lay buried in the ashes. Willis rekindled the fire and in a few minutes a warm glow pushed the shadows back. Austin shed his shirt with Willis's help, and in the firelight began taking inventory.

"Where do it hurt?" Willis asked softly.

"Where doesn't it hurt," Austin said through clenched teeth. He probed his chest. "Think he might have busted a rib—maybe only cracked it." He worked his jaw, wincing. "Not broken, but it will play hell to talk much the next few days."

"Yo' ought to bind up dat rib."

Austin looked around, but the people had left nothing useful behind. He used his shirt. Willis helped tie it tight. When they had finished, Austin stood under his own steam and walked back and forth, rotating his arm and arching his back.

Willis cringed with each moan and wince, but in the end Austin got his stride back. The exercise loosened tight muscles and forced bruised joints to begin working again.

"Time to go," he said finally.

"Go? Now?"

Austin took the hat and revolver Willis had rescued. "No time to waste." He gave the Sharps to Willis to carry. "They have a head start on us, and if we are going to get those people back, we can't wait around for me to get to feeling better."

Taking up a stick like a crutch, Austin started down the dark trail that the people had left behind.

Willis shook his head in amazement. All he could do was follow, and wonder if Austin had not taken one too many blows to the head.

It was not yet dawn when Calhoun rode up to the dark house and mounted the front porch. He rapped upon the door and waited while the men on horseback drove the slaves into a circle, huddled together, some near dropping for lack of sleep and too many forced marches. George was in a particularly poor state, sagging between two strong helpers who were themselves looking pretty ragged. Amy was clinging to her mother's skirt, half-asleep on her feet, while baby Robert was fussing in the arms of Violet, who was relieving Rebecca of the infant for a while.

"Whoever you are, you ain't welcomed here at this hour," a voice advised from the other side of the closed door.

"It's Sheriff Calhoun, Windy."

"Calhoun? What do you want?"

"Open the door."

The inside latch lifted, the door crept open a crack, and the two big eyes of a double-barreled shotgun peeked out. Then Windy. "So it *is* you. What's going on? Roosters ain't even commenced to talking." Windy noticed the gathering of black faces looking at him. "What's this all about?"

"We caught the man who wrecked your wagon. Unfortunately, he resisted arrest and was killed. But we got the runaways."

"I see." Windy looked back at Calhoun. "So what are you doing here?"

"My men are beat to a frazzle, and we need a place to keep these runaways until I can send a wagon for them. I was hoping you might help me out."

"What is it, Windy?" a woman's voice called.

"Sheriff Calhoun, dear. He caught the men who tried to steal our wagon, and the runaways he told us about."

Clutching a robe tightly about her, "Dear's" face appeared in the doorway looking sleepy and vaguely confused.

"Sorry to wake you, ma'am. But like I was telling your husband, we need a place to keep these niggers for a while."

Windy looked at his wife. "How about the root cellar? It's nearly empty now. It would be large enough."

She blinked a couple of times, still trying to clear her head of sleep. "I . . . I suppose so, if you think it will be all right. Why do you have to keep them here?" Her voice held a wary note, as if she felt that somehow Calhoun was implicating her in the slaves' crimes.

"It will only be three or four days, ma'am," he assured her. "No more than four at the most. Soon as I get back to Laconia, I will send a wagon and men to fetch them. In the meantime I can pay you for your trouble."

Windy nodded. "Just let me get dressed and I'll show you where it is."

"Does this root cellar have a good door?"

"We have bears in this country, Sheriff," Windy said as if that alone was explanation enough.

Morning found the men sprawled upon the front porch, asleep. Dear, whose name turned out to be Helen, never did go back to bed but got busy baking biscuits and collecting the chicken eggs hidden in bushes around the house—the chickens always laid them in the same places, and Helen knew every one. It was the aroma of breakfast that finally stirred the men from their deep sleep. They were still exhausted, but none could resist the fresh coffee, biscuits, and eggs she had prepared for them.

They ate breakfast and afterward sat around Windy and Helen's small table as Calhoun negotiated a fair price for feeding and keeping the runaways for four days. He was generous when he was provided with another man's gold and paid them out of one of Jim's saddlebags.

"Eighty dollars is kingly wages for feeding and watering them people," Calhoun declared.

Windy was inclined to agree.

"Now to a different matter. I need to leave someone here to keep an eye on them, just in case they get it into their heads to break out and run away all over again. I'll pay another forty dollars to whoever stays."

Helen said, "Is that really necessary? I mean, where can they go? Windy and I can see to them until you send someone back."

"I don't want to put you two out more than I already have, ma'am. And I don't want to lose these slaves neither." Calhoun looked at Leroy. "How about you and Cousin Teddy?"

Leroy grinned and shook his head. "I don't need forty dollars, Sheriff. I think I'll just take my nigger and go on home. It's been a real ordeal, and I'm ready for a hot bath, some easy sipping whiskey, and a soft, *dry* bed."

"I'm with my cousin, Sheriff. We'll be pulling out of here just as soon as we get our wench from the root cellar."

Calhoun shifted his view around the table, stopping on Mitch and Randy. "How about you two? I know you boys ain't so well heeled as to turn down forty dollars hard cash for an extra two days' work."

Mitch said, "We might be interested, but since there will be the two of us, make it forty dollars apiece."

"Eighty dollars? Don't make me laugh."

"How about sixty?"

"Done." Calhoun extracted three gold coins from the bag and slapped them onto the table in front of them. "I reckon that squares our business here." He stood and thanked Windy and Helen for their hospitality and the use of the root cellar. Outside they saddled the horses.

Leroy and Teddy removed Savilla from the cellar and took her to her horse while Mitch shut the plank door after them, dropping the heavy cross bolt back in place and locking it with an iron pin.

They left the farmstead and turned their horses down the lane toward the narrow country road. Laconia was a good fifty miles away and Leroy was anxious to be back—for the reasons he had already given Sheriff Calhoun—and for another that he kept to himself, one that was known only to Teddy. Leroy cast lusting eyes upon Savilla.

She glared at him and turned her head away.

Leroy grinned at the obvious challenge. Even in her bedraggled state, Savilla was easy on the eyes. Once bathed and dressed in decent clothes, she would be something else. Leroy was anxious to explore that something else—that mystery . . . without the clothes.

If she was willing, all the better.

And if she wasn't . . . ?

Leroy smiled to himself. He had ways of convincing even the most headstrong of women. Especially one who had no right to complain, and no one who would care even if she did.

NINETEEN

Austin needed to stop, needed to rest, but every time he tried, something within him would rise up and give him a shake and push him onward. At first he thought it was only concern for the people, but as the night wore on and that beast inside him kept pushing him along, Austin knew the reason was a bigger thing than duty, or even honor. This had become less a matter of the head and more a matter of the heart. And where the heart is concerned, there is no telling what a man might do, how many fires he might fight, rivers he might ford, mountains he might climb.

A man in love ain't worth a barrel of dry shucks!

That thought brought Austin's dogged steps to a halt.

Love? Was that what was driving him now? How could it be so? Was it more out of a concern for the one than the many? If so, he had no recollection of when it had occurred. Thinking it over, he knew it must be true, and he did not know if he ought to cry, or shout for joy. He was too tired to plumb such depths. All he did know for sure was that he had to find Savilla and get her and the others away from those men before they reached Laconia.

"Are we stopping here?"

Austin had almost forgotten about Willis. The young

man's words brought his thinking back to the job at hand. Austin had been following their trail in the dark. The sheriff and his men had simply left the same way they had come—the same way Austin and the others had come before that—and all that foot traffic had stomped a path of trampled ground and broken branches most of twelve feet wide. He could have followed it blindfolded.

"No, we go on." Austin heard the fatigue in his voice. He pushed off the tree upon which he had slumped, every muscle in his body raising its voice against the action. Time lost its meaning. The night lengthened, with Austin concentrating on putting one foot in front of the other. Sometime during those dark hours they hit upon the road. Here the moonlight came to his aid. It showed the tracks turning east . . . and so did Austin and Willis.

When morning arrived, they were still upon the road, dodging into the woods from time to time whenever a rider or wagon appeared in the distance. This was all familiar country to Austin now, and when shortly before noon the tracks veered off onto a little lane, he knew exactly where they would end up.

"They've taken them to the farm."

Willis frowned, clearly recalling the disaster he had made of their attempt to steal Windy and Helen's wagon and horses. "Dat's wonderful. I sure am not looking forward to going back der."

Now that Austin was certain the fugitives were nearby, a renewed vigor drove him on. He left the lane for the cover of the forest and hurried cross-country, knowing exactly where he was going this time. They made their way to the forest's edge, where the trees had been cleared for the tilled land beyond, and hunkered down to reconnoiter. There was the lean-to barn standing a little way away from the house. Inside it was the wrecked wagon, up on blocks. Its front wheels had been removed and Windy was currently beneath it on his back, working on the axle. To the left lay the farmhouse, a thin column of smoke trailing skyward from its chimney.

"See dem?"

"No, not yet." Austin scanned the little farm, at first see-ing no one but Windy. He began to wonder if he had been mistaken about the runaways being brought here, then he spied movement on the far side of the house. A man strolled into view. From his stance, his bull shoulders and thin brown beard, Austin knew he had been right.

At the sight of Mitch, his body revisited all the aches that that man had caused. His jaw throbbed and pain stabbed his chest with each breath. Austin pointed.

Willis nodded silently.

"They must have the people put somewhere. But where? And I don't see the sheriff and the others. Don't see but two horses."

"Inside de house?"

"Maybe." But Austin thought it unlikely. He watched Mitch cross the yard to a mound of earth Austin hadn't no-ticed before. There was a hole . . . or maybe a well . . . dug in front of the pile and the next minute Mitch had gone down into it as if descending stairs.

"The root cellar," he said.

"Can all dem people fit into a root cellar?"

"It is either a very large cellar, or they are packed in there tighter than cows in a St. Louis stockyard."

"What do we do now, Mr. Fandango?"

"Wait. Watch. See what happens."

"For how long?"

"Nightfall. It's a safe bet that nothing will happen before then."

"Yo' think so?"

"I think the sheriff went on to Laconia, leaving the slaves here. I think he will probably send back a wagon for them. Nothing will happen before tonight."

Austin and Willis moved deeper into the forest and circled around for a closer look at the cellar. They found a place to watch from just as Helen stepped from the house carrying a pail of something. Mitch and Randy took the pail from her and carried it down the steps to the root cellar.

"Feeding time. They are in there, all right." Austin leaned

back against a tree and pulled his head down over his eyes.
"Wake me when it gets dark."

"Yo' am going to sleep?"

"Nothing we can do right now."

"What if de others come back and take dem away?"

But Austin hadn't heard his question. Exhaustion flooded
over him and in a few minutes he was purring softly. He
dreamed about a man he hardly knew, one who had left his
life far too early. Sometimes the man's face was clear in his
mind, sometimes only a blur, and at others his dark skin
would fade unexpectedly and when it came into focus again
it was Big Jim Caywood there, not his father. Then a gentle
nudge stirred Austin from his deep slumber, and a soft voice
reached deep down into his unconsciousness, calling him
back.

The nudge grew firmer, the voice more excited.

"Mr. Fandango. It am dark. Can yo' hear me."

The sleep shed itself slowly at first, and in its place came
all the aches and pains again. Then Austin's eyes snapped
open and he was instantly awake.

"It am dark."

He sat up and groaned softly.

"Yo' hurt?"

"Like the south end of a northbound stampede."

Willis blinked, dumbfounded. Austin grinned in spite of
everything that grieved him. "What happened while I was
asleep?"

"Nothin' happened all day long, Mr. Fandango." In the
gathering gloom, Willis's eyes were wide and earnest. "Dey
bring water to de folks locked in dat cellar, but no one come
out." Willis held his nose and made a face. "It must smell
like a backhouse in dat cellar by now."

Austin and Willis moved to the edge of the forest again.

Mitch and Randy were lounging on the porch. Austin
could just barely hear their low voices, but could not make
out their words. Crickets chirped busily and fireflies were
making their first appearances for the evening. Already the
mosquitoes were becoming bothersome. A lamp burned in-

side the house, behind the curtains in the glassless window frames.

"It's time, Willis."

The young man stared at him. "Time for what?"

"For you and me to make trouble."

"But yo' am in no shape for to make trouble, Mr. Fandango."

"I suspect you are right, so I am going to have to rely on you, Willis."

"Me? Oh, but yo' know I don't never do nothing right, Mr. Fandango," he moaned. "I just make mo' trouble for yo'."

"I'm counting on you, Willis. You'll do just fine."

"Oh, I do't know . . ."

"Listen!" Austin's rasping command stopped the lad from going on. "You will do fine. Don't even think anything else. I'm counting on you. All those people are counting on you."

Slowly Willis nodded. "All right, what am I to do?"

"I'll draw those two away from the house. When I do, I want you to take it."

"Take it?"

"This is what you do. You go through that front door like a locomotive on a downhill run. You don't knock, you don't ask to come in, and you don't—I repeat—you don't take your eyes off of that man once you get inside." Austin glanced at the rifle. "My guess is they have no real stake in all this and they are not going to want to have their brains blown out over someone else's business. You just show them the business end of that Sharps and tell them to stay put. When I'm finished, I'll come for you. Understand?"

Willis said he did, but the uncertainty in his voice did nothing to put Austin at ease.

"Remember, there can be no hesitating on your part. And listen to me, don't let the color of their skin get in the way either. Once you start it, it's your game and you set the rules. Got that?"

Willis nodded.

"Just remember to wait until both those men have left the porch before making your move."

"I'll remember."

Austin stared at the lad. "I'm counting on you, Willis. I know you can do it."

"Yes, suh. I can do it," he repeated with little conviction.

Austin felt around on the forest floor for a weapon of some kind. He was in no condition to go hand-to-hand, and he only wanted to use his revolver as a last resort. His fingers found a stout branch and folded comfortably around it. It was oak, three inches thick and three feet long, a good, solid chunk of timber. He gave Willis a nod and watched the young man slink away toward the house, keeping well back in the deeper shadows of the trees. Then Austin moved off in the other direction and worked his way to the far side of the mound where the root cellar was buried.

Austin could see the two men on the porch from here. He leaned toward a nearby tree and gave it a solid *thwack* with the club. Across the way the two stopped their low talk and looked over.

Austin waited.

Randy and Mitch peered hard into the night. Eventually they fell back into their talk. Austin gave the tree another smack. This time Randy and Mitch stood. They exchanged glances and Randy stepped down and came across to investigate. He approached cautiously, his hand resting upon the revolver in its holster. First he looked down the dark steps to the door below. Seeing nothing wrong there, he peered out into the forest, which lay but a few dozen feet beyond.

Austin lay low, waiting. He heard Randy's footsteps come around the mound. Austin inched back until Randy was there, at the far side of the mound. Then he quietly stood and stepped into view.

Startled, Randy wheeled around. "You!"

"Surprise."

Randy grabbed the revolver from its holster. Austin swung. The oak club smashed into Randy's arm and the gun flew from his fist as he let out a yelp of agony. The movement had sent a lance of pain through Austin, too. Ignoring it, he drove the club into Randy's gut. Breath gushed out of the man. No time to hesitate now. Austin swung the club again, with all his strength, slamming Randy's head around. The man crumpled instantly.

"What's going on? Randy? What did you find out there?" A note of alarm was in Mitch's voice.

Holding his ribs, grimacing at the stabbing pain in his chest, Austin straightened and backed up against the mound. He glanced at the lifeless body at his feet. That last blow had finished Randy—maybe permanently.

"Randy?"

Austin peeked around.

Mitch started across the dark ground, drawing his revolver as he came. "Hey, what's going on out there? Randy? Answer me!" When he reached the mound he stopped and cautiously repeated his partner's name, this time whisper soft as he started around the back of it.

"Mr. Randy is in no condition to talk."

Mitch whirled toward the sound of Austin's voice. "You!"

Austin's fist shot out of the shadows. A fireburst of pain exploded before Austin's eyes as his fist connected. He could have just as easily used the club again, but this was something that needed doing on a more personal level. Back at the river Mitch had tried to kill him with his bare fists, and Austin intended to return the favor.

When his vision cleared, Mitch was flat on his back, stunned. Austin ground his boot into the man's wrist and bent for the revolver in the spread fingers. Another wave of pain momentarily blanked his vision.

This was plain stupidity. What made him think he could take Mitch hand-to-hand the way he was hurting now? Was it that temper of his getting in the way of common sense? Austin tossed Mitch's revolver aside.

Mitch rolled to his hands and knees, shaking the fog from his head as he stood. A left jab laid him out a second time, and Austin didn't know who hurt most from it. He sucked in a breath and hugged his side.

"You sonuvabitch," Mitch growled, shaking his head again.

"There is no one here to help you this time," Austin said, trying to hide his pain.

Mitch climbed back to his feet, keeping a safe distance. "Thought we killed you back at the Saline."

"You thought wrong."

The two men circled. Mitch lunged. Austin sidestepped and rounded, driving an elbow hard into his chest. Then they did another couple of turns, each measuring the other, looking for an opening.

Mitch said, "What keeps you up? You look like a dead cat I once stomped into the ground."

"Cats only have nine lives."

Mitch gave a laugh that sounded more like a snort. Still he kept his distance, circling carefully, and Austin hurt too much to make a try for the man. It was beginning to look like this could go on all night when something caught Mitch's eye. Austin noted the way the bearded man's view had shot past him and fixed on something at Austin's back side. At first Austin thought that Randy had regained consciousness. He dared not take his eyes off of Mitch but worked his way around in a circle. Then suddenly Mitch spun around and leaped to the ground. That caught Austin off guard, and before he figured out what the man had in mind, he saw Mitch grab up something from the ground. Metal glinted in the moonlight and suddenly Austin knew what it was Mitch had taken into his hand.

Austin threw himself to the left, hand stabbing for the revolver at his side. It cleared leather the same instant Mitch's own six-shooter took aim. Both guns fired at once, orange flame exploding blindingly in the darkness . . .

Willis's head jerked toward the open door at the roar of the gunfire. Sweat trickled into his eyes and tasted salty upon his lips. Immediately he swung back, the heavy Sharps rifle shaking in his slick palms.

"Don't move!"

"We aren't," Windy said. Helen squeezed his hand. "We won't move a muscle, boy. Just keep your finger offa that trigger."

"What is it you want from us?" Helen pleaded, her wide eyes staring at the big rifle.

"Just . . . just wait," Willis managed. Never before had he confronted anyone like this, let alone white folks.

"What are we supposed to be waiting for?" Windy asked. "Just what is happening out there?"

"I don't know!"

"You owe us some explanation for busting in here like you done and pointing that big gun at us. We never done you no harm."

"Don't talk."

"Boy, you're getting mighty nervous. Me and the missus would be obliged if you point that buffalo gun in some other direction."

Willis glanced at the door again. The night had grown silent after those gunshots and he wondered if Austin was alive or dead. If dead, Willis knew he would be in a whale of trouble for holding these two white folks hostage. All at once there were footsteps on the porch and Willis's heart climbed into his throat. Then the lamplight fell upon him standing there in the doorway.

"Mr. Fandango! Am I happy to see yo'. Yo' all right?"

Austin stepped through the door and glanced around the small farmhouse. There was only one other room besides the one they were in.

"What happened to dem two men?"

"They won't be bothering us, Willis." His view settling upon Windy and Helen. "Where is the key?"

"So, that's it. You come to free those runaways." Windy stood cautiously off his chair. "It's no business of ours."

Helen said, "We didn't want the sheriff to leave them here, but what could we do?"

"The key."

Windy reached atop a cupboard and put an iron key into Austin's hand. "Like I said, it's no business of ours. Do what you have to and then be on your way."

Austin gave the key to Willis and took the Sharps in return. Willis hurried outside. Austin pulled over a chair and lowered himself into it. Every muscle and bone cried out.

He ignored them. "Is the sheriff sending someone back for them?"

"Heard him talk about a wagon in a few days."

Austin spied the pile of gold coins on a crude sideboard. "Is that your pay for tending them?"

"Yes."

Austin pocketed Jim's money. "You won't be needing it now. I'll see that this is returned to its rightful owner."

"Whatever you say. Take the money. Just leave me and the missus be." Windy was obviously worried about provoking him. Austin judged that his appearance had a lot to do with that. He must have seemed a wild man, beaten and swollen, his chest bare and wrapped about with his filthy shirt.

"You have a bedsheet handy?"

"A bedsheet?" Helen looked at Windy. He gave a small nod. She went into the bedroom and returned a moment later. Austin took the sheet from her and slapped a gold coin onto the sideboard.

She stared at the coin. "You put one of these in my sewing basket, didn't you?"

"I borrowed a couple things from it."

There was the noise of an approaching crowd and Austin took the farmers out onto the porch. As the runaways filed up out of the root cellar and came across the yard, he searched for one face in particular. He was thinking that they now had a couple days head start to make it to the wilds of western Arkansas. In another week they would be home free in Indian Territory.

When the last of the fugitives climbed out of the root cellar Austin said, "Where are the rest?"

Helen said, "There are no more. That's all of them."

"There is one missing."

Windy said, "Oh, that must be the one they took with them."

"They took Savilla with them?"

"Those two young fellows claimed they owned one of them. Took her away when they left."

Austin stared at the people crowding in front of the porch just to be sure.

George said, "Dat's right, Mr. Fandango. Dat's just what happened. Dem men showed papers saying dey bought Miss Savilla at de auction. Dey done took her away wid dem."

TWENTY

He didn't feel a whole lot better, but he suspected he looked a mite more presentable. Austin buttoned his shirt over the sheet, which had been cut into strips and wrapped tightly about his chest. Violet seemed to know what she was doing, and between her and Rebecca they had done a proper job of binding his cracked ribs. He had a hard ride ahead of him tonight and his battered body was going to need all the support and care they could give him.

Outside, Willis brought one of Mitch and Randy's horses forward. "Dey ain't going to be needing it anymore, Mr. Fandango."

Austin said, "You did just fine tonight."

The young man beamed and Austin went on, "Now you are going to have to keep on a little while longer. You have Mr. Caywood's revolver, so it will be up to you to protect these people."

"I understand."

"Can you find your way back to the raft?"

"Yes."

"Then that's what you are to do. I'll meet you there if I can, but don't wait for me more than a day. If I'm not back by then, you take these folks across the river and strike south and west. Keep to the forest trails until you come to the Red River, then straight into the sunset. It's your only chance."

"Yo'll come back, Mr. Fandango. We all is counting on yo'."

Austin grimaced at the mighty weight of responsibility that had fallen upon his shoulders and wondered if Mr. Caywood had not been right in wanting to leave these people behind. Then he recalled the looks on their faces whenever they spoke of freedom. Austin knew he had made the right decision. "But if I don't, you know what you have to do."

"I know."

Austin groaned softly as he swung up onto the saddle. "Now all of you go on, get moving."

He waited there until the company of fugitives had disappeared into the night, then looked back at Windy and Helen standing there on the porch and inclined his head toward the root cellar. "Am I going to have to lock you two up?"

Windy shook his head. "We ain't going nowhere, mister. Like I already said, this ain't none of our business. But when the sheriff comes back, I'm going to tell him what happened."

"Fair enough." Austin turned his horse.

"Mister?"

Austin stopped. Windy said, "They mentioned Laconia. If that's where they are bound, you'll save yourself about four miles by taking the trail that runs behind my place."

Austin remembered the trace. It was there that Willis had first spotted this farmstead. "Thanks. But why tell me this? Why should you want to help a black man?"

Windy glanced at his wife. She nodded briefly. Windy pointed to the night sky, at one of the constellations. "See that? Know what it's called?"

"The Big Dipper."

"Yes, but it has another name, too. Some call it the Drinking Gourd. Some folks use it and the North Star to travel by. And sometimes when they are following it, they end up here . . . for a little while."

Austin stared at them. "You're a conductor?"

Windy shook his head. "No, our place is just a station

along the railway. This ain't the first time runaways have used our root cellar." He grinned. "Don't worry, I won't tell Sheriff Calhoun any more than is necessary. Good luck to you, mister."

Austin found the trace that ran along the back edge of Windy's property. Turning east, he put the horse into a lope and rode on through the night. The easy stride jarred his already battered body and he turned his thoughts to other matters—to all that really mattered to him now . . .

Savilla.

"We should be back home by this evening," Calhoun said, looking at the coffee that remained at the bottom of his cup. He paused and considered as he chewed a slice of dried peach that Helen had given them for the trip back. Then he glanced across the campfire at Leroy and Teddy. "I suspect you boys will be right pleased to get on home. Beating around in this here backcountry to chase down runaways ain't exactly what you two are used to."

Leroy nodded. "I can think of more profitable ways of spending my time." He grinned suddenly and tried to hide it, glancing over where Savilla was sitting, apart from them. "A lot more profitable ways."

His lurid look sent a cold shiver through her and she averted her eyes.

Calhoun chuckled. "Least you got *your* wench back."

"And you recovered those runaways, and all that *stolen* gold, Sheriff."

Calhoun cleared his throat, glanced back into the cup, then tossed back the coffee that was left in it, spitting out the grinds and wiping them from his lips. "Yep, I did all of that."

"Think you'll find the owner of that gold, Sheriff?" Teddy asked.

"I intend to try."

That was a lie and they knew it.

Matt Kelso came back into camp just then and poured himself a cup of coffee. "We should be getting a move-on, Sheriff. Sun will be full in the sky in half an hour."

Leroy took some of the dried peaches to Savilla. "Here, eat."

"Ain't hungry." Leroy was the last person on earth Savilla wanted anything from.

"Don't tell me that. I can see it ain't so. Eat it, dammit. Don't want you to get sickly now." He shoved the dried fruit into her hand. "Eat them up."

Savilla threw them away.

Leroy backhanded her. The crack rang in the early-morning silence alongside the road where they had camped the night before.

When Leroy returned to the campfire, Calhoun was grinning. "That's one stubborn wench. She needs a whip put to her backside."

"I've got a whip I'll be putting to her soon enough." Leroy reined in his anger and suddenly laughed. "And it ain't the kind that stings, though it will surely make her whimper some."

Calhoun glanced at Kelso. "Oh, to be young an' feisty again, heh, Matt?" He grinned and said to Leroy, "I reckon that me and Matt can find our way home without you boys." He gave Leroy a wink. "If you want, you and Cousin Teddy can linger here awhile longer." His view slid toward Savilla. She was holding a palm against her stinging cheek.

Kelso chuckled and stared long and lustfully at the woman.

Leroy said, "That's right thoughtful of you, Sheriff." He eyed Savilla, considering the proposition. "You two go on ahead. Me and Teddy are going to spend a little more time here, around this fire. Who knows what might come up?"

Teddy was grinning.

The sheriff and Kelso saddled their horses. After checking that the bags carrying the gold were securely tied to the spare horse, Calhoun stepped up into the saddle and peered down at Leroy and Teddy. "Don't you two boys enjoy yourselves too much now, hear?"

"We will try not to smile, Sheriff," Leroy replied straight-faced.

Calhoun laughed and grinned at the girl one last time. He

shook his head as if recalling some pleasant memories of his own and he and Kelso turned their horses toward the road.

When they had gone Leroy said, "Cousin Teddy, what do you say we have us some fun?"

Teddy leered at Savilla. "I'd say it was long overdue, Cousin Leroy."

Savilla stood and took a wary step backward when they came at her. Their intentions were plain and she wanted no part of it.

Leroy snatched her wrist, squeezing tight. "Let's the three of us move away from this road, heh? There is some grass over thataway. I saw it last night."

Savilla struggled to break free of his grasp, but Leroy easily overpowered her, pulling her along. Teddy followed them, prodding her with a pointed stick. Back among the trees Leroy threw her to the ground and ordered her to shed the dress while he hurriedly unbuttoned his shirt.

"No."

Leroy glanced at Teddy. The anxious cousin cocked his revolver and pointed it at her. Leroy said, "You're gonna give it one way or the other. I can hurt you real bad if you make it difficult. I can make it so bad you'll want to die. But believe me, wench, if it comes to that, dying won't come easy, or quick."

Cold fear shivered up Savilla's spine.

"Now get out of that dress and be snappy about it!"

As her hands went for the buttons, another voice spoke. "I don't think so."

"Austin!" Savilla cried.

Teddy and Leroy spun around.

"You!" Teddy cried, raising his revolver.

Austin fired. Teddy's gun went flying and the dandy grabbed at his wrist.

"He shot me, Leroy!" Teddy cried, staring at a trickle of blood from his hand. "The nigger shot me."

The cousins stood in stunned silence as Austin came from the trees, limping, his battered face a mask of pain and rage.

"I thought you were dead!" Leroy exclaimed.

"Not likely, not when there is still two strutting popinjays needing to be taught a lesson on manners."

"A lesson from you?" Leroy sounded dubious. "Look at you, boy, you can barely walk."

Austin fired again and the tall silk hat sailed off Leroy's head.

He shut his mouth and gulped. "What . . . what I meant to say was—"

"Shut up." Austin glanced at Savilla. "You all right?"

"Yes." She stepped around the cousins and stood beside him. "Dey told me yo' was dead."

"They tried at it all right." His face was swollen and he winced when he spoke. Savilla saw that talking hurt him real bad. "Where are the others?"

"Sheriff and his deputy just left."

"The gold?"

"Calhoun has it with him."

"What are you going to do with that gun, boy?" Leroy asked.

Austin thumbed the hammer and pointed it at Leroy's forehead. "What?"

"Err, I meant to say sir. Yes, that's what I meant to say. Sir." Leroy's eyes went wide, staring at the gun barrel.

Austin took another painful step forward. "Strip."

"What?"

"Out of them fancy duds."

"But . . ."

"Don't tell it's me not what you two had in mind for Miss Savilla."

"Well . . . but—"

"Now!" Austin growled.

Leroy and Teddy looked at each other. Savilla folded her arms and gave them a small grin.

"Hurry it up, *boys,* I'm developing an itch in my trigger finger."

Teddy and Leroy's fingers rushed to their buttons and buckles and in a minute they were naked as the day they came into they world.

Austin grinned. "What we have here, ma'am, are two

young bucks for your inspection. They got straight backs but kinda weak shoulders. Here, boys, turn around and show the lady your back."

Savilla shed her initial shock almost at once and said, "Dey is awful pink looking, and kinda puny, Austin."

"Aren't much to look at in their altogether, are they? Well, a couple weeks in the sun doing fieldwork will put some color and muscle on them. Turn around, boys. Let the lady have a good look. What am I bid for these two pinkies?"

"I'd not give a dollar for dem, even if I had a dollar to give. Dey is all shriveled up like a dead rose."

"Must be getting a chill." Austin shook his head. "Hear that, boys, the lady doesn't think much of you."

"I'll get you for this," Leroy growled.

Austin laughed. "That will be the day, sonny boy."

Savilla gave him a curious look.

"Fetch one of those fancy silk shirts while I keep them covered."

She brought one to him. Austin spied the silver case in its breast pocket and helped himself to a cigar and told Savilla to rip the shirt into long strips. Austin tossed a strip to Teddy. "Tie Cousin Leroy's hands, and make sure you do a good job of it." When Teddy was finished, Austin tied Teddy's hands. His bullet had only creased Teddy's finger. It had stopped bleeding by the time they were both bound. Austin marched them to the edge of the road and used the rest of the shirt to tie Teddy and Leroy's hands to an overhead branch.

"Don't look like much now, buck naked, do they?" He blew a cloud of smoke into their faces

"You'll regret this!"

"I doubt that. But if you want to come look me up in Texas, just ask for directions to the JC Connected, above San Antonio. Most everyone knows where it is."

Savilla was looking at him that way again.

"What?"

She shook her head. "Nothing."

Austin gathered up the pile of clothes. He tied their boots onto one of the saddles and carried the rest to the fire.

"What are you doing?" Alarm rang in Teddy's voice like a cracked bell.

"There ain't much travel on this road, so you two might be standing there for some time. It will give that pink hide of yours a chance to color up some. In the meantime I'll burn these just so that when you two popinjays are found, somebody is going to have themselves a good laugh."

Leroy glared at him.

Austin dropped the pile onto their campfire.

"Wait!" Savilla dove for the clothes, picking them out of the flames. She pulled an envelope from one of the vests and held it up. "Don't want to lose these."

"The receipts!" Austin shoved the envelope into his shirt for safekeeping. "These are your ticket to freedom, Savilla."

"Yo' know, Austin, you am beginning to sound a lot like Mr. Caywood."

"I am?"

" 'Popinjay.' 'Sonny boy.' 'Not likely'?"

"Did I say all that?"

She nodded.

"Hmm."

Austin came up over a rise in the road and spotted the sheriff and his deputy ahead. They were riding an easy pace, leading the single horse that carried Jim Caywood's gold.

He drew rein and watched them. "You stay here with the horses." He handed Savilla the reins to Leroy and Teddy's horses.

"I'm going with yo', Austin." The determination in Savilla's pretty brown eyes brought a grin to his face in spite of his body-racking agony.

"I have to get ahead of them and cut them off. You and these horses will only slow me down. Besides," he added gently, "I don't want to have to worry about you getting in the line of fire. Wait here."

She frowned, but understood his reasons. "Be careful."

Austin turned his animal into the trees alongside the road, keeping it just in sight. He pushed hard through the undergrowth, gritting his teeth against the uneven gait of the horse, ducking low branches, dodging trunks and deadfalls. The road made a bend. Austin angled through the trees and came back to the road a few hundred feet ahead of Calhoun and Kelso. He held back in the cover of the forest, and when the two men were almost abreast of him, he rode out onto the road and leveled the Sharps.

"You!" Calhoun's face was a mask of shock, slowly melting into apprehension as his eyes settled on the Sharps's big bore.

"Surprised?"

Kelso's hand reached back.

"I wouldn't do that," Austin warned, shifting the rifle.

Kelso stopped and carefully lifted his palms to the sky.

"What do you intend to do?" Calhoun demanded.

"Don't provoke me, Sheriff. I'm all done counting to three, and I've turned the cheek so many times I've got a powerful kink in my neck for it. So don't try anything."

"You're already in trouble, boy. Don't make it any worse for yourself."

"Sheriff, the way I see it, it can't get any worse and killing you two won't make any difference. I can only be strung up once."

Calhoun glanced nervously at Kelso.

"He's right, Sheriff. He ain't got nothing to lose by killing us."

"All right, what do you want?"

"First the guns. On the ground. Now."

Carefully Calhoun and Kelso dropped their firearms.

"The shotgun in the saddle boot, too."

It fell beside the pistols.

"Now you two."

They dismounted and stepped away from the guns. Austin told them where to stand. He stepped down off his saddle and, keeping them covered, bent for their weapons, groaning as he straightened. "The gold in those saddlebags belongs to Mr. Caywood. I'm taking them with me. And your horses."

"You going to leave us afoot?"

"Afoot?" Austin gave them a wide grin. "That's exactly

what I am going to do, Sheriff. Take off those boots.''

The men pulled off their footgear and tossed them into the road. Austin shoved the boots into Kelso's saddlebags.

''You can't leave us like this.''

''Oh yes I can, Sheriff.'' Austin swung a leg over his saddle, wincing. ''You left me for dead. Least you're still breathing. Anyway, I'm leaving you two a sight better off than those two dandies up the road.''

''What do you mean?'' Calhoun scowled suspiciously. ''You kill them, too?''

Austin just smiled. ''Kill them? I suggest you hike back up this road to where you parted ways. You'll see.'' He grabbed the reins to their animals.

''You're stealing our horses, too?''

''Stealing?'' Austin took gold from the saddlebags. ''No, sir. I'm buying them.'' He tossed a hundred dollars at their stocking feet. ''That should cover the saddles, too. If it isn't enough, you can come look me up next time you're down Texas way. Cousin Leroy and Cousin Teddy know where to find me.''

''I'll be coming after you, boy. You can count on it.''

''Do what you see fit, Sheriff. I'll be waiting. But first I recommend you get yourself home and buy new boots for your feet. Those stockings won't last long on this road and I wouldn't want you running around barefoot like a poor colored slave.''

Calhoun snarled, his fists bunching tight at his sides.

Austin laughed and left them standing there on the side of the road. Savilla was waiting where he had left her.

''I was worried about yo', Austin,'' she said. ''What happened?''

''Happened? Nothing much.''

''The sheriff . . . him didn't try to make trouble?''

''Trouble?'' Austin scoffed at the notion. ''No. In fact, he gave us his horses and another two pair of boots for the people to wear.''

''Austin! What did you do to him?''

He grinned, thinking that those wide, concerned eyes were just about the prettiest he'd ever seen. ''It's going to be a long, painful walk, but at least I left him and his deputy their britches.''

They passed Leroy and Teddy still tied to the tree, their lily-white skin beginning to redden under the bright sun glaring off the road. The sky was clear, without a cloud in sight, and Austin said, ''Looks like their cheeks are going to get sunburned, Miss Savilla.''

''Least cut us down,'' Teddy implored as they rode past. Leroy only glared at them.

Austin tipped his hat to the naked men and Savilla smirked, her eyes lingering long upon the two cousins just as their eyes had upon her that day at the auction.

TWENTY-ONE

The Texas prairie rolled away from the ranch house like great brown waves on a sea of winter grass. High overhead tattered clouds scudded across the gray sky. The feel of rain was in the chill wind that came from the north. It scattered the smoke from the chimney and kicked up swirls of dust at Austin's heels as he angled across the yard toward the house, clutching his leather jacket tight in front of him.

Movement caught the corner of his eye. He turned and peered hard to the west. A rider was coming, still too far off for him to identify. Austin stepped up to the porch and raised his fist to rap upon the door. Then he stopped. The squall of a baby beyond the door brought a huge grin to his face. He knocked.

"Come in, Mr. Fandango," Juanita's voice invited from the other side of the door.

Austin closed the door behind him and stood there feeling the warmth of the stove and the security of the heavy walls around him. It was a good house, one that would stand a hundred years, Austin thought, looking around the familiar place.

Juanita was sitting on the rocking chair, trying to comfort the crying baby in her arms. "Some coffee?" she asked.

"Yes, ma'am, Mrs. Caywood. Did I ever tell you that you make the finest coffee in all of Texas?"

She smiled, her dark eyes glinting in the afternoon light through the window. "Oh, at least once a day."

"Jim fussing again?"

By the stove, Savilla filled a delicate china cup. "I need to feed him," she said, bringing it to Austin.

"Thank you," he said, taking the coffee from her. Their eyes lingered a moment, their hands touching. Then she turned and lifted the baby from Juanita's arms.

Juanita stood. Savilla settled in the chair and started nursing their son. Austin grinned at the handsome baby in her arms.

"He looks like you," Juanita said, going to the kitchen table. "Every day he looks more and more like you, Austin."

He dragged his eyes off his family and pulled back a chair. "Made another count, Mrs. Caywood. The herd is up over three thousand."

Juanita frowned and shook her head. "What are we going to do about it?"

Austin shrugged. "Like I told you last spring, all we can do is keep an eye on them and put your brand to the calves. Don't have hardly enough men to work the place as it is, what with most the men off fighting. It's a sure bet we can't drive them to market."

"What market?" she scoffed. "With this awful war going on, it's either Abe Lincoln's soldiers or Jeff Davis's boys. And I don't know who I trust less. What would Jim do?"

Austin grinned. "He'd probably say something like, 'Let the popinjay bureaucrats have their war, and when it's over we'll start selling beef again.' "

A thin smile warmed Juanita's worried face. "He probably would say something like that, Austin."

There was a knock at the door. George stepped in and snatched his hat from his head. "Der is a rider comin' in, Mrs. Caywood. Looks like it might be that gentleman from over the other side of de river."

"Mr. Singleton?" Juanita stood and touched her hair back in place then smoothed her dress as she went to the door.

Duncan Singleton dismounted, wrapped his reins around the hitching rail, and came up the steps. He was the owner of the Bar S cow camp and he had been visiting regularly the two years since Jim's death to make sure Juanita was getting along, offering what men he still retained on his place to help her when work needed to be done. Austin would send men over to the Bar S when Singleton needed help.

"Afternoon, Mrs. Caywood," Singleton said, doffing his hat. He was a handsome widower with gray hair and a huge gray mustache. When he spoke, it was with a gentle English accent. He looked at Savilla and added, "Afternoon to you, too, Mrs. Fandango. How is the little one doing?"

"Growing big and strong, Mr. Singleton," she said, putting little Jim over her shoulder and patting a burp from him.

"Someday he will be as big as his father." Singleton smiled at Austin.

"Come in, come in. To what do we owe this pleasure, Mr. Singleton?" Juanita asked.

He turned to her. "I was in town last week and the postmaster had a letter for Austin. I told him I'd be coming out this way to check up on you, Mrs. Caywood, and he gave it to me to pass along." Singleton put the envelope in Austin's hand.

It was wrinkled and travel weary from months in transit. With the war on, mail often took months . . . that is, if it ever got delivered at all.

"Who is it from?" Savilla asked.

Austin studied the childlike scrawl then ripped the envelope and withdrew the single sheet of paper. "It's from Willis."

"What does it say, Mr. Fandango?" Juanita wanted to know.

Austin read the letter first, working his way through the tortured grammar and outrageous misspellings. It was short, and when he had finished Austin said, "Willis has joined the army."

"Read it aloud," Savilla said.

Austin cleared his throat and began:

Dear Mr. Fandango, and Mrs. Fandango, and Mrs. Caywood,

After I leave last year, Mr. War Eagle him take us north to Kansas Territory just like Mr. Fandango say him should do. Rebecca and Violet and Adaline go to gold camp and get job cooking and cleaning and they are getting paid a dollar a week! Adaline find herself a colored miner and her am married. Me and Isaac and Andy hear Federals am calling colored boys to join the army and fight for the freedom of all the slaves so we go and join the 1st Kansas Colored Volunteers. I am a private. General James G. Blunt is in command. A white officer named Kelly O'Toole am learning me and Andy to read and write. We ain't done no fighting yet, but we dig lots of roads and they pay us eight dollars a month! And they even give us clothes and shoes to wear! Sergeant O'Toole, him help me write this letter. I miss you all.

Sincerely,
Willis Black

"That is wonderful," Juanita said, busily dishing out boy-senberry cobbler and pouring another cup of coffee for her guest. Then she asked Austin to tell how he had led the runaway slaves out of Arkansas and brought them to the ranch until he was able to arrange for their passage north.

Singleton had heard the story already, but for Juanita's sake, Austin told it again from the beginning. Singleton laughed at all the right places, and he particularly enjoyed the part where Austin turned the tables on the two dandies. But everyone got quiet and thoughtful when Austin described the dangerous river crossing, and how the raft, crowded to its edges with people and horses, nearly overturned while grounding on the other side.

"It was those extra horses that really made the escape possible," Austin concluded. It was not his manner to take the credit for himself. "We ended up with ten animals after adding in the dandies', sheriff's and his deputy's horse, and

Mitch and Randy's. Once across the Saline, we put everyone on horseback, a few riding double, and in the next three weeks pushed our way through some of the deepest, most tangled and boggy forests I had ever seen.''

Austin grew somber when he recounted his torment from the beating Mitch had given him, and the festering shoulder wound that turned to fever and finally drove him to his knees, nearly ending the exodus right there in the wilds of Arkansas.

"If it wasn't for Savilla," he said over and over, taking his wife's hand and gazing into her eyes, remembering. "She nursed me back to health, kept me going. And when we finally spied the Red River, I knew we had made it, in spite of the odds.''

"Jim was helping you, too, from above," Juanita declared, and Austin knew it was something she truly wanted to believe.

"Yes, ma'am, he was. Once in Indian Territory, I figured we were home free . . . and that's when Willis spotted the Comanches.''

"We all thought we was on our way to Glory when them Indian ride up," Savilla put in.

"But it was only some of Chief War Eagle's warriors," Austin continued, "and they rode with us nearly all the way back to Texas.''

"A smashing good tale!" Singleton declared, taking a sip from his cup and finishing the crumbs on his plate.

The conversation turned to other things, but for Austin, his thoughts remained stuck in the past. Now that the war was on, there seemed to be little danger that anyone would be searching for the runaways, or for him, but he had not forgotten Leroy's threat. That had been over two years ago and so far no one had come looking. Laconia seemed mighty far away—another world away. A world embroiled in a bitter conflict of brother against brother—and maybe even cousin against cousin.

Later that afternoon, after Singleton had left, Austin stepped out onto the front porch and lit a cigarette. The winter wind snatched the smoke and hurried it away as he watched the clouds racing past. The reminiscing had brought back memories. Juanita had told him what she remembered of his father back those twenty or more years ago. She could not say where he had eventually ended up, only that she recalled him mentioning the New Mexico Territory.

The door opened behind him. Savilla stepped out with little Jim in her arms, bundled in a blanket against the chill wind.

"What are you thinking?" she asked, stopping close beside him and looking to the west, as he had been.

"Oh, nothing."

"Don't tell me dat, Mr. Fandango. I see it in yo'r face. I seen it come there after yo' read dat letter from Willis."

He stared into her wide eyes, so lovely, so perceptive. Then he laughed. "We've been married only two years and already you read me as if we've known each other all our lives."

"Well?"

Austin drew in a long breath and let it out slowly. He put an arm over her shoulder and drew her close. "He is out there somewhere. I just know it." He looked west.

"Your father?"

"When this war is over, when the men come back so that you and Mrs. Caywood won't be alone, I'm going to go look for him."

Savilla remained silent, her head leaning against his chest. He had spoken of this before and he knew she did not like the idea.

"It's something I have got to do."

"I know."

What kind of crazy notion was that? he wondered, searching for a father he hardly knew, a man who had walked out of his life almost a quarter of a century earlier.

No crazier than thinking I could lead fifteen runaway slaves clear across Arkansas to freedom.

Austin glanced up at the gray sky and had to grin. He could almost imagine Big Jim looking down on him now and shaking his head.

"Let's go home," Savilla said.

He took her hand in his and started across the yard toward their little house.